CW00517684

Tangle Tales 2

Oliver Barton

the
Deri Press

2023

Creation

First published by the Deri Press,
27 Brecon Road, Abergavenny NP7 5UH

This edition published by The Deri Press

Layout and cover design by Oliver Barton

Set in Times New Roman by The Deri Press

ISBN: 978-1-7391589-5-8

This novel is a work of fiction. Names, places, characters and incidents are the work of the author's imagination. Apart from the composers and their works, of course.

Prelude

Blind Bella, they called her. This was her bench, here in the Market Square, just outside Mr Bun the Baker's, overlooked by a solitary, rather sad rowan tree. Behind the bench was a narrow entrance into the Tangle, that mess of mediaeval alleys, dark and odd, in which it was easy to believe anything might happen and probably did. There were tales, there were rumours. Of course there were; it was very good for tourism. In contrast, the Market Square was open, bright and bustling, dominated by the clock tower, complete with public conveniences at the base.

Blind Bella had a reputation as a wise woman, a seer, philosopher, prophetess, an oracle. In earlier times, she would no doubt have been called a witch, though instead of medicinal potions, she dispensed words. Frequently cryptic words. But then, just as we all know a medicine can't possibly be effective if it tastes nice, so a prophetic utterance can't really help you if you think you understand it.

Every day, Stanislav Bun the baker, or his doleful, dreamy assistant, Merrylin, brought Blind Bella a cup of cocoa and a bun. An unbiased observer would say if Bella was lucky, the bun would be one of Mr Bun's renowned bacon rolls, at the creation of which, Merrylin, for all she gave an air of several geese short of a gaggle, was a genius. Blind Bella, however, did not consider a bacon bun lucky, for she had a sweet tooth or two. Not many more; several of her teeth had succumbed to rot over the years, leaving an alarming gap when she grinned. Which was rarely. But dicky teeth did make bacon a bit of an ordeal.

To be accurate, Bella did not frequent her bench every day. It just felt as though she did, for those who noticed her at all, that was. In fact, Bella was only there when the weather was clement. And when she felt like it.

It was doubtful that Bella was actually blind. Her eyes did not point the same way. If you looked at the skew one, as most people did, you could convince yourself that she was indeed blind, but it might be that whatever that eye saw was not the same as for normal mortals. Another dimension, perhaps. A parallel world, where past, present and future all co-existed. What else would you expect from a soothsayer?

A few people looked at the other eye when they met her, the straight eye. That was an unsettling experience. It seemed to see true, at you, even through you, into your core.

Given her disquieting appearance, it was natural that she had a reputation of being possessed of great wisdom. What she spoke must be true, if you could fathom it. Some of those who believed that ended to find themselves gravitating to her bench, to consult her, for advice, for comfort, or maybe to tell her their problems, not that she necessarily listened.

One such was Arthur Davison. He lived the other side of the Market Square in a second-floor flat. He didn't quite know why he consulted Blind Bella. The first time had been some years previously, on a particularly balmy Saturday morning. He had sat on Bella's bench, not because of her presence, but in spite of it. He was there to enjoy both Merrylin's attempt at cappuccino and the sunshine in melodious harmony. It was, after all, the nearest bench to the bakery. That day, he had looked at Bella, at her true eye. In turn, Bella's true eye saw his soul, perhaps his inner artist self. She spoke and prophesied:

'Tomorrow,' she had said, 'the walls will be wonky and nightmares will fly. You mark my words, young lady.'

Given his gender and getting-on-a-bit age, Mr Davison might have concluded that Bella was indeed blind or daft, or, since her other eye pointed elsewhere, that she was addressing somebody else. But there was nobody else within earshot, young lady or otherwise. Or she might have been talking to herself. Some people did, he knew that.

Whatever the case might have been, Arthur Davison took the words to heart. 'Oh,' he said to Bella. 'Do you think I should worry?'

'Depends,' she said. 'Are you a worrying kind?'

Arthur said he didn't think so particularly.

'Well then,' said Bella,

And that was her final word on the subject apparently, for she creaked to her feet, wagged a finger at him, and shambled off into the mysterious alleys of the Tangle.

After Arthur had finished his cappuccino, he wandered back through the market stalls and crowds to his flat diametrically opposite. There he noted down what he remembered of what Blind Bella had said. In case it proved important. "Walls wonky, nightmares fly," he had written.

Since that time, Arthur had consulted Bella several times. He had even been known to reward her, with a chocolate éclair on one occasion, a doughnut and a cream slice on others. They were gratefully received and demolished by Bella. The cream slice was not entirely successful. Seventy per cent of it squidged down her indescribable coats, though she seemed not to notice.

Each time Arthur consulted her, Bella uttered, and he made note of what she said, or what he could remember of it by the time he got home. He bought a thin, spiral-bound, reporter's notebook and labelled it in a slightly florid hand, "The Wisdom of Blind Bella". It now contained the following:

Walls wonky, nightmares fly.

You thinks you're there and then the pigeons arrive.

My feet hurt and nobody cares.

Look at the time. Look up, young lady.

Tomorrow is the mother of today.

He was not too sure of the last one; by the time he had reached his flat, he was a bit uncertain whether he might have made her prophecy up. Probably not. Or he might have misheard her. There was a risk with cryptic prophesies. Just because they didn't make sense could mean they were indeed actually complete gibberish. So far Arthur had failed to discern any hidden elemental truths in these, but he lived in hope.

Today, preparing his nightcap after returning from a rehearsal of the Chervil Choral society, in which he sang, he found himself for no reason looking at the thin, spiral-bound notebook while he waited for the kettle to boil. And it would in a moment dawn on him that the first of her sayings quite aptly described his Grand Market Square-scape.

But before we meet that, we must go back a while to another place in Chervil, to the bar of the Royal Hotel, no less. The present time must take its place in the queue, as Bella say in a more lucid moment.

1 Oscar

Nearly a year and half ago, Beryl Carson entered the unfamiliar portals of the Royal Hotel, into a time-forgotten mustiness.

It was empty but for a man at the bar, perched on a stool, head in hands. Beryl caught her breath.

'Oscar,' she gasped. 'Oscar Silvero.'

He looked up, heaviness in his eyes. She noticed they were a little bloodshot. He looked blankly at her.

'I'm...' she began. 'My mother is very fond of your music. I'm bringing her to hear you tonight.'

He sat up straighter, passed a hand over his remaining hair and tried to summon a twinkle to those eyes.

'My pleasure,' he said. 'Always glad to meet my public.' He looked wistfully at the empty glass beside him.

Beryl was distributing fliers for the Alzheimer Society's fund-raising coffee morning. Her next door neighbour was looking after her mother. It was a welcome break. After delivering to the Tourist Information Office, she thought she'd try the Royal Hotel, see if they'd take a few. After all somebody must stay there, though it looked unloved. And somebody clearly did. Oscar Silvero. The posters called this his Golden Goodbye tour, following his visits over the previous few years, which had progressed from the Farewell Tour, through the Final Farewell, to the rather desperate Leaving at Last.

It was now eleven o'clock. Coffee-time. Oscar was clearly not drinking coffee.

'My mother...' Beryl breathed deeply. 'My mother doesn't know what day it is. She thinks I'm her aunt or a nun, heaven knows why, or the manageress of some store or something. Never her daughter. But when she hears you, she's there, she's with you, singing along, all the words. When she hears you, I have my mother back for that little time.'

'I try to give satisfaction,' said Oscar. It was a pathetic response. Beryl closed her eyes and tried to force a flare of anger down.

'You shouldn't drink,' she said. The suppressed temper lent it a force that made Oscar pay attention. 'So much. For your own good,' she added, feeling she was being unforgivably rude. He looked at her with sudden fury too, ready to brush her away like a bothering fly. Then he sagged again, the effort too much.

'What else is there?' He looked again at the empty glass. 'This is my life, my living.'

A scrawny young man appeared behind the bar. Beryl struck before Oscar could speak. 'Excuse me, but can I leave some fliers for Alzheimer's here?' she said. 'It's a good cause.'

The barman scratched his neck. 'I'll have to ask the manager.' He took a flier and wandered off. Beryl knew it would go straight in the bin, but she had stopped Oscar asking for another drink.

'Settle down,' she said to him. 'Why don't you settle down.'

'Where?'

'Where are your friends? Or family?'

He sighed, a pitiful sight. 'My fans are my friends. They're everywhere. And nowhere,' he said, and sniffed. 'No family. Nobody. Not now. Time was...' A spread hand said it all.

'Why not here in Chervil, for example?' said Beryl. She had no time for self-pity. She had more reason for it than most, but it was not the answer.

'Gerbil?' Oscar seemed puzzled.

'Chervil. Like the name of the herb. Say it again.'

Oscar got it right.

'It's where you are now. It's where you're performing tonight, for heaven's sake. In the Lyric Theatre.'

'Right,' said Oscar. 'Yes. Yes... Oh God.' He put his head in his hands again, the same forlorn figure as when she came into the bar.

'Settle here in Chervil. You could sing my mother to sleep. Help her. Help me, too. That's better than this.' She waved at the empty glass. She was being bossy, and she didn't care

Slowly he raised his head, looked at her. Their eyes met for a long moment.

'Come and help me deliver fliers. Fresh air'll do you good. You'll see what a lovely little city this is. Where's your coat?'

Oscar shook his head. 'In my room.'

'Fetch it. I'll pay for your drink.' Surprising herself, Beryl banged on the bar and cried 'Service!'

Oscar slid off the stool, and Beryl realised he wasn't nearly as tall as he looked on stage. 'Hurry up!' she said. He tottered off. She felt a small glow. The barman reappeared, a startled rabbit. 'We're leaving,' she told him. 'How much for the drink?'

'Drinks,' mumbled the young man, and started punching the till.

'Never mind,' said Beryl. 'I'll pay.' She looked round the bar, now revealed as drab and peeling in the light leaking in from outside. She thought of how her mother shackled her life. Wasn't that price already too much? And yet... She sighed. 'Oh yes,' she said to herself, 'I'll pay.'

The Royal Hotel had had its day. Presumably it was new once, but to Beryl the fading, dark-red, heavy curtains, the sticky carpet, the nicks and tears and stains all contributed to a desire in her to run away into the limpid clarity of the open air and some familiar car fumes. Perhaps Oscar was drawn to the place as though it was a sentient fading creature. Or maybe he first came here as a bright young crooner, and they had both degenerated in synchrony.

And here he was, back again. Beryl quite expected he would chicken out, but here he was. Long, black coat, shabby, homburg hat, for all the world as if he had stepped out of a black and white classic film.

Without a word, Beryl led the way outside. It was not that the sun was shining and the air balmy, but it felt as if it was so. In truth, it was overcast and tending towards light drizzle. Beryl looked at Oscar. He looked at his shoes. Then he looked up.

Beryl was sometimes struck by the way you could see the boy in the man. Looking at a male politician or captain of industry on the tele, she saw the sullen, podgy toddler, sulky at being denied a sweet or a toy, or the know-all schoolboy who irritated other children and teachers alike.

In Oscar, as his eyes meet hers fleetingly, she saw a small, underfed urchin pleading, 'Please don't tell me off again.' Who had told him off in his life? His mother? His doctor, perhaps, when he presented with evidence of poor diet, excess of alcohol and little exercise? 'Be kind to me,' was the message in those eyes.

'Come along,' she commanded. 'Too nippy to be hanging about.' All right, it was bossy, but Oscar obediently followed her as she made her way to Mrs Tenby's tea-rooms, which always carried an array of fliers to educate and amuse muffin-eaters.

'What are you singing tonight?' she asked as they meandered through the alleys of the Tangle.

'Oh, this and that,' he muttered. 'Usual stuff. Standards from the days when a tune was a tune. Something to make you laugh, something to make you cry. Step back into yesteryear.'

'You're just quoting your publicity blurb,' said Beryl.

'Yes. It's all I know.'

It was not all he knew. Beryl was well aware of that. She had taken her mother to hear him a couple of times, and one thing he did know was how to perform, how to sell a song, to milk its emotion.

They set off along Eastgate, Beryl as sergeant-major, Oscar her troop. 'Do you know Chervil well?' she asked. Silly question.

'No,' he said.

And so there was silence as they turned left to plunge into the gloom of a particularly narrow alley. Ahead, round a couple of contortions and beyond an intersection or two, lay Not Martins Square and Mrs Tenby's Tea Rooms. Or at least the square was usually there. You never quite knew with the Tangle. Beryl could think of nothing to say, so they forged on, almost on tiptoe, because the buildings, nearly touching above their heads, seemed in private conversation. There was a sound other than their footsteps, however; Oscar was humming. Beryl couldn't make out the tune. She looked at him. He seemed altered in a slight way, almost in another world.

And then quite unexpectedly they burst out into the oddly named Not Martins Square, which was a space, yes, but certainly not square. There were four or five alleys leading in or out, or both. Never trust your senses here, nor your ability to count. These days, the square was largely deserted in the daytime, with locked shutters on frontages. Except for Mrs Tenby's Tea Rooms, which were a portal into an earlier era, one in which tea-plates had flowery patterns and waitresses frilly aprons. At night, Not Martins Square was rumoured to become a very different place, but it was a stout constitution that went there to find out. Beryl felt it was home to nefarious practices; she shied away from further delving.

'I've been here before,' cried Oscar. He looked like a little boy, his chubby face lit up with joy. Except Oscar's face was anything but chubby. It was ravaged by age and alcohol, but now it seemed somehow radiant.

Beryl was still in charge. As they went in, she said, 'You've been here before on your other tours, probably.'

'No, no... Yes... No. Before... before that... I don't understand.' The little boy lost.

The tea rooms were a bit seedy these days, that's what Beryl saw. There were only two people seatet at the tables, the lace cloths were slightly grey. She deposited some leaflets and pushed Oscar outside again. He turned and gazed at the facade of the café, at the square. Little boy puzzled.

What it was, decided Beryl, was the Tangle getting to him. It did with some people. Not her, of course. She was matter-of-fact. She did not hold with suggestible malarkey. And yet... And yet she did take Oscar out of the Tangle by the quickest route, which led out onto the High Street. There, opposite, was the Lyric

Theatre, where Oscar was to perform that evening. They'd take a few fliers, surely. She shepherded Oscar across.

'I know this place,' he said. Of course he did, silly man.

After that, she must get back home. It didn't do to take advantage of kind neighbours in the business of mother-sitting. So she led Oscar to the end of the High Street, turned right into Eastgate, and there they were, back at the woodlouse graveyard of the Royal Hotel.

'Wait,' said Oscar as Beryl turned to leave. He ferreted about in an inner pocket. 'Have you a piece of paper?' he asked, and after a moment of fruitless delving. 'And a pen?'

She had. She was sensible Beryl, after all. He wrote on the back of the flier that she produced. 'Excuse me asking, but what is your name?' he said, 'I'll reserve two seats for you for tonight. Is it just the two?'

Beryl told him she already had tickets. 'Front row,' she said.

Oscar looked so disappointed. 'Oh well,' he said, 'one tries to give satisfaction.' Little boy rejected. He turned and entered the Royal Hotel. *Back to the bar,* thought Beryl, and hoped not.

She took herself home. Annoyingly, the neighbour who had been mother-sitting said her mother had been a perfect darling, chatting away as though dementia was an unvisited foreign country from which spotty dogs came. As soon as the neighbour left, Mum burst into tears for no reason and waved her arms about as if she was swatting wasps away when Beryl approached her.

'Come on, Mum, lunch-time. Come into the kitchen. Baked beans on toast with a poached egg. You like that.'

Her mother brightened. 'And soldiers? You must have soldiers.'

'Not with a poached egg, Mum. That's with boiled eggs.'

'Oh. Who's coming to dinner?'

'It's lunch, Mum. Nobody's coming, it's just us.'

After lunch, she settled her mother in the front room with a cup of tea and the television. It seemed to be a programme in which a couple were trying to sell their house, but it would do.

Beryl went upstairs to the spare room. As she opened the door, she felt a little quiver, a frisson, shoot down her spine. It was always so. She had no idea why. Probably a psychic would say it was the spirit of a person who died in that room many years ago, but she had no truck with that kind of nonsense.

No, she ignored it. The spare room was where she practised. A pile of music lay on the bed, beside it a longish rectangular leather box. She opened the case and reconstructed her flute, her Gemeinhardt, her companion since schooldays. She breathed down it to warm it up while sifting through the music with the other hand.

She chose the volume of Karg-Elert studies. Challenging, good for limbering up. She limbered.

Her mother had always seemed to be in denial about Beryl playing the flute. In all her life, Mum had never once referred to it, nor told Beryl how brilliant she was. At least, Beryl liked to think she was brilliant. She told herself she was used to her mother's indifference, but it still hurt, even now Mum was the way she was and she should feel sorry for her. It was Dad who had encouraged her to learn the flute, because she had shown some slight aptitude for the recorder in primary school. In some way, Beryl suspected that her mother was jealous of Dad's attention to Beryl and chose to pretend the flute-playing didn't exist. In later years, before Beryl's own husband was felled in his prime by a catastrophic stroke, he too had been at best sniffy about her flute, and referred to it scathingly as a penny whistle. Now these negative influences were gone, the one confused, the other dead, she was making a renaissance, she told herself. A Phoenix, or rather, a Syrinx, rising from the ashes.

In her oh-so-sensible moments, which were many, Beryl knew she was competent but actually never had a hope of being brilliant because she had never been prepared to practise, at least, not in the way that led to total technical mastery. And a tip-top technique was a prerequisite to brilliance. But she was lucky enough to play in the CSO, the Chervil Symphony Orchestra, which was, like her, competent. For an amateur band, that was. In other words, pretty good considering. For years she had played second flute to aged Cyril, trying not to dwell all the time on how much better she reckoned she could play any solo bits, but just last year, after a scare or two, Cyril decided it was time for less stress and handed the mantle of first flute over to her. So now she was taking it all a bit more seriously.

At the moment, the orchestra was rehearsing Beethoven's Leonora No.3 amongst other things, and that had a rather showy passage for the first flute that Beryl thought she played exquisitely. It would be nice if others thought so too. Particularly the tuba player, with whom she was very slightly obsessed. The trouble was, the brass only usually came in at a fairly late stage in rehearsals and she was not too sure whether Leonora 3 had a tuba part, or anything else in the programme for that matter, so he might not be playing at all. If he wasn't, maybe he'd come to the concert anyway, to listen. And be impressed. He had a voluminous moustache. Not that that had anything to do with anything, but she rather wondered if it would tickle.

She lived a fantasy while she played, a reproduction of the Laughing Cavalier on the wall an appreciative audience. The time passed, and then it was into the routines of a cup of tea and preparing Mum to go out in the evening, and then supper, and then persuading Mum into the car and driving the ridiculously short distance to the car park beside the Lyric Theatre, and getting Mum out and in and up and down and, at last, sat in their seats in the front row of the stalls. The stage reared a couple of feet in front of them. It would feel like Oscar was singing to them alone. That was what Beryl hoped.

The theatre was not full, the average age considerable. Why on earth would a young person want to hear a has-been like Oscar? Oh, that was cruel. His voice could get through to her mother as little else. That was a blessing, a great blessing.

Oscar's backing band assembled on stage, all well into their third age like Oscar, who must be in his seventies. They were seasoned veterans, they could probably do the whole thing on autopilot. Maybe they did. They twanged and banged and chatted a bit and looked only to need pint jars at their elbows to be ready for a good session down the pub.

Then the house lights dimmed and they started playing, slipping into the act like a seal into the sea. Oscar entered. He turned his smile on as he emerged from the wings. His hair was slicked back, what there was of it, his once snazzy suit seemed too big, his cravat an anachronism. He plucked the microphone from its stand and was away.

"Blue moon," he sang, "you saw me standing alone..."

Beryl saw him there standing alone, alone but transformed. Although physically he was a poor specimen these days, moving into the husk stage, inevitably to be followed in years to come, she imagined, by reverting to a chrysalis and then back to a caterpillar and the earth, although she could see all that, there was a radiance about him, a halo of a voice, that reached out and nurtured the audience. She could sense Mum relaxing next to her, drawn as moth to candle.

He moved from song to song, and in no time at all, it was the interval. Beryl bought two ice-cream tubs from the usherette with her tray at the end of the row, keeping Mum in view in case she decided to go walkabout. Her mother managed the ice-cream rather well. No spillage, no need for dabbing with tissues moistened with spit.

'I prefer strawberry,' announced Mum when she was done.

'It was strawberry,' said Beryl.

Beryl was not a patient woman by nature. She had learnt patience through years of her father succumbing to dementia and eventually dying from pneumonia, and now her mother going a similar way. She had learnt it, but underneath she still seethed and wanted to scream and it was hard not to feel sorry for yourself and that life was unfair, but there it was. And Oscar would be back soon.

Halfway through the second half, Oscar started on *My Funny Valentine*. He was looking directly down at Beryl, then at her mother. Next thing, he was coming down the stairs at the side of the stage and making his way along the front row, until he was directly in front of Beryl's mother and was singing to her, to her alone, just to her. Beryl found tears in her eyes, to her shame and embarrassment.

"Don't change your hair for me, not if you care for me," he crooned, "each day is Valentine's day."

And then he was moving back onto the stage and pressing something into Beryl's hand as he went, and he had seguéed into *Night and Day* and the magic moment had passed.

Beryl looked at her mother, who was staring open-mouthed like a lovelorn teenager. 'Thank you, Oscar,' Beryl said to herself, and her eyes moistened again. She looked at what he put in her hand. It was a business card. "Oscar Silvero," it said, "available for weddings, bah mitzvahs, soirees, etc. 'England's Sinatra'" And his mobile number. On the back he had written, "Yore right, I should settle down. O."

When they reached home and Mum was safely in bed, at least for the moment, Beryl poured herself a gin and tonic and sat down in the living room, gazing unseeingly at the blank television screen. She thought. She thought long and hard. Then she reached for her journal.

Beryl called her journal Hattie, long for HAT, "*How Are Things?*" The question nobody ever asked her, meaning "How are things *for you, Beryl?*"

People used to ask "How are things?" of Jim, her husband, aka the Selfish Shit, when she looked after him after the major stroke he'd had in flagrante delicto in one of his students' rooms, that stroke that left him a dependent baby for five long years before he had the decency to die. God alone knew how many of his students' lives he tainted with his attentions. During that time, nobody said to Beryl, but how are things for *you*? How does it affect *you*, how are *you* coping? Certainly not at his funeral, when it was all fond reminiscences of how he was the life and soul, and such an inspiring lecturer. Nor when dementia really began to affect her mother just after that, not even giving Beryl a chance for a recuperative sabbatical. From carer to carer. 'How are things with your Mum, Beryl?' they asked. Downwards, that's how they were, ever downwards. Slowly, inexorably.

At some point when "good old" Jim was her dribbling baby after his stroke, Beryl started Hattie. Intermittently. Hattie asked her how things were for her, and Beryl told her. Hattie was endlessly patient. Hattie listened; she didn't judge. And because of Hattie, Beryl managed to remain strong.

When Mum replaced Selfish Shit Jim as dependent, Beryl acquired a cat, because she read somewhere that animals were supposed to be calming for dementia sufferers. Her mother however regarded the cat as some manifestation of hell. To give the cat a purpose in life, Beryl decided maybe she could take on the role of confidante in place of the journal Hattie, so she called the cat Hattie instead. Alas, furry Hattie proved unsatisfactory. She tended to wander off in the middle of Beryl's therapeutic rant, or fall asleep, or start her washing contortions. So Hattie the journal was reinstated and the cat renamed Victoria after the Queen of that name whom she resembled not in the slightest. Hattie the journal helped, though Beryl was inclined to be rather flowery in her prose style.

Dear Hattie,

How are things today, Beryl?

Not so bad, thanks for asking. There is a glimmer of hope, a faint possibility that my Burden might be shared. Nothing more than an errant ray of sunshine momentarily slipping through the dark cloud cover. Today we went to OS's final final final tour recital and I spoke to him before & he came leafleting with me and I lodged a little thought in his mind... At least I think I did. I hope I did. An acorn, a seed. And who

knows, an oak may grow, strong and reliable, on
whom I can hang some of my Burden. I dare not spell
it out, because that might put a jinx on it. I know you
are a true friend, Hattie, and my secrets are safe with
you, but who knows what ethereal djinns or will o'
the wisps are floating about unseen and watching
what I write? Enough of such disquieting thoughts.
There is a glimmer of hope, let that be all for now.
    Good night, dear Hattie.

And Beryl drained the last of her G&T, locked up and went to bed. Victoria, the cat, joined her at the foot, so if a djinn or will o' the wisp was watching, they might have observed that Beryl resembled a noble knight of old on a tomb in a church, resting his feet on a faithful lapdog. Noble Beryl. Faithful Hattie. Jury was out on Victoria the cat.

As it happened, Victoria was easily offended. Being used first as therapy for Beryl's mother and then cast as a dumb comfort blanket for Beryl to dump all her anxieties and troubles on was frankly beyond the pale. It insulted her pride. However, now the journal Hattie had been reinstated and Beryl's mother had cast Victoria as a devil in fur, a view that Victoria had taken trouble to instil, the cat was prepared to reconsider. She decided that perhaps Beryl was worth keeping as a pet, not just a convenience for food, warmth and so on. For yes, it is cats who choose humans, not the other way round. "Pet owner"? Not so. Illusion, carefully fostered by cats. There are contracts, unilaterally drawn up by the cats. Humans are to provide the necessities and comforts of life; in return the cat might, just might, live up to human expectations of affection: purring, chasing bits of string, sitting on knees, ripping the furniture, bringing in dead or partially dead rodents and birds as gifts and so on. If they feel like it. They treat their humans according to their perceived worth.

For Victoria, being named Hattie was an indignity beneath contempt, but this was partially offset by acceptable feeding and general lack of restriction on places to sleep, and access to the wider world (in the form of a cat flap). She was also expected to put up with the stuff, the angst, the negative feelings, the anger that Beryl should have reserved for a therapist. The cat acted therefore. It was a doddle for Victoria to convince Beryl's mother that she was a evil malign influence. Any cat observer will know of their ability to transform from a soft, purring, adorable, fluffy ball into a vicious, claw-and-tooth, bristling cacodemon in the twinkling of an eye. So when Beryl was out of the room…

It worked, of course. And Beryl, good soul, adjusted the cat's name to Victoria, which, although not her real name (which was unpronounceable and unspellable, as Mr Elliot observed in his poem), yet had dignity and respectful resonances. Thus the cat was left coping with the good bits and habits of Beryl, in her view, and Beryl went back to writing her feelings down in the original Hattie, the *How Are Things* journal.

2 The Wind Quintet

It was about a year later.

'Oh, Mum, Mum, Mum, what are you doing?' Beryl tried to wrestle the kilo bag of frozen peas from her mother, who was attempting to empty them into the washing-up bowl.

Her mother fought back, wild-eyed. 'No, no, I must get on,' she cried. 'So much to do.'

Beryl won. Her mother looked suddenly very old, deflated, and Beryl felt a wave of sadness sweep away the annoyance.

'It's all right, Mum,' she said. 'It's far too early to start getting supper. Let's go into the sitting room and you can watch tele with Oscar. He'll be back down soon. And I've got the quintet due in ten minutes. You'll enjoy that.'

The older woman turned her uncomprehending gaze on Beryl.

'Come on, Mum. I've got to get ready in here for the quintet. I'm your daughter, Beryl, Mum,' she added, forestalling the inevitable question.

Her mother allowed herself to be led out of the kitchen door just as Oscar Silvero came down the stairs.

'She was trying to cook frozen peas in the sink,' said Beryl.

Oscar took her mother's arm from Beryl. "My funny Valentine," he sang softly, "sweet comic Valentine." Beryl's mother smiled, for a moment a young girl, and they went into the sitting room. Beryl followed and stood in the doorway.

'I'll close the door so the quintet won't disturb you too much. When we have a break, I'll bring you hot drinks. Will you be all right?'

Oscar looked at her. He was so different from when she encountered him in the Royal Hotel a year ago. Not physically, but now there was a peacefulness about him, a sense of coming home, of meaning something. She hadn't really thought what she was doing when she invited him to move in as a lodger, to settle down. He took so readily to Mum, and she responded so well to his singing. They were of an age, after all. He seemed to have inexhaustible patience and tolerance with her, crooning old songs when she became upset or confused, and she calmed and smiled, sometimes joined in. That was of enormous value to Beryl. She could go out without making irksome arrangements or worrying. At least about Mum. She had to keep an eye on Oscar though. He was only a few drinks away from the slippery slope to maudlin depression again. She knew that. The cupboard in which she had a few bottles was firmly locked. He was well behaved and seemed happy ensconced in the spare room. He did not seem to experience that strange tingle she used to feel when she entered that room. Either she imagined the feeling, or she was sensitive to things he wasn't. She didn't like that thought. Her view of herself was of a forthright, practical woman who got things done, not some fey psychic. Certainly not.

'Don't you worry, Beryl,' Oscar said. 'Dorothy and me, we'll be right as tuppence, won't we, Dotty?' And Dotty beamed up at him, and then looked daggers at Beryl. Beryl was used to that, but it still hurt. She picked up her flute and stand and music case and went back to the kitchen, closing the sitting room door behind her.

She collapsed the table and moved it against the wall, arranged five chairs in an arc, and sank down on one of them. There were aromas lingering from lunch, but they weren't too bad, not that anyone would notice like as not.

The quintet were all members of the Chervil Symphony Orchestra. Beryl considered that they were, like her, all pretty competent but not brilliant. It was just a bit of fun. They had no intention or desire to perform in public. But then, who knew?

Beryl liked to think that the quintet was all her idea, but she suspected it was actually Mel's. Mel played the French horn, and was young and dynamic and a bit of a whirlwind. Perhaps Beryl sowed the seed of the idea of a quintet once in the pub after a CSO rehearsal, and Mel nurtured it to germination and flowering.

The doorbell rang, and before long three of the others were there. They assembled their instruments, and the air became cacophonous from limberings up – raucous seagull noises from Evelyn's oboe reed, Mel burbling away impressively with the opening flourish from *Till Eulenspiegel*. Beryl trying out her top D, for which she had only recently discovered the fingering and wanted to show off, not that anyone reacted other than wincing at the piercing noise. Only Fred was silent, fiddling endlessly with his clarinet reed. Beryl had always felt the flute was a pukka instrument, not depending on fallible things like reeds, just the skill of the player. On the other hand, that meant if you messed up, you could only blame yourself.

'Where's Stan?' demanded Fred.

'Where indeed,' replied Beryl.

As if on cue, the bell rang once more, and there he was, Stanislav Bun, lumbering his bassoon case, gushing apologies. 'I am sorry, so very sorry for my tardiness,' he said. 'It is stupid thing. My wife, in the middle of the roasted English lamb, she says I am ruining her career, it is heartless of me, I am a veritable *dzik*, a wild boar. They are pest in Poland,' he explained.

'My wife,' he went on, 'she is hostess at Pink Pyjama club. What am I supposed to have done that is so evil? I have brought bread into the house. To be sure I have. I am baker. Do I not bring bread home? Why is this bad? I do not require her to eat the bread. But she, she say it is temptation. She cannot resist. Well, I say, it is very good bread. Do you want me to bake bad bread?

'We have the row. The blazing row. And so I am late. Is it my fault, I ask you? The roast lamb, he is sawdust in my mouth,' he finished sadly.

'Never mind all that,' said Beryl. 'The others only beat you by a few minutes. What have you managed to get hold of, Mel?'

Mel dug in her bag and produced some music. 'The Danzi we tried last time, and I've splurged out on Malcolm Arnold's *Sea Shanties*. They only cost a tenner.'

'We must split the cost, dear,' said Evelyn, the oboist.

Mel waved a hand. 'No, no, it's okay. I like the idea of building up a library and they're only a tenner as I said.'

Stanislav Bun looked askance. 'Who is this Malcolm Arnold?'

'English.'

'Oh, English. Well.' It was a dismissive "well".

'They're hilarious,' said Mel.

Stan frowned. 'If you say so… But the English music, well…'

'Oh really now…' started Evelyn.

'Come along,' said Beryl. 'No arguments. Thank you, Mel. Let's get going.'

And going they got. The Danzi trundled along respectably. It was not difficult; they had looked at it last time, they were confident.

When they stopped for a break, Beryl made tea. The others chatted away, Evelyn stalwartly defending all British composers (she did not like to be provincial by restricting herself to English ones, she said), Stan banging on about Chopin, and did they realise that Otto Klemperer was born in Poland?

As she waited for the kettle to boil, Beryl looked at them and thought what a disparate bunch they were. Mel, half anyone else's age, probably young enough to be Evelyn's grand-daughter. Evelyn, the picture of a precise English spinster. But she played a mean oboe. It must be those pursed lips of disapproval. And Fred, who used to play in a cruise ship's band. Clarinet and saxophones and goodness knows what else. He was an old stager, nothing fazed him, apart from his reeds which seemed eternally to be found wanting and out to get him. And Stanislav Bun; while he could be a bit fiery, he was very serious about bassooning. Baking too. And Poland, which was the cradle of everything revolutionary in the arts, if he was to be believed.

Beryl took a small tray through to the sitting room, where she found her mother and Oscar both fast asleep, the television spooling on unwatched. Victoria, the cat, was stretched out in front of the fire. At least the quintet playing hadn't disturbed any of them. She gently shook Oscar and silently indicated the tray. A sleeping Mum, like sleeping dogs, was someone to let lie, in her opinion. After a moment of bewilderment, Oscar understood what she meant, and made a face like a repentant school-boy at his having nodded off. Victoria woke as well and yawned enormously. Somewhere in her mind, Beryl thought she heard a voice: '*You see how tolerant I am. Sleeping while your lot wail out there. Am I magnanimous or what?*' Victoria looked at Beryl. It was a look of great meaning. Cat to human. A shiver coruscated down Beryl's spine and she went back to the kitchen.

Back in there, they seemed to be arguing over whether a saxophone was a "serious" instrument or not. Silly. Beryl sat down with her tea and a rich tea biscuit and listened. Given their ages, it seemed curious to her that the one who managed to dampen the argument so that it didn't get out of hand and acrimonious was young Mel. She was an extraordinary girl. She told them that while at school she played flugelhorn and then tenor horn in the local silver band where she was brought up.

'Flugelhorn. Vaughan Williams used one in his ninth symphony, didn't he?' said Evelyn, clearly intending to reassure Mel that it was a "serious" instrument, unlike the saxophone.

'Yes,' said Mel, 'absolutely, and three saxes as well. Instruments are, like, instruments, if you ask me. It's what you play on them that matters, yeah?'

And so they progressed to Malcolm Arnold's *Sea Shanties*, which proved trickier than they expected. Despite his disparagement of English composers, Stan attacked them with cheerful gusto. It was good. Beryl saw them out afterwards with that uplifting glow that the mental and social tussle of playing with others gave you. All except Mel, who stayed on a bit at Beryl's request.

'I want to ask your opinion, Mel dear, if you can spare a moment,' Beryl said. 'Would you like a glass of wine? I know it's a bit early...'

'Better hadn't. Driving. But don't let me stop you. What's up, B?'

Beryl went to a secret place in the kitchen of which Oscar knew nothing, and retrieved a bottle, from which she poured herself a good glass of red cheer. 'I have to hide it so that Oscar... He's... he has a little weakness. Hence my having a glass when he's out of sight. Now Mel, you know I work part-time at the Motley Brew?'

'The café in Three Geese Alley or something? Of course I do.'

'Well, Mary Bellamy... Do you know Mary? The Motley Brew is her business.'

'No. I've only ever been there when you're there.'

'Well, she's getting on and finds it's becoming too much, so she's asked if I'll take over as manager.'

'Do you mean, like, run it full-time? Buy the Motley Brew?'

'Yes... no... at least maybe in time. That is, she wants me to run it, and maybe I could buy the business later on. But not the premises, they're rented. I'm not sure who the landlord is. Anyway, now that Oscar is looking after Mum, there's no reason why I can't take on the café full-time. Mary would be happy to come in occasionally if I needed her, and I could get others to help out. I just wanted to see what you thought, Mel, because... because... Well, you're a level-headed young woman and might see drawbacks I don't...'

'And because you're, like, ancient and doddery? Oh come on, B, you could do it standing on your head. Hey, this isn't a smart way to try to get me to take up waitressing, is it?'

'Oh, Mel, no. You've got your life, writing and so on. But on the other hand, if you wanted to, part-time...'

Mel raised her hands. 'No. I'm going all out on this writing thing at the moment. Maybe later, like when I've published a dozen or so books...'

Beryl laughed. 'You'll be off doing book signings and appearing at Literary Festivals and that sort of thing. So you reckon I should go for managing the Brew, then?'

'Why not? But what do I know? What if your mother gets worse?'

Beryl paused. 'Yes… yes, quite. Yes, that could be a problem. She's pretty stable at the moment. But I know things aren't going to get better. And Oscar might get fed up and wander off. I don't know. I suppose the next thing will be a care home. I know that. It'll come. I just don't like to face up to it. But having said that, I have actually done a bit of research, finding out which places are well regarded and that sort of thing. I suppose I ought to try getting Mum to visit some to see how she reacts. It would be nice if she could be part of choosing. I'll talk to Oscar and see if we can make it some sort of game, so Mum doesn't think we're trying to get rid of her. And she's managing fine here at the moment. With Oscar's help. Oh, that man is a…'

The door opened and there was that man, as large as life. His eyes, like a dog sighting a rabbit, immediately zeroed in on the wine glass. An embarrassing pause. Then he looked away, trying to look virtuous, and said, 'Have you finished playing, Beryl? I want to pop out for… for a few things.'

'It's all right, Oscar. I'll look after Mum. I'm not going anywhere. Will you be back in time for supper? Half seven?'

'Oh. Yes, yes, I'm only… I'll be off then. Dotty's still sleeping at the moment.'

Oscar went out of the kitchen, leaving the door open.

Mel leaned over confidentially, and said, 'Is he going…?'

'I don't know,' whispered Beryl, 'I don't know. Leopards don't change their spots. But what can I do? He's not my responsibility, even if he lives here and looks after Mum. If he… But I've no evidence. Nothing I can pin down. He might have taken up betting?' she added, hopefully.

'Would that be better?'

'Well, he's got plenty of money. If he wants to throw it away... Better than drinking yourself into an early grave.'

'How old is he?'

'I don't know exactly. Early seventies, I think. Not that much younger than Mum.' They heard the front door bang shut. 'Do you know what he told me the other day?'

'No,' said Mel, agog.

'His real name isn't Oscar Silvero, it's Bill Bunion.'

'Bunion?'

They both dissolved in giggles.

'You know he sings to Mum and she's like a little lamb? The other day I suggested to him he joined the Chervil Choral. It's a bit different from what he's used to, but he would meet lots of people. Friends. It might help him. He says that as a child, he was in some cathedral choir or something, a chorister. There's no better training for a singer. And he hoped at one time to be a professional baritone. A solo career. But it's a difficult business, and he started doing spots in a club to make ends meet, and then... then it all took over, and lo and behold, the creation of Oscar Silvero, crooner. So anyway, he would be perfectly competent in the Choral Soc. Perhaps he could do a few solo spots with the choir, get himself known as a classical soloist.'

Mel laughed again. 'Beryl, you're like a Samaritan, you are. Digging people out of the gutter and making upright citizens out of them. You can call the café the Motley Brew and Rehab Café. You'd make a pile, I reckon. What did Oscar say to your idea?'

'He smiled and said nothing. But his eyes, his eyes, I could see them flitting about. I think I've planted an idea in his head. Oh, for God's sake, Mel, he's not a bad man, he's brought lots of pleasure, he deserves friendship and a place in society in his old age. If I can help a bit... Anyway, for now, he's a godsend as far as Mum's concerned, so it cuts both ways. Just keep him from the demon drink...'

Later on, after she had cooked supper and Oscar had returned – she was not sure if she could detect alcohol on his breath or not –

and they had eaten and fed Mum and put her to bed and Oscar too had retired, she assembled a gin and tonic and sank down in the living room in front of the fire and sprawling cat.

Thank God she had the flute and the orchestra. It kept her sane. This term it was a Scandinavian programme – Grieg and Sibelius. An upbeat selection. She sighed. From the hearthrug, Victoria, stretched out and partially upside-down, blinked lazily at her. Again she felt that shiver and imagined she heard a voice in her mind: '*And you have me. Count your blessings. And before you go all introspective and sorry for yourself, write it down in that bloody journal thing. Just don't dump it all on me.*' Beryl shook her head and obediently got Hattie out of the drinks cupboard. She locked it in there. She didn't want Oscar reading it.

Dear Hattie,

How are things, Beryl?

Yes, well... I realise I am wrong about one thing. Mel asks me how I am. She alone. Not out loud, not explicitly she doesn't, but she cares, at least a bit. I feel I can talk to her. And so young! So fair dos.

But OS. God he makes me angry. Why doesn't he just say he's off for a drink? It's the pretending he isn't that gets to me. I can try and make sure he doesn't in the house, but outside... Oh, I know, people will say I can't have everything: someone to help care for Mum and who's also a paragon of virtue. I knew what he was when I suggested it to him. And he does help. A lot. He does.

There are times I just want to scream.

But positive things. Hattie, I'm resolved. I'm going to take over as Manager of the Motley Brew. I will, I will. It's what I need. I'll tell Mary Bellamy tomorrow.

*By the way, I think Victoria can walk through
walls. I'm sure she wasn't in the sitting room before
the practice, and yet there she was when I took
drinks through. Is she supernatural? Spooky, as Dame
Edna would say.*

Hey-ho.

Good-night Hattie, sleep tight.

Signed: Beryl, Manager of the Motley Brew

She returned Hattie to the drinks cupboard, and locked it up and checked that all was well downstairs before going to bed. Victoria was not in evidence now. The door of the room was shut. How? But Beryl had no intention of worrying. It was not unlikely the cat had gone upstairs and walked through the closed door into Oscar's room and was now snoring away in unison with the great entertainer. Bill Bunion, indeed!

3 *The Chervil Choral Society*

It was some six months later still, in the bar of the Hippocampus, that sprawling watering hole on the banks of the river Cher, just downstream from Chervil Castle. It was a favoured resort of some of the Chervil Choral Society after rehearsals. And a few of the Chervil Symphony Orchestra as well for that matter, also on Thursdays, though neither group was particularly aware of the other. Different camps.

This Thursday, the group of choristers was small and, as usual, they were grumbling. With them was Arthur Davison, perched on a seat on the periphery with a small glass of dry sherry; with them, yes, but not really part of them. It was a source of puzzlement to him. He came to the pub in order to make an effort to appear sociable, but rarely was his presence acknowledged. In truth, the others talked so much, he would have had a job to be heard if he tried to join in more. Arthur was a long-time member of the bass department in the choir, known, if known he was, for having a discrete voice. Small but accurate, he liked to think.

Sometimes Arthur wondered if he had sung with the choir so long he had become part of the furniture, a fixture or fitting. Now, that was a question to ponder: if you were to be an item of furniture, an interior design feature, what would you choose to be? He decided he rather liked the prospect of being a brass curtain rail. You didn't often find them in choirs. It would be distinctive.

The others were getting critical. It always happened, and as usual, Bernard Pontdexter was their prime target. Bernard was the conductor of the CCS, the supremo, the maestro, the jumped-up second-rate musician in the view of one or two of them. Moira, one of the sopranos, forthright and opinionated, in Arthur's view, was asking rhetorically why his downbeats at the beginning of bars were upbeats, and why when he got excited all his beats were upbeats, so you had no way of knowing what beat of the bar you were on if you should happen to get a little bit lost. 'Listen to the other parts,' said Diana drily. Arthur had decided long ago that Diana couldn't stand Moira, for what it was worth. They both still came to the pub.

'I sang under this Russian conductor once,' Mike, another bass, said, 'and he sort of waved his arm around in a circle, and at a certain point the Russians – he was here with a Russian octet, including a sub-bass – my God, you could feel the floor shake when he turned it on – and anyway, they all came in at a certain point in the circle, so we just followed them a split second later. But I never worked out which bit of the circle was the real downbeat.'

Moira said she thought Bernard was just lazy and complacent and nobody had the guts to tell him.

'And,' said Fergus, 'it's high time he re-auditioned everybody. I mean, there's dead wood. I don't want to name names, but Charles, I mean, always turning up late because he pooh-poohs warm-ups…'

'Which Bernard often forgets,' interrupted Moira. 'If they're important, do them every time. If not…'

'I do my own in the car on my way to rehearsals,' said Diana. 'Any good singer would.'

'When you condescend to turn up, Diana. Look…'

'Moira, dear, perhaps some people need more rehearsal than others. Besides…'

Fergus had been trying to get back in. 'Look at… I mean, I've got to say it, look at old Walter. I mean, you don't have to stand next to him. He barely knows what day of the week it is, let alone which piece he's supposed to be singing. I know he doesn't make much noise, but, I mean, he's wobbly and it sort of clouds up the tenor line. An audition…'

'He's Rupert's uncle' said Moira. 'Rupert is chair of the choir, if you hadn't noticed. Rupert's got Bernard like putty in his hand.'

'Oh, I don't know...'

Arthur Davison lost interest. They could dissect Bernard Pontdexter as much as they liked. But they should remember that he had brought the choir to pretty decent concert standard. And poor old Walter. Walter was a decent chap, and we all got old. You couldn't just throw people out with the rubbish when they got on a bit. 'Would they be able to find anyone better than Bernard?' he asked himself as he finished his sherry and left the Hippocampus, an exit unremarked by the others.

Conductors did not lurk round every corner, he observed to himself as he walked. Bernard could be irascible, certainly, but he had a lot to contend with, what with Rupert and Charles, not to mention the women, some of whom could be equally argumentative, look at Moira. So, 'Let him be,' said Arthur Davison to the ducks out for a last swim along the River Cher before turning in.

From the pub, Arthur liked to take the path along by the river on a clear evening if the moon was up. It felt safe enough from muggers and the like. It was longer than simply going along Southgate, but there were the ducks, sometimes a couple of swans, and the trees, with the wind gently soughing through the branches. It soothed him, for he had to admit choir rehearsals could be stressful. As indeed the pub could be afterwards. Maybe he shouldn't bother with the pub. After all these years, he still felt excluded.

After passing beneath the bridge taking Eastgate over the river, he continued a bit, turning left along a path that came out beside the Lyric Theatre. When did he last go to anything there? He had a vague memory of going to a pantomime. That must have been years ago. With his sister, Constance, and her family, when they visited. They kept their distance these days. Apart from Mel, his niece. She lived in Chervil for a while a couple of years back, but went off to university or college or somewhere. She was only a girl at the time of that panto visit. The show had probably been an exciting experience, reflected through the eyes of young children, but his recollection was still hazy.

On the other side of the High Street from the theatre was the Tangle, that maze of mediaeval alleys at the heart of Chervil. In its midst was the Market Square, where Arthur Davison lived in a second floor flat. The route from the High Street to the square was mercifully quite wide, short and well lit. Even though Arthur had lived there for years, he did not care to tread the alleys of the Tangle proper after dark. You could never be sure of anything in there. It defied maps and logic.

His flat was his sanctuary. The living room had a long dormer window divided into little panes overlooking the square with what was usually a sea of parked cars. There were no cars on Tuesdays and Saturdays, however. On those days, the square boasted a bustle of stalls selling vegetables and shoes and wonder-mops and so on. At present, the place was dark, of course, it being night-time, with spasmodic bright puddles from street lights splattered through the space. A mere handful of cars were still there.

Arthur filled the kettle. He wandered back into the living room and stood by his table looking down at work in progress. He was engaged on an intricate pen and ink drawing of the square outside on one of those market days. His Grand Market Square-scape. A new venture for him. He was trying to be literal, to recreate the actual. Usually he drew imaginary craggy landscapes, castles with spiky turrets, odd contorted trees, and in among them, little chubby dragons, cute, wide-eyed, appealing. And other creatures, unicorns, garden gnomes, gryphons. A fairy-tale illusionary world. Doodles, really. But this time, inspired by the wonderful over-arching view he had from his window, he was doing something different: a panorama of a busy and quaint bit of the world from the point of view of a benevolent god in a second floor flat looking down on his creation. Or, if you had that sort of mind, the view of a nosey voyeur.

At least, he was trying to be realistic in his Grand Square-scape. But the perspective was distorted. Although Arthur was well skilled in accuracy, a perverse streak ran deep in his veins. His version of the scene was dominated by the clock tower, too large and slightly awry. It was as though it was quivering, like a rocket about to launch into space. The buildings around the square curved outwards as though they didn't like each other very much. The market stalls bustled and clustered, seemingly on the move, their produce and goods spilling impossibly over their margins. He couldn't help but create worlds of strangeness and magic.

Today, he looked out of the window. Naturally, what he saw today was different. It was currently neither market day nor daytime. There was, however enough light in the sky to silhouette the clock tower. On top, rising above its spurious crenellations, was a shape, hunkering. Arthur shuddered. There, in that place in his drawing, he had tentatively inserted a vulture, a hunched-looking undertaker of a bird. In pencil. It wasn't a serious addition, just a tentative whimsy. Now it appeared evil. Almost violently, he rubbed it out.

Outside, from the dark cut-out of the tower, the shape unfurled wings and flapped clumsily away.

As he prepared his usual nightcap of a cup of lemon and ginger infusion, Arthur's thoughts turned to Blind Bella, prophetess, fixture of the Market Square when she felt like being there. He dug out his spiral-bound notebook containing her words of wisdom, few and enigmatic as they were. And suddenly the one of them seemed to have meaning. "Walls wonky, nightmares fly" he had written. What were the buildings in his Grand Square-scape if not wonky? What was a vulture if not the stuff of nightmares? He shivered. His nightly infusion of lemon and ginger was meant to induce a calm and refreshing night's sleep.

On this night, it failed.

About three o'clock, he rose and took his seat at the drawing in front of the dark window. Outside, the clock tower's top looked reassuringly normal as far as he could tell. No more vultures. No more. He took up his pencil and sketched in an antidote. A small rabbit among the market stalls. Cuddly, friendly, a Flopsy Bunny of a rabbit, the stuff of warm, homely dreams, not of nightmares. Then he drew another, peeking round a vegetable stall. Rabbits needed something to eat, after all. Be kind to your creations and maybe they would let you sleep.

He drew breath, squinted at the drawing, picked up his pen and inked them in. No going back now, no rubbing out. The rabbits were here to stay. And then he drew something else, sitting on a bollard swinging its legs. It was not man; too small. It was not dwarf, nor was it elf. It was – how would he describe it? Arthur tilted his head to one side, his tongue protruding forgotten a little from his mouth. Whatever the creature was, it was humanoid and a bit cheeky. He never meant to draw it. It seemed to draw itself, and it was in ink. He couldn't rub it out. Well, well. Perhaps he should christen it. He decided it was called a Dwelf. It felt better with a name. He was pleased with it, his newest and most unexpected creation.

His sleep after that was untroubled. Next thing, the radio alarm rudely interrupted and it was morning. He dressed and surveyed his masterpiece. The rabbits gazed back cheekily. The Dwelf looked cheerfully unconcerned. Arthur smiled at them, and made himself breakfast.

As he passed through the Market Square on his way to the office, the ancient space felt comfortable, an area immune to the coming and going of cars and market stalls and parades and all the other things people could throw at it. It simply was. Over it, the clock tower was a benevolent dictator, or better, a father, watching over his children and making sure they knew what time it was. Or a mother hen, looking after her brood of small appealing rabbits. With momentary alarm he looked about, but thank heavens, no rabbits were in sight, nor little chaps sitting on bollards. Why should there be? They were in his drawing, they were his little whim, his fancy. They had no real existence. Did they?

It was with blithe step that he finished his commute in the bland anonymity of the upper room of Buffalo Building Supplies, where he was accountant. Although he did not know a gromit from a soffit board, accounts were accounts, and he did know about them. They were a safe world, one where rules applied, procedures must be followed. There was no room for improvisation. So he was content, if bored, and left his imagination to take wing at home and in the world of music. Accountants would always be needed, if only because most people were bored stiff by financial affairs and tended to go brain-dead when they were mentioned. So Arthur was safe and employable. If he looked like a fastidious, fussy little man, that was because he was when at work. He did not draw little rabbits on his notepad. He did not hum the bass line of *My Heart is Inditing*, one of the pieces the Chervil Choral Society was currently rehearsing. Oh no. He practised that *pianissimo* along with a CD at home.

It was going to be a very non-Christmassy concert this year. Maestro Pontdexter had announced that they would all benefit from a moratorium on abiding shepherds, snowy stables, little donkeys, not to mention red-nosed reindeers and sleigh-bells. Next year, he said, they would embrace them with renewed gusto. So for some perverse reason, this year he had chosen a Coronation theme. In addition to a couple of Handel's anthems for George II, they were singing Purcell's *My Heart is Inditing* for James II, and other Coronation anthems by Blow, Clarke and Croft. Undiluted joy, plus regal pomp and circumstance. *Pity the audience,* thought Arthur Davison. *Might they not welcome a touch of gloom? Would they have to stand respectfully throughout?*

Oh dear, he realised, he was becoming as grumpy as the other members of the choir back in the pub. He smiled to himself in his corner of the office. His own little world. It was not peaceful, for the active personnel of Buffalo Building Supplies seemed to like to wear hefty boots with steel toe-caps, even if only working at the sales desk downstairs or on paper-work in the office, and the noise of them tramping up and down stairs was thunderous. But there he was. He had to make a living somehow, and Mr D was content.

Perhaps he should not have been. If he had had a crystal ball...

4 The Chervil Symphony Orchestra

It was a week later. The Chervil Symphony Orchestra were at rehearsal. Their conductor was Clifford Hope-Evans, head of music at Chervil College.

They were progressing nicely through Morning from *Peer Gynt* when Clifford stopped them. 'What's that banging?' he demanded. 'There're no timps here.' He glared at Sid, the timpanist, who at that moment was doing a crossword and clearly not hitting anything.

Beryl heard the banging as coming from a different direction anyway. She looked down the line of woodwind and as the banging resumed, thought she could see Stanislav Bun's music-stand shaking to and fro. There seemed to be a little shower of white dust coming from it, and then the music fell off.

'Stop,' cried Stan, 'stop it.'

'What are you doing?' said Clifford.

Stan raised an arm in the air. 'Nothing, nothing. Sorry, sorry. It is… Oh, please to excuse me.' He stood up and rushed out of the room, clutching his bassoon to him like a fragile baby. All eyes followed him.

As the door swung to, Clifford seized the moment before they all started talking. 'Okay, okay, take no notice, folks. Let's take it from the top again. No, from letter A. And…' He brought his pencil down and off they went, Sid struggling to grab a stick to play one note before his thirty-odd bars rest. With Clifford at least, a downbeat was a downbeat, no mistaking it. And you didn't monkey about with him. He had a well-honed line in sarcasm that could whittle the stoutest heart down to a stub in a moment. But in the beating line, he was a model of clarity.

They were only a few bars into letter A when Stan returned. He resumed his seat and picked up the place with no trouble. Clifford did not refer to this odd episode again during the rest of the rehearsal. Beryl, though, was frantically curious, as indeed probably most of them were. What was it all about? What was the white powder? Thoughts of poltergeists and cocaine whizzed through her mind and did not help her playing.

As they packed up at the end, she approached Stan.

'No, no,' he said. 'I tell you later. Not here. In the pub. I see you there. First, I have something I must do. I go by the bakery.' And off he hurried.

Beryl and Mel repaired to the Hippocampus. Stretch their imaginations as they might, they could come up with no sensible explanation of the Stan incident.

'How's your Mum?' asked Mel to pass the time until Stan appeared.

'She went to Restawee Home for the Elderly last Monday,' said Beryl. 'Like a lamb, Oscar singing *My Funny Valentine* in the car on the way. No problem at all. He's been visiting two or three times a day since. I go in once. She seems not really to notice she's not at home. It's early days, though. But she's really quite docile on the current medication.'

'Restawee. That's gross. What sort of name is that?'

'It's heaven, dear, believe me. Such a load off my mind. And Oscar's too, probably, though he never complained. Mum was becoming impossible. It was back to nappies and that sort of thing, not to mention tantrums.'

Stanislav Bun materialised at their table. He had his bassoon case in one hand and something resembling a small stone in the other. He plonked it down on the table in front of Beryl and Mel.

'Hey, hey, Stan,' said Mel. 'What's that?'

'Wait. I tell. Is crazy. Crazy.' Stan went to the bar.

'It looks a bit like a rock cake' said Beryl. She prodded it with a finger. 'It's certainly rock hard. I can't believe Stan baked it. His bread is amazing. I use it all the time at the Motley Brew. First big improvement I've made since taking over.'

'Crazy,' said Stanislav again as he returned. He took a long draught of beer and wiped his mouth with the back of his hand. 'Is crazy. Before orchestra, I go by the bakery because I have left my wallet there. I go in, and there is this little person. He is covered in flour and kneading a lump of dough. Pummel, pummel, pummel, he is, as if his life depend on it. Standing on chair because he is little, little. Is he a man, is he dwarf? I do not know.

'"Oh," he says, when he see me, "You'll regret it." "Regret what?" I say. "Threatening me," he say. I say I am not threatening him. He say I am about to. Me, I am late for rehearsal, I have no time for arguing. I pick up my wallet. The little chap leap on the table and grab hold of it too. "What you do with that?" he yell at me. I tell him it is mine and I need it for buying beer after rehearsal. He say, "Can you prove it yours?" I show him my driving licence and he lets go.

'"What you doing here?" I ask. He say he is making bread, like I am idiot, and he say because I am not there, why do I mind? I am late; I must go. I say at ten o'clock I return and he must not be there and the bakery must be clean and spotless. And I go to rehearsal.' Stan took another swig from his glass.

'What about the banging and that?' asked Mel.

'I come to that,' said Stan. 'Do not hurry me. In rehearsal, the little person appears, covered in flour – my flour – and he bang my music stand with wooden spoon and shout "How do you light oven?" in his high high voice. I take him outside and he say he can't light oven. I say why are you in my bakery. He say it is something called St Botolph's Binge tonight and he must make buns and he can't light oven.

'I ask him is this a thing that only happen once, or will it happen again and again. He say it is the one time, he is going to stick to things like foxglove crisps or hot newts or stewed rat tails next time. What is "newt"?'

Mel said, 'Never mind that. Get on with it, Stan.'

'Me,' said Stan, 'we Buns have saying, "Don't drop the egg". We try to make all nice and calm, no fighting. I tell him how to light oven. He goes away, I come back to rehearsal.

'Then,' he went on, wagging a finger in the air, 'then I go in bakery after rehearsal. It is quiet, it is dark, it is clean. On the table is this.' He pointed to the rock cake, if that was what it was. 'He leaves it for me, I think. I think I do not want it. I think I will break teeth.'

There was silence a moment. Beryl said, 'I didn't see any little man.'

'Nor me, Stan,' said Mel.

Stan looked at them in turn. He held his hands up as if they were about to attack him. 'Okay, okay,' he said. 'Believe me. There was little chap. I do not know if he is man or what, but he is there. But then,' he added, 'we Buns, we Slavs, we are, how do you say it, we are sensitive. We see what others cannot. Ghosts, goblins… You have heard of Baba Yaga? Chernobog? Kikimora?'

Beryl and Mel shook their heads.

'Rum baba?' tried Beryl.

'Chernobyl?' suggested Mel.

'No, no, no. There you are,' said Stan. 'You see? I am sensitive. You are not. Is not your fault.'

Beryl had an idea. 'Stan, tell me. Have you ever heard a cat speak?' Immediately she regretted opening her mouth. It sounded like she was going gaga. But Stan was immediately interested.

'Perhaps I am wrong about you, Beryl.' He raised a lecturing finger and wagged it. 'If a cat talks, listen to it. That is what I say. That is all. Listen.'

Mel snorted. 'Are you two bonkers or what? Perhaps you'd both be better off at Restawee.'

There was a pause. 'That's not funny, Mel dear,' said Beryl.

'Sorry, B. Forget I said it.'

'What is Restawee,' asked Stanislav.

'Oh nothing, nothing, Stan,' said Mel. 'Let's change the subject, yeah? Do you know what we're doing in the Orchestra next year?'

'I do,' said Stan. '*The Creation* by Mr Joseph Haydn. Is with the Choral Singers, so Evelyn says. Evelyn is on committee. She knows these things.'

'You mean the Choral Society?" said Mel.

Beryl switched off. She was smarting inside from Mel's silly joke about Restawee. Over-sensitive? Perhaps she *was* going bonkers. It was time she forged new friendships. Perhaps a special friendship. After all, what was stopping her? But who did she meet in her life? It would be tricky chatting up a customer at the Motley Brew. Not ethical. Well, not that exactly, but – oh, for heaven's sake, she didn't know how to. No. Better to have a shared interest, perhaps. Was there anyone in the orchestra? That tuba player with the splendid moustache, for example, who tended to feature in her dreams rather often. How could she, how did they put it, effect an introduction? She should stop dithering and make a move. But how? What?

Her trouble, she realised was that exactly the time she should have been honing her dating technique was long long ago in student days at Teachers' Training College, and instead, psychology tutor Jim Carson – the Selfish Shit – had seduced, or possibly raped her (as they might say these days. Had she been willing? It was so long ago), precipitating the events that resulted in marriage and the birth of ungrateful and luckless son Algy. She'd never had a chance. And she'd never finished her training. What a waste. But now, proprietress of the Motley Brew, she was somebody. And she needed someone to share that with her. With or without moustache.

Dear Hattie, she wrote back at home.

How are things, Beryl?

Mel asked if Stan and me were bonkers. Stan is, no doubt about that. Lovely bonkers. But me? Am I? I think I'm perfectly normal, but maybe everyone thinks they are and it's other people who are mad. But I look at other people and my own life, and I reckon I've been put upon more than my fair share. Bringing up Algy, which was a thankless task, then Dad's decline (OK, I didn't have to look after him directly much, but he was a great worry), then the Selfish Shit, then Mum, and now Oscar. Perhaps Oscar will see he should move out and get a place of his own. I can't very well throw him out. "Now Mum's safely in a home, you've served your purpose. Now kindly bugger off."

Anyway, that's enough for one lifetime, and now I want something for ME! Oh, all right Hattie, I admit I've got the Brew, and I'm first flute in the CSO, and those are big plusses. But I want more. Let's face it, Hats, I want a soul-mate. Not anyone. The right one. One to make me feel good and important and worthy. Tuba and moustache optional. But I don't know how.

Enough of whimpering. I'm good old capable Beryl. I can cope. I always have. There must be a way, and I'll find it.

Good night, dear Hattie. Sleep tight.

5 Arthur Illustrator

About a month later, Arthur Davison was sitting at his window with a cup of tea, drawing a little cute dragon sitting on top of the clock tower. Maybe he had forgotten about the vulture he pencilled in a while back, maybe he was exorcising it. He shaded the dragon with cross-hatching to give its round stomach protuberance, and added a little shadow.

He looked out of the window down onto the Market Square. There was no dragon sitting on the clock tower, not in reality. Only in Arthur's meticulous wobbly drawing and in his imagination. Now too he had added other chubby dragons serving fruit and veg at a stall, drinking tea and eating crumpets outside the Market Cafe, and even one on its way into the gents at the bottom of the clock tower. They were in addition to all the rabbits dotted around the square, of course, who seemed to have proliferated in his drawing. That was the way of rabbits.

None of these creatures featured in the view when he looked out of his window. Nor did the market stalls, but that was because Tuesdays and Saturdays were market days, and today was a Sunday.

Mr Davison sighed. He was, in truth, a little bored. It was not that he hankered after excitement. Just a little stimulus.

As if in response to his thoughts, the doorbell buzzed. He went to the intercom. 'Uncle Arthur, it's me. Mel. Can I come up?' said the speaker.

Momentarily he couldn't fathom it. Then, of course, with a shock he realised it was his niece. Melisuavia, daughter of his tyrannical sister Constance. Mel used to live in Chervil, he never knew why, but had gone away to college or something.

'Come up,' he said, and pressed the button to unlock the street door two floors below.

He opened the door to the stairs and waited for her to climb up. She burst upon him with the vigour of youth, reached up, flung her arms round his neck and kissed him on the cheek. It was disarming and charming. It was Mel all right.

'I'm back, Uncle Arthur,' she said. 'Are you pleased to see me? I've finished my Master's, and I came back to Chervil oh, about a year ago.'

'Master's?'

'My Master's degree. I'm an MA now. Aren't you impressed?'

'Well, I never.' Arthur Davison still considered her a little girl, an impression helped by her elfin stature and boyish haircut. 'Does that mean I have to call you Doctor?'

'No, don't be silly. That's a PhD. So, an MA means, well, it doesn't mean anything very much. It just looks impressive on your CV. But that doesn't matter because I've decided to become a writer. Justin's earning pots so I can take the time. It's cool.'

Mr Davison was confused. She went so fast. What had writing to do with it? Who was this Justin? He began with, 'Your MA, your Master's…'

'Semiotics,' she said. 'But look Uncle, I'm sorry I haven't been in touch for so long, only now I want to drag you out for coffee. You'll grow roots rotting away here in your garret. We can catch up and that, and I've got something to ask you.'

'I'm not rotting. Oh dear, there's a lot of Constance in you.'

'Leave Mummy out of it, Uncle,' cried Mel. 'Look what she's achieved.'

And he, Arthur, had got nowhere and achieved nothing. Was that the implication? Sister Constance was a force to be reckoned with. She always had been. Early on, he had learnt to take the line of least resistance. He did as she bid. And now Mel. He fetched his coat. Those who failed to flex with the wind, he told himself, they were the ones who snapped.

Mel led him through the contortions of Chervil's Tangle. 'So you could become famous,' she said to him as they trod with care over ancient patches of cobbles between half-timbered buildings. 'It's a matter of luck and who you know. And, like, genius,' she added, skipping out into a patch of sunlight before them.

'But,' objected her uncle, 'I don't want to be famous. And in any case, how? I'm afraid, my dear, I don't know what you're talking about.' Was that true? Arthur often found the Tangle made him doubt things, like his own name for example, or left and right. It was a confusing, unmappable place.

She stopped him outside a café, all mellow browns. The Motley Brew. 'Have you been in here?' she asked. 'You'll like it. I want you to meet Beryl. I think you'll get on.'

More mysteries. But Mel had thrown the door open and was pushing him in. 'Hi, B,' she said, going up to the cake-laden counter. 'This is my Uncle Arthur. He is going to do the pics, but he doesn't know it yet. He sings with the CCS. Give him your special.'

The woman at the counter glanced at Arthur Davison, who shrank a little from the direct female gaze, albeit from one essentially homely-looking. 'What's my special, Mel dear?' she said.

'You know.'

'No, I don't.'

'So make one up. I want Uncle to be, like, impressed.'

Arthur decided to be assertive. 'A cup of tea would do,' he said.

Mel exploded. 'Would do? Would do? Beryl doesn't do "do". Beryl does awesome, don't you, B?'

Beryl ignored her. 'What kind of tea would you like, Mel's Uncle? I've lots of kinds.' She waved a hand at rows of jars and boxes on the shelves behind her.

Suddenly Arthur felt mischievous. 'Do you have broken orange pekoe tips?' he asked. He had read the name in a book somewhere.

'Well, no,' she said. 'I do have orange pekoe, as it happens, but as far as I know it's not broken.'

So he settled for that. Mel chose hot chocolate with whipped cream on top, and they picked cake from the array – mocha éclair for her, flapjack for him.

'You're my first customers,' said Beryl. 'First on my first Sunday opening I mean. This is on the house. How did you know I would be open, Mel?'

'You told me on Wednesday.'

'Did I?'

'Yup. Between the Danzi and the Ibert.'

Mr Arthur Davison, meek and self-effacing, was finding all this a trial.

'For heaven's sake,' he said, 'what are you talking about? I feel I ought to be told since you brought me here.'

Mel laughed. 'Wind quintets,' she said. 'We, Beryl and me, are part of the Famous Five. B's flute, I'm horn of course.'

'Is that what we're called?' asked Beryl, squidging whipped cream. 'The Famous Five?'

'No,' said Mel. 'I just made it up.'

Arthur was still confused. 'You play the horn? The French horn?' How little he knew his niece.

'Sure do, Uncle. Ever since the cradle. I'm the David Pyatt of Chervil.'

'Who?' Would this ever become clear to him? 'May we sit down and suppose you start at the beginning of whatever this is all about, my dear? Then perhaps I'll understand.'

Mel looked at Beryl and raised her eyebrows in what looked like a private signal of exasperation. Uncle and niece went and sat in a cosy nook surrounded by burnt toffee panelling.

'Right, Uncle. Do you remember sending me birthday cards when I was young?'

He did. Why did he stop? He had drawn little scenes with cute animals on them. Probably he decided that she would find them embarrassing after a certain age. 'Yes,' he said cautiously.

44

'Well, I'm writing this book.'

'Yes?'

'So, it's for kids.' Mel seemed almost shy.

'Yes, for children. How old?'

'Quite little. I think. Thing is, it's, like, a bit dark.'

'Dark?' Why didn't she get on and say it?

'Well, kids might be frightened. A bit.'

'I thought children liked being frightened. All these horror films they seem to make.'

'Well...' Mel said. 'Thing is... Do you know *Struwwelpeter*?'

Uncle Arthur didn't.

'So, it's a German book of stories for kids. They're really scary. And then there's Grimm's fairy tales – they're dark, dark, dark. So I thought...'

She petered to a halt.

Uncle Arthur Davison came to her aid. 'You're wondering if I might draw some pictures...'

'Yeah. Yup. Thing is, Uncle, the animals you drew then were cute, yes, but I remember I was a little frightened of them. As though the cuteness was only... like, superficial, but underneath...'

'I see.'

'Don't be offended...'

'I'm not offended.'

'Oh, please forget it, Uncle. It was only a thought...'

Arthur did feel a little offended. He thought his little creatures were utterly innocuous. This suddenly introduced the appalling thought that perhaps his drawings unconsciously said something about him, his inner self, his soul. Was he exposing his deepest feelings by accident? It was completely ridiculous. Any such interpretation was entirely in the mind of the beholder, and anyway beholders of his drawings were very few and far between. And did he care? Everybody had hidden angsts and troubles; why would anyone suppose he didn't? Not that he knew what they were. He didn't dwell upon such things. Furthermore, if his drawings were to appear in a book, he could use a pseudonym and then nobody would know. But was his true being really somehow revealed in cute dragons and lovable bunnies?

While all this ran through his mind, Mel sat there gazing at her éclair with a look of anguish. She looked up. 'Maybe I'm reading things into my memories, Uncle. So, the thing is, I've invented these creatures that are outwardly sweet and nice, but are mischievous and eventually evil underneath. They look like little fluffy ducklings, but they've got arms. They're called Gnoxies.'

'Gnoxies.'

'Yes.' There was a pause. 'It's a sort of mixture of gnome and pixie, you see…'

'Yes, of course. Ducklings with arms, you say? I wonder…'

He found a pen in his jacket pocket and drew on a paper napkin. And there, in a few lines, was indeed a fluffy little duckling with arms. Arms akimbo. Its big eyes glared at the viewer. It challenged. The tiny beak looked capable of a nasty nip.

Mel was delighted. She leapt to her feet and hugged her uncle. She kissed his forehead. She cried, 'B, come and look at this.'

Beryl came over from a table she was wiping. 'What is it?' she asked.

'It's the first ever Gnoxie,' said Mel. 'It's wonderful, it's awesome.'

Beryl said, 'It looks like a duckling with arms.'

'Well, yeah,' said Mel. 'So, do you get any vibes from it?'

'Vibes?'

'Like is it nice or nasty? Good or bad?'

'It's a nice drawing, if that's what you mean. Very… economical. It says a lot with very little.'

'Says, like, what, would you say?'

'Oh, I don't know. Something like, "I'm a duckling with arms."'

Mel threw up her hands in despair. 'B, you're priceless. Never mind. It's a start, Uncle. Are you interested?'

Arthur thought for a bit. 'Perhaps I should read your story and then think about it.'

Mel said she would email it to him.

Arthur left the Motley Brew in a strange state of perturbation. There was a frisson of excitement, like that he'd felt as a child when anticipating his birthday, tinged with the knowledge that sister Constance would do her best to spoil it. And yet, rather like a sprinkling of pepper on strawberries, it increased the buzz. Undoubtedly that was the prospect of becoming a bona fide illustrator. But something more too. Was it something Mel's friend, Beryl, did or said? What had she said?

Enough, enough. For the moment, he'd plenty on his plate. The Grand Market Square-scape. Practising for the Choral Soc. Living. Those sort of things. And a spot of accounting at Buffalo Building Supplies to keep body and wallet together.

6 The Man with the Moustache

The next Thursday, Beryl knocked on Oscar's door three times before he replied. 'If you want breakfast, Oscar, you stir yourself now,' she cried.

'I'm ill,' came the voice.

'No, you're not. Get up and get downstairs. You can't spend your life in bed. Remember tonight...'

He would get himself up. Beryl's diagnosis was that ever since her mother had gone into Restawee Home for the Elderly – elderly being defined as those who had dementia, mental problems, or were just indeed very old – since Mum had gone there, Oscar had lost his primary reason for living. He was depressed, she reckoned. To be sure, he visited her Mum daily, but otherwise he had little to do except sit in front of the tele or stay in bed. And probably sneak out to the pub on the pretext of getting some fresh air.

But Beryl had a campaign going to get him to join the Choral Society. The company, the something to look forward to, the buzz of performance, these should revitalise him. That was the theory. So she had sown seeds, planted ideas. And today... today he had agreed he would go along and sample a rehearsal with the choir, and be auditioned afterwards. She was sure he would sail through, what with his being a chorister as a child and everything.

That was part of her plan. Another part was that he would, with the renewed self-confidence that this would bring, find himself a flat or house and move out. For now that Mum was safely in a care home, she could realistically consider herself in the market for a new relationship. But it needed Oscar out of her house. He was not a hindrance in the same way as Mum was, but he gave the wrong impression.

And there was the resolution that she sort of came to in the Hippo a month or so ago. That she should look for a new mate. What an awful way of putting it! A partner in life. A partner of *her* choice. Moustache and tuba or not. Her husband had been pretty much obliged to marry her after he impregnated her at Teachers' Training College. When he was her Psychology tutor. Nowadays he would be sacked for that, so she believed, but at that time it seemed pretty much par for the course, tutors and students. If you wanted the grades… He married her when the fruit of their liaison, Algy, was born, and so made it respectable, but his habits stayed with him. Dalliances, as they were called in earlier years, with students hither and yon. Beryl reckoned she only knew the half of it. It had its comeuppance on him in the end, though. Notably the severe stroke in the act in a student's room. After that she had five years of caring for him, now another helpless baby. Their actual son, Algy, Algernon – whose idea had it been to christen him that? – had disappeared into the world when he left school, pursuing his own profligate way, no doubt. She'd reared him to that. Now she reared her husband to death, so it transpired, five long dependent years later. And then her mother moved in, unsafe to live alone any more. A lifetime of shackles. No more.

With these thoughts in mind, she allowed herself to consider – just consider as a possibility – the eligibility of men she met. Not Oscar. Heaven forbid. He was at least twenty years older than her and, let's face it, pretty decrepit as examples of manhood go. Ravaged by time and booze. She needed somebody with a bit of zest for life. But where did she meet men? Oh yes, some came into the Motley Brew, but you couldn't go round chatting up your clientele on the off-chance that they included a soul-mate. And were unattached. And interested in some of the things Beryl was.

Well, it came down to someone in the orchestra, didn't it? Obvious. And the man with the moustache. She had got as far as finding out his name by the simple method of looking on one of the concert programmes. Gerald. Her excuse for not having made the effort even to talk to him was that opportunities were few; a tuba wasn't often needed in pieces and even if it was, the brass players only appeared for the last few rehearsals. As a result, so far, her only contact had been a wistful gaze across a crowded rehearsal room. Unreturned. She must, must, must make an approach.

And tonight she had a strategy.

If Gerald was there at the rehearsal, she'd follow him home afterwards, like in spy stories. Then, when she knew where he lived, she could contrive to bump into him accidentally one day, and that would be a start. It was a chance. He might be married, after all. Or gay.

It was silly, she thought. Actually, she had being trying to ignore it, but there was a voice in her mind seeming to say *'it is lunatic and probably disastrous and will end in tears believe me.'* If that was Victoria speaking to her – and Stan Bun had thought it not unreasonable, apparently – she did not agree. Stan had said to listen to the voice. Well, that was silly too. She could make up her own mind, thank you very much. 'I shall make up my own mind,' she said aloud. At that exact moment, Victoria came into the room and exited again straight out of the cat-flap without even acknowledging her presence. A snub. Beryl clenched her lips together in obstinate defiance. After all, one of the reasons she had joined the orchestra was to meet people. But she was woodwind, and he was brass, and on the few rehearsals the brass were there, they seemed to be outside the rest of the orchestra, and talked only to each other. Very loudly, usually. Though she thought he seemed different from the oh-so-cool, laid-back trumpets and the brazen trombones, as if his moustache set him apart. But the next concert, which as well as the *Peer Gynt* music, included *Finlandia* and *Karelia,* both of which had tuba parts. So he should be there, for the brass were deigning to join the rehearsals from today. Why did they get away with so much less rehearsal? Were they so brilliant they didn't need it? Were brass players so rare they could dictate the terms on which they would come and play? Beryl enjoyed rehearsals. Usually. Looked forward to them. The team-work, the conviviality in the pub afterwards. That was part of the point of playing in an orchestra, surely?

She heard Gerald before she saw him. From outside the hall, she could hear the mellow, resonant blop blop blop as he warmed up. Ever since she first saw him, she had wanted to ask how you can play the tuba with such a fulsome moustache. She'd wanted to find out other things about moustaches too.

So he was here, and therefore according to her strategy, tonight was the night. She was distracted in the rehearsal. It showed. Clifford, the conductor, even lost it with her. 'For God's sake, Beryl,' he burst out. 'If you can't be bothered to watch me, listen to the flaming tuba; it's defining the tempo there. You can't miss it. It's that big brass thing over there.'

She couldn't miss it, that was for sure. She actually wanted to be the tuba, cradled in those arms. She struggled through as best she could. The trouble with high flute parts was that they were terribly audible. If you were a bit out with the beat, or played a wrong note, everybody noticed.

At the end of the rehearsal, she was packed up and ready to go in double-quick time. Gerald took a while to envelop his beast in its cloth bag.

And then he went out, and she followed. And her heart sank. She had imagined him walking home down the streets, with her tracking him, skulking well back, pretending to look in shop windows if he turned around. She never thought he'd have a bicycle. Not with a bloody great tuba! It did explain why he spent the rehearsal with his right trouser leg tucked into his sock, though.

Gerald swung his tuba in its bag onto his back like a rucksack, and scooted away. But Beryl had her strategy; she wasn't going to give up now. She started walking, faster and faster, then running, making no effort at concealment. At first she was grateful that a flute was so light to carry, then the stitch started, and she wished she'd taken games lessons at school seriously, and she panted and she wheezed, and she nearly knocked people over, and she was stared at, and she felt terrible, and she thought she would lose him, and then, just as she thought she couldn't go any further...

...he glided to a halt outside the Duck and Grouse. Beryl stopped short, gasping. Gerald chained his bike conscientiously, and he and his tuba disappeared into the pub.

She stood there, breathing like a walrus, flushed, aching, and trembling. She couldn't burst in like this. He clearly wasn't going anywhere for a while. She would wait until her heartbeat was back on the scale, and then she would wander in vaguely nonchalantly and feign surprise. The first thing she would see, she thought, would be the enshrouded tuba perched on a chair.

The second thing would be she would hear a voice that said 'Hello! Beryl, isn't it? Will you join me? Can I get you a pint?'

And the third thing would be she would have a sudden conviction that today, or very soon, she would find out whether a big, bushy moustache tickled.

So, after five minutes, although she knew her cheeks were still terribly rosy, she clenched her fists, took a deep breath, and in through the door of the Duck and Grouse she went.

Gerald was at the bar, perched on a barstool, amid a group of other men on barstools with whom he was talking animatedly. He was evidently a regular.

A sense of unbelievable foolishness swept over Beryl. What did she think she was doing, chasing after a man like a lovelorn schoolgirl just because he had a moustache? As though he didn't already have his own life. She left the pub and started to walk home. Slowly. Then, as it began to drizzle, faster.

She arrived back home bedraggled and dispirited. The house was morgue-like. Oscar must still be out at the choir. Even Victoria the cat was nowhere to be seen. No welcoming mew or purr from her. Beryl unlocked the drinks cupboard and extracted the bottle of gin. The line she had drawn on it coincided with the level of the liquid. At least that was a positive note. She poured herself a large measure, drew a new line, added a splash of tonic and locked the cupboard again.

By the time Oscar returned, she had washed up the glass and was sipping a cup of tea. Oscar almost bounced in, ebullient. It was probable he had been to the pub. Beryl knew some of the choir also went to the Hippocampus after rehearsals, like she and Mel and Stan did. She'd seen them there. Noisy crowd.

'Hello,' he cried. 'I'm in.'

It was a moment before she realised what he meant. 'You passed the audition?'

'I did,' he said. 'They are a fine bunch, a fine bunch. I look forward to joining them after Christmas. I will be an asset, Bernard says. Bernard is the MD, the musical director. A fine chap, a fine chap. Not before Christmas, he says, because the balance of a choir is a fine thing, it needs to be fine-tuned, he says, and it needs the whole course of rehearsals before a concert to achieve that. Of course, I know all about this. It is the same with bands. My own band, if one dropped out – like Tiger, the bass man, he dropped dead in a concert in, where was it? Milton Keynes, I think. A real bummer, that was, which I remember saying at the time. We found a replacement but it didn't click, you know what I mean, didn't click for months. The band, that is. But he was a fine bass man. The new chap, that is. And Tiger. One in a million. Two in a million.'

'Oscar,' said Beryl with force, 'I am pleased for you. Now go to bed.'

Oscar stopped still. 'Yes. Yes, of course. Sorry. Going on a bit. But it's good news, isn't it? Things were going downhill on the performing side for, I suppose, years now before I called it a day, and it's good to know I can still cut the mustard. Yes. I'll leave you in peace, then. Some fine folk in the choir, you know. I was just saying to, what was his name? Mike or Charles or something. I was saying…'

'Oscar. Go to bed. You can tell me about it in the morning.'

'Yes, yes. Of course. Yes. I'm off. Good news, though, eh?'

'Yes, Oscar. Good night.'

'Good night, Mary.'

He went. He called her Mary. Who was Mary? Beryl realised she knew nothing much of his previous life, least of all any relationships with women. For all she knew, he was married, or had been, many times perhaps. She thought of the man with the moustache and sniffed. Then she went back to the locked cupboard, opened it, extracted the bottle of gin, and looked at it for some time. She put it back again with a sigh. It was not the answer. Instead, she removed Hattie, her journal, and found a pen.

> Dear Hattie,
>
> How are things, Beryl?
>
> Oh God, Hattie. It's sooo embarrassing. I feel about an inch high. Soiled. What was I thinking of? You don't go around chasing after men. Not at my age, not that I ever did. But I didn't know. Nobody's ever taught me. Selfish Shit Jim never gave me a chance. I don't even know I ever even liked him. But you know... No, you don't. Nobody does.
>
> And worse, if that was Victoria talking to me before the rehearsal, she told me it was a bad idea and I ignored her. I defied her. Stan said to listen. I'm sorry, Victoria. Next time I will listen. I will, I promise. Except now Vickicat seems to have run away from home. At least, she's not around now. I haven't seen her since she went out in high dudgeon just before I went to orchestra. She's usually here at bed time, campaigning for a last snack...

'It's not "campaigning". How vulgar. You only give me a treat to make yourself feel good, magnanimous, that sort of soppy human thing, and then you sleep better and don't toss and turn and disturb my sleep – which I need. That's why I accept the treats. I don't put in all those hours of shut-eye for pleasure, you know. They're necessary. But I don't expect you to understand.

Anyway, this time, I hope you've learnt your lesson. And next time, like Stan says, whoever Stan is, listen to me, okay?'

And there was Victoria heading for the hearth-rug, having materialised through a closed door as seemed to be usual. Beryl sniffed and said, 'Sorry,' in a small voice.

It's all right. She's here now. Am I going mad imagining my cat is talking to me? I don't know. But Stan seemed to think...

Anyway, is it any more mad than thinking I could chat up a tuba player I've never even spoken to? Oh God.

Well, I'm going to have that second G&T now. I am. I am going to treat myself. So there, World. And Cat. And Tuba Man. Put that in your pipes and smoke it.

Good night, dear Hattie.

She looked at Victoria, who now appeared to be totally dead to the world, curled up, paw over face. But Beryl saw an ear twitch as she closed Hattie, and heard a tiny, tiny voice in her head saying *'I should think so too.'*

When she did retire, half an hour later, after the promised second G&T and paying a forfeit to Victoria of several over-priced cat treats as an act of contrition, the cat led the way upstairs, curled up at the foot of her bed and was instantly asleep. So there things were. Beryl reckoned she'd learnt her lesson. Next time, listen.

7 The Little Man

A couple of weeks later, when he arose, Arthur Davison found he was out of bread. He liked toast for breakfast. On the other side of the Market Square was Mr Bun the Baker's, and so Arthur repaired there.

Merrylin, Stan's dreary, dreamy assistant, greeted him with a "Yeah?" In that moment, any resolutions to be kind to his waistline evaporated, and Arthur said he would like one of Mr Bun's outstanding bacon rolls, and coffee rather than tea to complete his breakfast indulgence.

While Merrylin got to work, Arthur could see that Mr Bun himself was in the further depths of the bakery waving his arms about, his baker's hat flapping. He appeared to be arguing. With whom, Arthur couldn't see. The baker's bulk obscured his view.

And then he saw Mr Bun extend a forefinger and heard him cry, 'Go. Is nothing to do with me. Out.' A small figure moved into view, started waving its arms about too, then clasped its hands to its head, turned and stalked off out of the front door of the bakery.

Mr Bun followed and slammed the door. He wheeled on Merrylin. 'This door. Is shut, okay? Keep it shut.'

Young Merry looked astonished. 'Yer what?' she said, ''Snot what you said…'

'Shut,' yelled Mr Bun and was about to return to the depths when Arthur intervened.

'That little chap,' he ventured. 'Who? What?'

Stanislav Bun stopped stock still, staring at him. 'You see him? You see the little rat? Tell me it is so.'

'The chap you just ordered out? Yes, I saw him. I've seen him before, but not in the flesh, not real…'

'You are sensitive?' demanded Stan Bun. 'You see him, like I see him? Are you Slav?'

'Slav?'

'Slav. From the heart of civilisation, from Polska, Słowacja, Transylwanii, or...?'

Arthur said sadly, 'No, I'm afraid I'm only English. Or British, if you like.'

'Is not what I like,' said Mr Bun. 'What I like is you can see little men, you are sensitive. That, my friend, is rare. Like a baker bassoonist is rare.'

'I'm sorry?'

'Is no matter. You and I, we must talk.' Stan looked pointedly at Merrylin, who was poking at some bacon on the griddle and looking gormless. 'She, the girl, she cannot see.'

'See what?' said Merrylin.

'Is no matter,' replied Stan. 'On with your work. Make the best bacon bun for my friend. Is on the house.' He turned back to Arthur Davison. 'Would you do me the honour of meeting me to talk? Is important, I think.'

'What? Talk about what?'

'This evening, is possible? At the Hippocampus public house? Do you know it? By river. This evening. You are free?'

'Well, yes, but...'

'Is good. At the Hippocampus at seven o'clock. You will be there?'

'I... Well. Yes, I can be there. But what is this about? I must tell you that that little chap, I...'

Stan Bun interrupted him with a raised hand. 'Not here, not in front of the girl. Tonight in the pub, you tell me, I tell you. We understand each other. Some things must not be shouted in the street. No. Is matter of being sensitive. Tonight, then. Enjoy your bacon bun. Is best in Chervil, believe me, and we Buns know our buns.' He turned to Merry, 'On the house, remember?' and rounded the counter back into the bakery.

Merry, despite her dreamy demeanour, turned out a crisp, butter-oozing delight of a bacon roll and a more than acceptable cup of coffee. Arthur sat on a stool at a shelf along the bakery window, and ate and sipped while gazing out on the square and wondering where the little chap the baker had been shouting at went to. From his vantage point, his attention was caught by a hopping motion. It looked like a small winsome rabbit. He could swear it turned and looked straight at him before disappearing behind a parked car. It was Friday, not a market day, so there were cars parked in the square, which consequently lacked the charm the market stalls brought. The square merely lurked, biding its time until the traders made it live. Cars were inanimate, reflected Arthur Davison. *Is that the most profound thought you can come up with?* he asked himself. It was early in the morning. He hadn't yet finished his first cup of coffee. Could one reasonably expect deep and meaningful reflections about life under such circumstances, even with the inspiration of a Bun bacon bun?

The rabbit did not appear again. His fast broken, Arthur continued onwards to Buffalo Building Supplies to his little corner in the office and a scintillating day of playing with accounts.

That evening, at five to seven, he was pushing open the door into the Hippocampus, the pub where some of the choristers of the Chervil Choral Society and he went post-rehearsal. There were quite a lot of people in the bar. It was, after all, Friday evening, and many a worker thought a drink or two before going home would set them up for the weekend. Arthur Davison was uncertain what to do. If he went to the bar he would have to order a drink, and then what? Did he loiter there like a bar-fly until Mr Bun appeared? Did he find a seat and risk Mr Bun not seeing him? The pub was large and had several rooms and odd bits and pieces. So he dithered.

There was a smack upon his shoulder. He turned to face the baker himself, though he didn't instantly recognise him without his baker's hat on. The man was entirely bald. It was not expected. However, Stanislav Bun would have had no trouble recognising

Arthur since he looked exactly the same as he had that morning. Stan bought them both drinks and they retired to a secluded alcove.

'My name is Bun,' the baker said. 'Call me Stanislav, or Stan if you like. People here think I take the name Bun from some card game for kiddies, but is family name in Poland. I am proud of name, so I call my bakery "Mr Bun the Baker's". Is sense, not so?'

'I am Arthur Davison,' said Arthur. 'I'm pleased to meet you.'

Introduction over, Stan started the business of the day. 'The little man. You see him. You are sensitive.'

'Ah yes,' said Arthur, 'the little man. It's a funny thing. You see, I'm doing a drawing of the Market Square – I live in a flat overlooking it – and, I don't know why, I drew that little man some time back, sitting on a bollard. I don't know why I drew him. Anyway, it was definitely the same little man you sent out of your shop this morning. Isn't that odd?'

Stan leaned forward. 'What is odd, my friend, it that you see him. Most people, they do not. I know this because the little man came into a rehearsal of the orchestra and made chaos and nobody saw him except for me. I am, you understand, sensitive to the little people, the spirits. I am Polish, I am Slav, that is why. We Slavs, we can see them. It is special ability. So do your Celts, like the Irish, they see the little folk. But you, you English, you are mongrels, you are bits and pieces of races and tribes and cultures and so you are blind. Except you, Mr Arthur Davison, are not. You are special.'

'Oh, I don't know…'

'I tell you what that little man was doing in my bakery. He has appeared in the bakery before, a month ago. I go back there after work to pick something up. He is there, busy with flour and so on, baking in my bakery. He says I am not there so why should he not use it? Then I go to rehearsal – I play the bassoon in the Chervil Symphony Orchestra – and he comes in and makes chaos, banging my music stand with a spoon and so on, because he cannot light the oven in the bakery. I tell him how to do it, and he goes away. But nobody else in the orchestra, nobody sees him except me.

They hear the noise he makes, but they do not see him. I don't know what they think. Maybe they think me a little mad. Probably that is so.

'Then today the little man appears in the bakery this morning and shouts at me that he and his people – I don't know who his people are – have been sick since the day he bakes in my bakery. He makes buns for, what does he call it, St Botolph's Binge, he says. He says all his people are sick afterwards. He has just got better and comes to shout at me. He says it is my fault, my bakery is dirty. My bakery is not dirty. It is clean, clean, clean. I am scrupulous, I tell him. He shouts and shouts and I throw him out.'

Stan stopped, leaned back, and swallowed a copious draught of beer. He glared at Arthur.

Arthur said, 'I see.' He couldn't think of anything else to say.

'You say you draw the little man in your drawing?' asked Stan. 'When is this?'

'I don't know exactly. A month or so ago.'

'And you do not know why?'

'No. I drew some rabbits at the same time, and then I just found I had drawn the little…' A thought struck Arthur. He saw a rabbit in the square that morning. A little shiver of cold ran down his spine. He tried to put the thought aside.

'Rabbits?' Mr Bun the Baker picked up on the word. 'There are rabbits in the Market Square. You do not expect rabbits. They appear in the last few weeks. I can see them.' He leaned forward again and thrust an index finger at Arthur, who flinched. 'You, Mr Arthur Davison, you who can see the little man, you draw the man, you draw the rabbits, and they appear in the square.'

That was the thought Arthur did not want to think about. 'It's ridiculous,' he mumbled. It was. It was simply coincidence. Of course it was. He had often drawn cute little dragons in the past, and they didn't spring out of the page into life, did they. Did they?

Stan Bun was merciless. 'You draw, they appear. You create them. Is obvious. I do not like this little man. He makes untrue accusations about my bakery. If you create him, then you can get rid of him. I ask you to do this, Mr Davison.'

Arthur spluttered, 'How can I? He's in ink. It's Indian ink. It's meant to be permanent. Sometimes you can scratch out a line with a scalpel but it's very difficult not to make a terrible mess. I couldn't erase a whole figure.'

'Destroy the drawing. Burn it. Is obvious. Burn it and no more trouble with little men and rabbits. They eat vegetables on market day. The traders, they cannot see them, they think it's people stealing. Burn the drawing.'

'I... years of...' Arthur couldn't take this in. It was ridiculous. You didn't just leap to conclusions and do drastic things because of a coincidence, a mere coincidence.

There was a cry of 'Hey, look who's here.'

Stan and Arthur looked up to see Mel standing over them. If Arthur wasn't utterly flummoxed he might have observed that she resembled a pixie, a mythical creature, and wonder of wonders, he could see her.

Mel dragged up a stool and plonked down at their table. 'You look like I'm a ghostie or something. It's only me.'

Stan was the first to recover. 'Hello, young Miss Remington. Do you know our Mel, Mr Arthur Davison? She is French hornist in orchestra.'

Mel laughed. 'Course he does, Stan. He's my uncle.'

'Uncle?'

'You know what an uncle is, yeah? I bet you have them in Poland.'

'Of course, of course. Is surprising, that is all.'

'Is that meant to be an insult?'

'No, no. No, I mean... I don't know. I'm not suspecting.'

Mel laughed again. 'So, this is Uncle Arthur, my mother's brother. How do you two know each other?'

'I have bakery,' said Stan, spreading his hands wide. 'Many people come there. Mr Arthur Davison, he is regular.'

'Of course.' Mel turned to Arthur. 'So what do you think?'

'About what?'

'My book.'

'I am sorry, but I don't have your book.'

'But I sent it you, like, two days ago.' Mel suddenly smote herself on the forehead. 'Oh sugar, I remember now. I was going to, and then Jason suddenly threw up all over the sofa. Never mind. Cool. I'll send it when I get home. Well, ciao guys, better go. I'm with some guys. Great to see you.'

And off she zoomed to a knot of people round the bar.

'Is this Jason a cat, do you know?' Stan asked Arthur.

'I think he's her boyfriend or partner or something. I'm not certain of how she lives. It's all very...' Mr Davison waved a hand vaguely. 'It's all so frantic.'

They both sat quietly a moment. Arthur had this distinct feeling, not only of often being invisible, but of being behind. As though the world was charging away somewhere, and he was struggling to catch up in the rear, crying out, 'Where are we going? What are we doing?' and nobody took any notice.

He dragged himself back into the here and now. Stanislav Bun, next to him, was a reassuring presence, someone happy to sit still, it seemed. And to pursue a profession with a name. A baker. You knew where you were with a baker. Mel's generation seem to have jobs whose titles or descriptions were wholly incomprehensible. Semiotics. Logistics. Cleansing operatives. Still, Mel was trying to become a writer. He knew what a writer was. And he was about to work on some illustrations. Which brought him back to his Grand Market Square-scape and Stan Bun's insistence that he destroy it.

'Do you really think I should burn my picture?' he asked Stan.

Stan shrugged. 'What else? That little man, he is big problem.'

Arthur thought the little man was more like a small problem and probably only a problem to Mr Bun the Baker, but it would be rude to say so. And he had only drawn one of him. Now the rabbits, on the other hand... But nobody was complaining about them, at least not to him. Then he remembered the vulture incident.

Lesson for Mr Arthur Davison, he thought. Sketch creatures and people in pencil first so you can rub them out if they misbehave.

'I see,' he said. 'Well, I'll do what I can.'

'Thank you,' said Stan. 'I am being appreciative. Now to serious affairs. You are Miss Mel's uncle. Do you play an instrument? You know I am bassoonist.'

'No, no. I had piano lessons for a while when I was young, but I did not have an aptitude. I do sing. With the Chervil Choral Society.' He suddenly felt bold, that he could confide in Stan. After all, Stan said they shared this odd sensitivity. 'And I enter the competitive music festival each year, though I don't tell people.' *Not that people would be interested*, he thought. 'I go in for the Oratorio class.'

Stan Bun looked impressed. 'You are brave,' he said. 'Do you win?'

'Oh no, no. I receive kind comments from the adjudicator and usually a mark of about 72 out of 100.'

'That is very good.'

'I'm afraid not. The marks they actually award range from about 70 to 95. I know they do that so it doesn't feel too harsh on weaker competitors. They want to encourage. My voice is weak, I acknowledge that. In their comments, the adjudicators tend to exhort me to project a little more, but I don't like to disturb the neighbours.'

'The neighbours?'

'When I practise at home. So I sing quietly, and I suppose I'm used to doing that. But I don't mind.' Arthur looked wistful nonetheless. 'It's a little challenge for me each year, the festival. And I do have my brief moment of singing a solo in public. Not that the audience is anything much more than the other competitors.'

'It is however brave for you. Now playing bassoon, there are moments in pieces where I have a little solo. That is my chance to shine. I become very nervous.'

As they chatted on about orchestras and choirs and the state of the world and amount of litter in the streets, Mr Arthur Davison realised he was feeling very comfortable. This was rarely the case in company. But Stan treated him like an individual, someone whose thoughts counted, who was a person of interest. And vice versa, of course. Arthur might be self-deprecating, but he considered that he was not bad at taking an interest in other people, given the chance.

Arthur reciprocated the buying of drinks, and in due course they parted on the best of terms. Arthur walked home down Southgate, Eastgate and the High Street. The river path was not for the faint-hearted on a moonless night, and the Tangle in the mediaeval heart of Chervil best avoided. The Market Square felt safe enough, though. There was wide enough access and good enough lighting to feel reasonably benign. Arthur looked around as he crossed the square. Not a rabbit in sight, no little tiny men with big tempers. He reached the haven of his flat and stood at the control tower of his front room looking out over the square. He gazed down at his drawing. It had taken him years. Stan wanted him to burn it.

How did you burn a large piece of paper in a flat? There were smoke alarms. They were loud, as Arthur once discovered when he burned some toast. Mr Bun's bread, of course. But Bun bread or not, it still set off an almighty clangour which shortened Arthur's life by several decades. Traditionally, he imagined, one would put the paper in the bath and burn it there, where you could douse it with water if things looked like triggering the ghastly alarm. But what an awful mess that would make. Also, he didn't have a bath, only a shower.

Gazing at the masterpiece, Arthur decided it was worth giving the scalpel a go. Scrape away the little man. It was not a wonderful method of removing unwanted lines, tending to leave the paper over-absorbent so that future ink feathered out instead of making a neat precise line. You could also actually make a hole if you weren't careful. But in this case, the alternative was to destroy the whole thing, so it must at least be worth having a go. He looked at the little bollard-perched fellow with contempt. 'Die,' he said to it. 'Vanish. Go back to the hell from which you came.'

But after a couple of drinks, it was well to be circumspect. It was prudent to wait until the morning, when his hand would be steady and he could concentrate better. So he made his mug of lemon and ginger tea and retired to bed, to dream, strangely, of being a bumble bee.

In the morning, before breakfast even, Arthur was at his table, scalpel in hand. It was still dark outside – nearly the shortest day, after all. The problem was where did you begin to expunge a small manlike creature sitting on a bollard? Which bit first? He started with the left hand. The right hand was hidden, and he felt that even if things went horribly wrong, a one-handed little fellow was kinder than a headless one. It was crazy, he told himself, to take all this seriously, despite what Mr Bun said. But then, he did see the creature in the bakery. Or did he? Was it a trick of the light? Easier to think that, than that there were creatures romping around that only he and Bun could see. Probably others too. Stan Bun did not say how common this being "sensitive" was.

This whole idea, that the act of drawing a creature made it come to life, was hard to take seriously. After all, he'd doodled and drawn little fantastic creatures most of his life, and as far as he knew, the world wasn't overrun with them. And what about other artists? Did Hieronymus Bosch's extraordinary creations escape from his paintings and haunt the world? Did Tenniel's drawings of the Jabberwocky? He shivered at the thought. He wasn't given to going for walks in the countryside, but if he ever did, he'd give tulgy woods a miss.

If bursting into existence needed more than simply being drawn, what was the extra factor? And could they always be eradicated by erasing them again?

Enough of wondering. The picture would be no worse off without the little chap on the bollard. The Dwelf, that was what he christened it. So on with the scalpel, gently, gently. The hand disappeared, only a little barely detectable roughness of the paper left. Next, the arm. Then, biting the bullet, the head. Did it glare at him as he scratched? No, it did not. It was a good idea he had decided to do this in the morning, not last night. Things always looked more fanciful late at night.

The head vanished. Just the body to go.

In a few minutes, there was only a missing bit of bollard that had been hidden by the Dwelf. Arthur burnished the paper where he had scratched with the rounded end of a pen. He then tried to fill in the rest of of the bollard. Only the slightest of feathering. A triumph. Altogether a triumph.

Arthur stood and looked down at a Dwelf-free Market Square-scape and nodded his head. A good job. Now the proper thing to do was to go over the square to Mr Bun the Baker's for breakfast and to tell him the success of his mission. If Stan told him he should have burned it, he would say: Pooh, pooh, this was as good, if not better. To burn the whole thing would be letting the terrorists win.

Mr Arthur Davison felt smug.

As he crossed the vaguely lightening market square, where Saturday stall-holders were beginning to arrange their wares, did he see any rabbits? Was it too dark? Did he try not to look? Whatever the case, he reached the bakery without anything to alarm his sensitivities, and entered the light and cosy warmth with its yeasty atmosphere plus coffee overtones.

'My usual,' he said to Merrylin, cock-a-hoop as he was.

'Yer what? What's that?' she said.

So he itemised a bacon roll with coffee option. 'Is Mr Bun here?' he asked.

At that moment, there was a cry from the far end of the bakery. Stan Bun appeared, a barrel on two flimsy legs. 'My friend,' he cried. 'Mr Arthur Davison. You are welcome.'

He wiped his hands on his apron, skirted the counter and grasped Arthur's hand in his own. It hurt. Doubtless bakers had very well-developed hand-grasping muscles, with all that kneading and what had you. Arthur squeaked in surprise. 'It is done, Mr Bun,' he managed.

'What you say?'

'You-know-who is deleted, wiped out,' Arthur amplified.

'You burn him?

'No, I scratched him out. He is no more.'

Merrylin was frozen, spatula in hand, mouth open in horror.

'To work,' Stan commanded her. 'Best bun for my friend, yes? On house again. To work.'

She scuttled to obey with a frenzy driven by total fear, shooting terrified glances at Arthur every couple of minutes.

'You are good man, Mr Arthur,' said Stan. 'I owe you, as you say. But I too must work. Nose to the millstone as also you say. We meet again soon, yes?'

Arthur nodded overmuch. 'Yes, oh yes. Thank you, um, Stan.'

'No, no, I thank you.' Stan said as he returned to the depths.

The bun when it came was as buttery and crispy as the day before. Merrylin managed to slop some of the coffee into the saucer as she served it. She burst into tears and turned away, sniffing like a small steam engine.

Arthur settled on a stool at the shelf along the window, looking out at the stalls materialising in the growing daylight. It was a sight of which he never tired. Hence his drawing, hence his pleasure at having avoided burning it. Today, he reflected, was Saturday. Today he would treat himself. He would go out and buy a CD of Haydn's *Creation*, which was next term's programme for the Chervil Choral Society. He would buy it and listen to it. All afternoon. He already had a score from the library, though he cautioned himself that it might not be the right edition. Nevertheless it would be a start. He would sing along with the CD, pianissimo, of course, and even attempt the solos. Maybe there was one he could try at next year's competitive festival. Killing two birds with one stone. Killing two Dwelves with a single scalpel.

To this end, when he left Mr Bun's Bakery, Arthur headed off into the mediaeval tangly heart of Chervil, the alleged haunt of ne'er-do-wells and shady types, not to mention cacodaemons and harpies. None of which he proposed to draw in his Grand Market Square-scape. Chervil was lucky enough still to boast a music shop selling sheet music and CDs that was hidden down one of the more angular alleys, and since the tendrils of day were wriggling their way down to the cobbled passages, the Tangle felt benign enough. At least Arthur, having lived in the Market Square for some years, knew his way around. When he first moved there the Tangle seemed unfathomable, unmappable, a place where missing persons had been wandering for years totally lost, a place of claustrophobia where the echo of your own footsteps bouncing back from ancient shop fronts and off the cobbles told you you were always being followed by the unseen. Either Arthur was now used to it, or he had learnt to walk softly.

He came to a halt before the shop, the regrettably named Notes4U, to be met by a notice in the window that said it opened at ten. It was barely nine o'clock. Momentarily nonplussed, he turned and trudged his way back to the Market Square. As he burst out of the Tangle, the growing clangour of the market stalls was a physical assault. He skirted around the periphery to the door up to his flat.

Inside, with the door closed, the stillness was a different world. Arthur Through the Looking-Glass. Returning to his flat, his eagle's nest perched above the bustle, was always a moment to reflect, to freeze for a moment, in awe of the petrified stillness of his little fortress and wondering how to wake it. Usually that meant putting on the kettle. But today, as he was full of Merrylin's finest, he settled instead for turning the radio on to Radio 3, where Record Review was getting into its Saturday stride. Too much to hope that *The Creation* should be the Building a Library selection of the week. That would wonderfully inform his choice of recording when he returned to Notes4U, if they had a copy. But it was not to be.

Arthur stood vacantly and gazed at the bollard, the site of the late Dwelf, on the panorama of his drawing spread on the table. If you didn't know, you'd never guess there had been a little man there. Good job. And then his gaze trundled out of the window and onto the activity below, constant movement, comings and goings. Dimly he recalled reading somewhere once about something called Brownian motion, a sort of aimless fidgeting that particles or molecules or whatever got up to in a fluid or some such. In a solution, they called it at school, the voice of Mr Stinks his chemistry teacher floated across the aeons to tell him. What was his real name? Perhaps he didn't have one. Did teachers ever exist outside the classroom? He was sure they didn't when he was at school. They were locked into the staffroom at night to prepare exquisite torment for their charges and let out in the morning to begin the torture over again. Like Sisyphus. Or maybe not. Random squiggles in a solution; that was the activity in the market. But a solution to what? What was the problem?

The problem, he told himself sternly, was what to do with the next hour, until the music shop opened. More like forty minutes now, actually. He could stand and gawp, his brain in the free-fall of suspended animation. Or he could do what modern people did, fire up the computer and let the worldwide web spin itself into the flat. Yes. He would do that.

And so he did, and miracle of miracles, there was an email from niece Mel. Little Melisuavia.

'Hi Unk,' she wrote. 'Here UR. Only the 1st 2 chpts, cos Jase says its too violent for little kids after that so I'm revising. Good luck!! M.'

And there was an attachment, which Arthur opened. And read...

8 The Gnoxie

Poppy and Cuddles

Poppy has lots of toys. They are mostly people. Teddy-bear, Giraffe, Sheep, Penguin, Aardvark. There are so many, she can't remember all their names.

They live in a big toy box.

One day, Poppy finds one she has never seen before. She's sure she has never seen it.

'Hello,' she says.

He looks like a fluffy duckling, but with arms and hands.

'What are you?' asks Poppy.

'I'm Cuddles,' he says. 'I'm a Gnoxie.'

Poppy is surprised Cuddles can talk. Usually she has to speak for her toys.

She has never heard of Gnoxies.

'What is a Gnoxie?' she asks Mummy.

Mummy doesn't know. Daddy doesn't know. Daddy asks Google. Google doesn't know.

Poppy sits Cuddles on the table in her room and looks at him. Cuddles sticks his tongue out at her. It does look funny. A tongue sticking out of a beak!

Cuddles picks up an orange and throws it at Poppy. It hits her on the forehead.

'Ow!' she cries. 'That hurt.'

The orange falls to the floor and goes splat. Cuddles laughs. He thinks it is very funny. His laugh sounds a bit like quacking.

Poppy is angry. 'You're a bad Gnoxie,' she says. 'I shall put you back in the toy box.'

She reaches out for Cuddles. He flaps his wings and flies up on top of the wardrobe. He sits there and laughs at Poppy.

Poppy bursts into tears and runs for Mummy. When Mummy comes in, Cuddles is back on the table. He looks sweet and cute. His big round eyes have lovely long eyelashes. He blinks them at Mummy.

'Oh, what a darling duckling!' says Mummy.

'He threw an orange at me,' says Poppy, sniffing.

'Don't be silly, dear,' says Mummy. 'Ducklings don't throw oranges. Now play quietly, because I've got things to do.' Mummy leaves Poppy's room.

Poppy looks at the floor. 'Where's the orange?' she asks.

Cuddles says, 'I ate it. I was hungry. It was horrible. I prefer slugs and snails. Fetch me a slug,' he demands, 'or else...'

He picks up a sharp pencil. He looks as if he is going to throw it at Poppy, like an arrow.

Poppy is frightened. She can't talk to Mummy about it. She must go into the garden and find a slug. She hates slugs.

Daddy is always complaining about slugs eating his lettuces. Poppy goes straight to the vegetable patch where they grow.

In one of the lettuces she finds one. It has eaten a hole in the leaf. It is only small, but she is nearly sick. It is slimy.

She goes to her room. Cuddles is swinging from the light shade. He flies down to the table.

'Gimme, gimme, gimme,' he says, and pecks the slug from Poppy's fingers.

'Ow!' she cries, because he has pecked her.

'Gross,' says Cuddles, and spits the slug back at her. It hits her on the nose. 'It's covered in dirt,' says Cuddles. 'You should wash it.'

Poppy runs out of her room and slams the door and goes to Mummy.

'I can't go in there,' Poppy says. 'I'm frightened.'

Mummy says, 'Oh, for heaven's sake, don't be such a baby.'

She puts down what she is doing and marches into Poppy's room.

Cuddles is sitting blinking on the table.

Mummy picks him up and throws him in the toy box. She closes the lid. 'There,' she says. 'Let that be an end to it.' And off she goes.

But it isn't the end. Oh no, not by a long way.

• • •

It went on for another chapter. Not the sort of thing Arthur usually read, of course, but this was work. He read on.

It seems Cuddles and Poppy go down to the kitchen early the next morning, where Cuddles persuades Poppy to open the fridge. He eats a whole bar of chocolate he finds in there. Poppy's mother comes in and sends Poppy to her room without breakfast, thinking she's eaten the chocolate. Cuddles flies out of the window to get Poppy some food, comes back with a bowl of cereal, spills it all over the carpet, then goes back and returns with piece of toast with a bite out of it. 'Oh no!' cries Poppy. 'You must have stolen Daddy's toast. Now there'll be real trouble.'

Arthur looked up from the computer screen. This, then, was the beginning of his new role. Book Illustrator. Serious stuff. He rose and wandered over to the window and his masterpiece in all its Dwelfless majesty. Beside it was the paper napkin on which he drew the little sketch he made in that café of the Gnoxie. Of Cuddles, it transpired.

Could he see that, that little feathery bundle, throwing oranges at little girls, slurping up cornflakes from the carpet, and then looking cute and oh so innocent for Poppy's mother?

Well, yes, he could. He could draw Cuddles. Small adorable creatures and wobbly buildings, those he could manage splendidly, he reckoned. Little girls and mothers, however, they were another world. Poppy was just a little girl. Mel had provided no description, nothing to make her different from any other small girl. It would be up to him. And he must draw her, because obviously Poppy was going to feature a great deal. To date, his familiarity with little girls had been very sketchy and mostly one of annoyance. Along with little boys, they seemed to make a lot of noise accompanied by whining and bawling, and get in the way when you were going somewhere. Poppy, he supposed, had to be a sympathetic character, or at least one a juvenile reader could empathise with, and he must make her distinctive. Like Thelwell's pony-riding tots or Ronald Searle's Trinians' monsters. Or Tenniel's Alice, or Quentin Blake's Matilda. Arthur was surprised he knew so many. He had to be different from them. He had to be original. His streak of confidence was waning fast.

Have a go, he told himself. Be daring. Study the little girls he encountered, or rather, passed in the street. He could sit on a bench in the square on market day and observe. No. Perhaps not. Not a good idea. These days you were liable to be frog-marched off to the magistrate for doing that.

Arthur sighed. It was going to be distinctly problematic.

In the mean time, after all that Poppy and Gnoxie-ing, it was time to return to Notes4U, which should now be open. He zigzagged his way across the square, holding close to his wallet and purse against the pickpockets alleged to frequent both there and the alleys of the Tangle beyond, according to the Chervil Gazette. Like the muggers, slave traders and drug traffickers who were also supposedly lurking. Lawless violence. That was a bit of a feature in Mel's book so far, it seemed, and like to get worse, from what she said Jason said. Was this fitting fare for formative minds? Perhaps in this world of death-dealing computer and online games it was entirely normal. Arthur seemed to remember some terribly frightening characters from his own childhood, in fairy stories, for example. Not to mention his dear sister Constance, Mel's mother, of whom he was fairly permanently scared when little, simply because she was a frightening child. She still was frightening, or was last time he saw her, though now he would charitably describe her as formidable. Unless she had in the last few weeks become a Buddhist nun or something. If Buddhists had nuns.

Such musings brought him to Notes4U's door. Inside, the unlikely proprietor, a morose individual who resembled a retired night-club bouncer or bare-knuckle pugilist, showed a glimmer of enthusiasm at his request and produced two different versions of *The Creation*. Except one was called *Die Schöpfung* and was sung in German, which was, the bouncer assured him, the original language that Haydn wrote it in, though he did himself also do the English version. Arthur wasn't sure this was correct, but he was certain the Choral Soc. would be singing it in English. Apart from anything else, there was usually a collective groan from the choir members when they were asked to stray from their mother tongue, though they seemed happy enough to cope with quite a lot of Latin. Even that invoked arguments. Mostly, thinking back, from Rupert, choir chairperson. But a whole concert in German would be beyond the pale.

So English it was. Christopher Hogwood and the Academy of Ancient Music. Should be good.

Arthur toddled homeward, trying to keep an unprurient eye out for little girls, but their mothers, nannies or other guardians seemed to be keeping them safely locked away. It was only when he was climbing the stairs to his flat that the lightning bolt of inspiration hit him. Of course! Use Mel herself as the model. She was generally elfin and didn't look anything like her age, not that he knew how old she was. And wasn't it so, that authors were often writing about themselves, maybe in disguise? So Poppy could have close-cropped hair and pointy features like Mel.

How Mel came to look like that when her mother Constance was, at least to Arthur's eyes, more like a Valkyrie was inexplicable. "All women become like their mothers," wasn't that what Oscar Wilde wrote? If so, Mel had a lot of metamorphosing to do. But for now, she could be his model. He wouldn't tell her, he thought. See if she saw the likeness. Mind you, if she didn't, it wouldn't say much for his drawing skills.

And so, geed up with enthusiasm, he put the kettle and CD number one on, and equipped with paper, pen and tea, settled down to see what happened.

He drew and drew and screwed up pieces of paper and drew again. Meanwhile, thanks to Haydn, on the CD, God was busy creating the heaven and the earth and adding light. At which, so the archangel Uriel sang, "Affrighted fly hell's spirits black in throngs: down they sink in the deep abyss to endless night."

How prophetic, Arthur might have thought if he could read the future.

9 *Jess the Jester*

Meanwhile, while Arthur was drawing and then singing (quietly) along with Haydn's *Creation*, Beryl was doing an in-depth clean in the kitchen at the Motley Brew, when Irina came in from the café. 'Mrs Beryl,' she said, 'there is man which ask for you.'

'Who asks for you,' corrected Beryl. Irina was keen to improve her English.

'No,' said Irina, 'he ask for you, not for me.'

It was a strain at times. Today was a Saturday and maybe having Irina in was an unnecessary expense, because Beryl didn't make cakes on Saturdays and could perfectly well man the front of house herself. She had recently taken to opening for a bit on a Sunday, but as for cakes, the punters just had to make do with whatever was left over. The place was closed on Mondays, though Beryl did come in and do some baking for Tuesday. But having Irina in on Saturday meant she could really give the kitchen a thorough going over.

Wiping her hands on her apron she preceded the girl out into the café. By the counter stood Oscar. If he had a cap, she reckoned he would have it in his hands and be wringing it. He seemed wretched.

'I'm sorry, I'm sorry, Beryl,' he said. Oh God, what had happened now? Was he pissed? He didn't really look it, but you never knew, not with a habitual drinker, so she was led to believe.

'Come and sit down, Oscar,' she said, moving towards a table.

'No, no,' he replied. 'I don't know why, but please, come with me. I don't know why. It's… It's…'

'Look, I'm busy, Oscar. I'm working. Tell me what it's about.'

'Oh God,' he said. 'Oh God, oh God, oh God. No. You must. Important. Don't ask me more. Please.'

She had never seen him like this before, and she had seen him in some pretty wretched states. It was almost as though he was possessed. But there was a look in his eyes. A beseeching. Like it or not, it called to her. After all, she had rescued him from his downward spiral, or at least she thought she had. If he was to revert and do something stupid, it would make her feel awful, never mind what it did to him. Oh, that seemed brutal, she thought.

'Will it take long?' she asked.

'I don't know. I just don't know. But please…'

Beryl couldn't see an option. If she didn't go, she would spend the rest of the day wondering and worrying. Hey-ho. 'Oh, very well,' she said. 'Irina, can you hold the fort for a while if I go and see what Oscar wants? I'll make sure I'm back for locking up.'

'Hold the fort?'

'Look after the café.'

'Oh yes. Of course, Mrs Beryl. You are safe with me.'

'Thanks. I hope I won't be long. Right Oscar, lead the way. Where are we going?'

Oscar said nothing. He turned and went out, waiting on the pavement for her to get her coat and join him. He led her out to the High Street, then along a bit and down a short bit of alley into the Market Square. Being Saturday, there were plenty of stalls, still buzzing with activity. In among these he went. She followed. She was rather annoyed.

'Where are we going?' she repeated. 'To Stan's?'

'Stan?'

'Stan Bun. The baker, the bassoonist. You've met him.'

'Oh. No. We're… I don't know why.'

He threaded through the stalls, not the confident figure he cut on stage performing, not the wizened depressive when in the drink, no, now she thought he looked like an eager puppy following a scent, no, not eager, not at all, more like he was driven. Or perhaps pulled. Yes, that was it. As though an invisible retractable lead was being drawn in.

The direction, hither and thither among the stalls, averaged out as towards Mr Bun's Bakery, hence Beryl's question. But as they drew near, Oscar veered off to the corner of the square, a place of a rowan tree and a solitary bench in front of a travel agents. "Twelve nights in the Baltic," the shop window proclaimed, "from only £3299 including flights.*" That little word "from." Aye , there was the rub. And an asterisk. Always an asterisk. "Terms and conditions apply," it probably meant, or something similar.

But in front, by the bench, was a person. An extraordinary person. Beryl couldn't imagine how it was only when they were close by that she noticed him. He... or was it she?... had a sign, on an A-board, like a street evangelist. "Jess Jerkin, Jester," it read. "Tortuous Tours Through the Tangle. Just for you."

The person was presumably Jess Jerkin himself or herself. Beryl decided she would assume it was male. Whichever it was, it was dressed in motley, diamonds in coloured quadrants on the jacket, pantaloons, cross-gartered yellow stockings, three-corned pointy hat with bells at the tips, the lot.

'Just in time,' he said. 'Off we go.'

Beryl looked around. There was just them. Nobody else waiting. 'You arranged this?' she asked Oscar, but his eyes seemed miles away.

Jess Jerkin the Jester set off down the nearest alley, capering over the cobbles in a strange zigzag manner, so that Beryl and Oscar could follow at a leisurely stroll and still keep up.

As was usual for her in the Tangle, Beryl felt an ominous sense of claustrophobia. Stupid, she told herself, but the way the buildings on each side crept out towards each other floor by floor as they went up shut her in, cut off the light. It was as though they wanted to touch and kiss if only they grew high enough, while down at street level, there was enough distance between them for a cart to pass. A hand-cart it would have been, back in mediaeval times. Appropriately, Jess the Jester turned an elegant cartwheel in front of them and they broke out into…

…into Not Martins Square. And yet…

That was not surprising. There were several alleys leading to or perhaps from Not Martins Square. Because of the unease she felt in the narrow streets, Beryl, if she needed to reach Not Martins Square would usually go along the decently wide Northgate or High Street, and then cut in by the shortest alley.

Why would anyone go to Not Martins? The Square boasted Mrs Tenby's Tea Rooms with Bellis Books. To Beryl, proprietress of the Motley Brew, it was important to keep an eye on the competition, hence she visited once in a while. Besides, Bellis Books specialised in second-hand cookery books. In the square, other than Mrs Tenby, there was Provocation, a restaurant boasting foraged food that was rumoured to use road-kill. Beryl had absolutely no intention of ever going to that. She could remember reading a review in the paper. For the rest, the buildings were shuttered shops or clubs or whatever, which apparently only came out at night. Like stars. Or teeth. Again, Beryl did not wish to know. One did not venture into the Tangle at night. It was bad enough in daylight.

Not Martins Square, sure enough; but now it was wrong. That was what was surprising. Somehow wrong.

'Whoosh,' cried Jess Jerkin, and flung a hand up brandishing a stick with a miniature replica of his head and hat on the end. And the buildings, which normally grew towards each other as they rose, floor by floor, all seemed suddenly to consider they were encroaching each other's personal space, and bent away, as if they all smelled rather bad, rather mediaevally with open drains. As if someone had drawn them with a whimsical distaste for vertical straight lines.

'Chervil Cathedral,' cried the Jester, waving his stick at Mrs Tenby's Tea Rooms with Bellis Books. 'A fine example of Early Peculiar architecture. Note the net curtains in the upper windows, so typical of Romanesque sensibilities.'

Dutifully, Beryl and Oscar looked up. Beryl thought the net curtains looked like cross-hatched renditions of ordinary curtains. Indeed the shadows on the buildings – for some weak sunlight did penetrate the Square – also looked like cross-hatching rather than shadow. And the whole place seemed to be in a kind of sepia monotone. It was indeed Peculiar, Early or not.

She looked for the name plaque; could this really be the Not Martins Square she knew? The name was there, but the "Not" seemed to waver and wamble as if it was not too sure of itself.

Jerkin the Jester saw her looking. 'The name,' he said, 'does it trouble you?'

It did. It always had. It made no sense. Should there be an apostrophe? "Martin's"? And why "Not"?

'Why not?' said Jess Jerkin, though she had said nothing. 'I could tell you, but you might not like it.'

Like it? Like it? It was not a question of like. Beryl needed to know. Beryl wanted an explanation, a factual, logical, in-the-cold-light-of-dawn, down-to-earth explanation.

Oscar was singing *Just One of Those Things* quietly. Beryl looked at him. He seemed content, at ease, untroubled. Perhaps younger, his hair less sparse, with more body. Had he been using Not Martins Patent Shampoo and Conditioner, guaranteed to restore lustre and life? Beryl started giggling. Honestly, this was ridiculous.

The Jester said, 'Would you like an ice-lolly, missy?' and proffered a drooping artificial daffodil. 'No? Well, come along now. Chop, chop.' And off he capered up another alley, the buildings shying away from each other as he went.

Beryl and Oscar trotted after. At least, Beryl trotted, in a state of total puzzlement, and yet not in a state at all. Oscar seemed to float, happily singing the while.

The Jester pointed out the Houses of Parliament and the University and the Gallows Tree as they passed, though Chervil had none of these. Suddenly he turned and faced them. From nowhere he produced a veteran car horn, honked it and proclaimed, 'Hold hands, I prithee, for time presses and we must skip the next bit.'

And skip they did, Beryl and Oscar, hand in hand, like eight-year-olds in a school crocodile, without a care in the world, and then, then...

...they popped out into the Market Square again, and there were passers-by looking at them as though they were totally bonkers.

'I thank you,' cried Jess Jerkin the Jester. 'That is the end of this Tortuous Tour. Please recommend us to your friends and enemies. Every day, every hour on the hour when I happen to feel like it.'

And Jess Jerkin was suddenly a tall, elegant middle-aged man with a top hat, a frock coat and a silver-headed cane. He bowed deeply, doffing the hat as he bent. 'Felix Appleby at your service,' he said. 'Giving you a nudge.'

From behind them came a voice. 'Madame Beryl and Señor Oscar, come, take a glass of coffee and one of Stanislav Bun's famous bacon buns. Is nonpareil.'

And there was Stan Bun himself, tree trunk on twiggy little legs, pleased as anything with his command of languages, inviting them into his bakery.

They complied. Of course they did. Looking back, Beryl could see no sign of the Jester or the top-hatted man, whichever it was. 'Did you see...' she began, but Stan raised a hefty hand to stop her.

'Naturally I see,' he said. 'I am Pole. We see.' He tapped the side of his nose. 'But it is not good always to tell. Some things are without explaining. Like my Bacon Buns. They are beyond belief, as you say. On the house,' he said to Merrylin, who sighed deeply and creaked into action.

'But Stan,' said Beryl, 'it's three o'clock. Not the time for bacon rolls. And high time I was getting back to the Brew.'

Oscar had emerged from whatever dreamland he had been in, back to impersonating a small dog, this time agog at the prospect of a biscuit. 'Well, I wouldn't say no,' he said. 'Thank you, er,

Stan.' He turned to Beryl, his eyes so sad, so pleading. 'Stay, Beryl, I beg you. I need to talk. It is better here than at your home.'

Her home. Not just "at home," or "their home." Were the words important? It was after all *her* home. He was only a lodger. Well, she really didn't need to return to the café for another half-hour.

'All right,' she said. 'Merrylin, dear, can you give me one of Stan's Danish pastries instead of the bacon roll? It's still a wickedness, I know, but not quite as bad.'

Merrylin sniffed. 'There ain't none left. Like, it's Saturday, yeah?'

So a bacon roll it was, and wondrous, and odes could be written to Stan's bacon buns, she had to admit. Meanwhile, Oscar...

'I must go,' he said.

'But I thought you wanted to talk? And what about your roll and coffee?'

Oscar sighed. 'No. I mean leave your house. I realised, back there in the... what do you call it? Where that, that chap... Where he took us...'

'The Tangle?'

'Yes. I thought... It came to me... Now that Dotty is in the home, I'm just in the way. I don't want to be an... an encumbrance. I should move on. Get my own place. I know I'm just a sad old has-been, but...' He petered out.

Beryl wished exactly that too. Now that he said it, she felt contrite, as though it was her wish that was forcing him. 'I see,' she said. 'If you feel like that. Of course you *could* stay... After all, you're paying as a lodger. It helps my finances a bit. But if you want to go...'

'Yes,' he said. 'I should. I realised back there, when he waved that stick thing. Like a conductor, almost. I wonder...'

Again he paused.

'Yes?'

'I wonder, was that why I led you there? Was it? Tell me, Beryl?'

'Don't ask me, Oscar. I don't have a clue. And yet I feel it was the right thing that you did. Not just for you. I don't know why...'

For someone so sturdy of trunk, Stan Bun moved very quietly. Maybe it was his tiny feet. Whatever the case, neither had noticed that he was now standing by them, three plates of Bun's Bacon Buns steaming in his hands. 'I join you,' he said, and drew up a chair. 'You two. You are not sensitive. I am Pole. I see things. I do not know what happen out there. Something did, that I know. So I tell you this for free. Do not ask questions. Go where you need to go. Do what you need to do. If it is right, it is right. I know these things.'

There was silence, apart from Merrylin half-heartedly cleaning her area. Beryl thought: *I'm at sea here. I haven't the remotest clue what's going on. But for some reason, I believe Stan to be wise in a way I don't understand. And hey... If it all results in Oscar finding a place of his own, what's not to like, as they say?*

'Is exciting, yes?' said Stan Bun, beaming like a benevolent uncle.

And it was. Strangely it was. And not just because she might soon be rid of Oscar – and she was awfully grateful to him for helping out with Mum, and of course he was still visiting Mum in the home and singing to her – the staff told her so, and Mum responded, unlike when she, Beryl, visited, and she might as well be any old sod for all the reaction she got, yet still she went, out of duty really... But if he moved out, Oscar could perfectly well visit Mum from wherever he was living, assuming it was still in Chervil, and if not... Oh well. Early days. It was a hopeful start, that was the thing.

But apart from all that, she too was excited. For herself. And she had no idea why.

The three of them sat there, butter oozing down their chins, nearly as happy as pigs in a pool of muck. Which was, Beryl thought, an unfortunate comparison giving that they were eating bacon. She felt a giggle rising up, like a bubble in a bottle of pop, and she was a child again, and resolved that when she got home, she'd open a bottle of wine, get the flute out, and indulge in a favourite fantasy since a girl of being a great virtuoso invited to play a concerto with the Chervil Symphony Orchestra, no, let's be outrageous, with the Berlin Phil. What should it be? Mozart? Quantz? Nielsen? Except she didn't have the music of the Nielsen. How about the Poulenc Sonata; she believed it had been orchestrated. By Lennox Berkeley, she thought. But the flute part'd be the same. It was a pity Weber didn't write something spectacular. Perhaps he did?

Oh, she was well away. Then her down-to-earth self caught up with her. She looked at Oscar. He was lost in his thoughts. Stan was still beaming. But time, like a dripping tap, was gradually filling the day up, and she had an Irina back at the Motley Brew who didn't know what to do to lock up. The Motley Brew, the Jester in motley – what was his name? Already she couldn't remember. But were the motleys coincidence, or did it all mean something? Maybe Stan could tell her, but, alas, she must go. Back to Irina. Back to the Brew.

And go she did. As she left the bakery, she looked over at the bench beside which she seemed to remember the Jester waited. There was no jester now, nor a top-hatted man. There was a bundle of rags sitting on the bench though. Blind Bella. Everyone knew of her. Some said she was a soothsayer. Others that she was simply a pathetic old woman. Once, on a particularly bad day with the Selfish Shit Jim, wandering round the city in a cloud of I-must-get-out-of-the-house-or-I'll-do-something-terrible depression and anger, she'd sat on that bench. Probably because Stan Bun's bakery was nearby, and Stan was a comfort. But there was no way she could talk to him and cry on his shoulder when he was at work, even if it had occurred to her. So she had sat there on the bench, enveloped by the warm and distasteful aroma emanating from old Bella. The woman had turned one eye in her direction and said, 'Why does the canary in a cage sing? Answer me that, young lady.

And if you could see your way to a silver sixpence, I'll tell you me life story. Maybe.' And Beryl had given her a pound, but all that happened was that Bella rose and meandered away into the dark alleys of the Tangle.

The Tangle, wherein was the cathedral and the Houses of Parliament and the Gallows Tree. Why did she think that? Already she could barely remember anything of whatever his name was did or said.

She turned and set her steps back to the High Street, the safe route to the Motley Brew. She was Beryl Carson, sensible, rational, dependable Beryl. And unrecognised virtuoso flautist. One who shortly would discover whether Irina was competent or could not be trusted to be in charge for a minute.

10 Drawing Cuddles

'Bring the sketches,' said Mel. 'Go on, bring them. All of them.'

It was a couple of weeks since Mel had sent her two chapters. Arthur Davison had quite a few drawings in pen and ink. He had a lot more in the waste bin. But now he felt he had developed a cartoony version of Mel to portray Poppy and he had sort of worked out how to make her recognisably the same person whatever angle he drew her from. He had tried to cheat a bit with Poppy's mother and father by having their heads out of the picture, like the humans in Tom and Jerry cartoons. You just saw their lower body and maybe hands when holding something. Could he keep this up? Time would tell. And now Mel was here and was looking at them. She was strangely silent. Rapt even. Arthur hoped so. She went back and forth between them. And now she was taking him somewhere with them.

Arthur carefully put the folder into a plastic carrier bag. 'Where are we going?'

'We're going to see Beryl. She's the most level-headed person I know. I want to see what she says.'

Arthur was at a loss. Mel had come round to his flat, wanted to drag him off to this Beryl, whoever she was. She was bossy, that was what Mel was. Took after her mother, his dreadful sister Constance. 'Beryl?' he asked.

'You know, at the Motley, yeah?'

'Oh dear, Mel, you've lost me.'

'Come on, Uncle Arthur. You know, the Motley Brew? The café? Where you drew the first-ever Gnoxie on a paper napkin? Last month? Here, in Chervil?'

'Yes, yes, I remember. I remember the Motley Whatsit. But Beryl, you said?'

'She runs it. You met her then.'

'Did I?'

'Yeah. And she plays in my quintet. Or perhaps I play in hers. I don't know who thought of the idea first. And she plays in the CSO. Flute. You must have seen her when you came to our Christmas concert?'

Arthur thought for a moment. 'No, I can't say I remember the flautists.'

Mel pulled on a bright green bobble hat, making her look even more the pixie. 'Oh, never mind. You'll recognise her when you see her.'

He trudged carefully through the square and through the Tangle. There were icy surfaces where the sun couldn't reach, which was most of the narrow cobbled alleys. Mel bounced along with the sure-footedness of youth. Somehow her presence made the place benign, almost friendly, instead of the usual unnerving, unworldly effect it had on Arthur. Ah, youth!

At the Motley Brew, as they entered and the aromas and ambiance tried to sneak out of the door, indeed Arthur remembered the occasion well, the creation of the first Gnoxie. As for the person currently clearing a table, a young woman with a doll-like face and her hair tied back, she rang a vague bell in his mind.

'Hiya, Irina,' said Mel. 'Beryl around?'

So this wasn't Beryl.

The girl said, 'In the kitchen.'

There were people at two of the tables. Mel led the way to an empty one in the corner under a light. 'Sit here, Uncle, and I'll go and see if Beryl's free, okay?'

As she vanished behind the plastic curtain that presumably led into the kitchen, the doll-like girl came over to take his order.

Arthur said, 'I'd like, no, I'd better wait for… for my niece. She's…' And at that moment, Mel reappeared and came over. They ordered. Coffee and cake, naturally.

'She'll be out in a sec,' Mel told Arthur. 'She's just putting a cake in the oven.' She glanced at the girl, Irina, who had retired behind the cake-laden counter and was playing steam trains with the coffee machine. 'Irina seems okay. Beryl says you've got to be so careful who you get in to help. Either they are ignorant or they break stuff or they screw up your customers so they give the place one star on Trip Advisor.'

'Does that matter?' Arthur had heard of Trip Advisor but had only a vague idea what it was or what it was for.

'Yeah,' said Mel. 'If you're, like, visiting Chervil, you know, you look up places and if there's a one-star review all about cockroaches and rude staff and stuff, you go somewhere else. Even if there's only one one-star and hundreds of five-stars, you think, well, there's no smoke without fire. Well, I wouldn't and you wouldn't, but other people do, and the other thing is, B says, that if you're the one running the place, it hurts. You know, you take it personally and you can't argue back or that makes you look bad too. And you might want to review the customer, if you can remember them, and say how ghastly they were and dropped food on the floor and had these ghastly children who ran about screaming and so on and so forth...'

She stopped as Irina delivered their coffee.

'Oh,' said Arthur Davison.

Then he said, 'Have you written any more since last...'

'Yeah,' interrupted Mel. 'Yes and no. I mean, yes sort of. The last thing I sent you was the chapter where Poppy runs away from home, wasn't it? And the Gnoxie steals a scooter? Well, I decided to bin that. It was getting, you know, sort of out of hand. But I haven't really decided what happens instead. But that's progress, isn't it? Even if it looks like going backwards. Here she is.'

She was Beryl, emerging through the plastic curtain like a butterfly from a chrysalis, wiping her hands on her apron. She saw Irina was about to take cake over to Mel and Arthur, so relieved the girl of the plates and advanced with them to the corner table.

Arthur did remember her, now he saw her. Mel's friend. Of course. Played what was it? The flute, she'd said. A comfortable woman. A friendly woman. Not threatening, like he often found women – perhaps biased by memories of sister Constance when he was of a formative age.

'Who's the coffee and walnut?' asked Beryl.

'Guess,' said Mel.

The other was an Eccles cake. Beryl scrutinised the faces of the two. It was a test of her professional judgement. Then she proffered the Eccles cake to Arthur.

'Wrong,' cried Mel. 'Me Eccles, Uncle Arthur, cake.'

'Ah well,' said Beryl, smoothing her hair back. She drew up a chair from another table. 'Get me an Earl Grey, Irina dear,' she called across to Irina at the counter. She offered a hand to Arthur. 'Hello again, Mel's uncle. I remember that what-d'you-call-it you drew on a napkin. So Mel has sweet-talked you into doing illustrations for her great work?'

'No, no,' said Arthur, 'I'm more than happy. It's new ground for me...'

'Show Beryl your pics, Uncle,' Mel burst in. 'He's got a knack, B. He may look like a dry old stick, but you know what, he's got this streak of wickedness. Anarchy sort of thing. Nothing's quite straight, it's all a bit quirky. Here, look.'

Arthur had produced a picture of a Gnoxie coming through a young girl's bedroom window and a bowl of cereal flying out of its hand. The window and room were indeed slightly awry, as though they had had a little too much to drink.

'That's the Gnoxie spilling Poppy's breakfast,' explained Mel. 'Isn't it, like, dynamic? Like it's exploding?'

Beryl put her specs on, which had been dangling round her neck, and frowned. 'I can see the spilling bit, and I recognise the duckling thing, like the one you drew on that napkin. But why is it coming through the window?'

'Because Poppy's been banished to her room,' said Mel, 'because the Gnoxie ate the chocolate bar and dropped the wrapper and Poppy hasn't had any breakfast, and so...'

'Enough, Mel dear. I don't understand what you're talking about. I need to read the story, I think. But it's a lovely picture. Very vivid, full of life.'

Not too full of life, hoped Arthur. He reckoned he was on safe ground drawing odd creatures in a purely fictional setting. The trouble with that little man on the bollard was a real creature in a real place. He had drawn the Dwelf in a representation of the real Market Square, even if it was wobbly and distorted. That was, if all that little man and Stanislav Bun business actually happened. But if Gnoxies started appearing as a result of his drawing them, it would be in a fictional world, the world of Mel's imagination. And that was safe. Surely? Anyway, the whole thing was too fanciful. He reckoned he'd be seeing fairies next, and then they'd have to lock him away.

'So you reckon they're cool, B, do you?' said Mel. 'Would you buy the book?'

Beryl whipped the specs off again. 'How much is it?'

Mel looked startled for a moment, then realised Beryl was joking. 'I've not finished it yet, see, 'cos my Jason says it's way too violent, like bloody, for little tots. It would turn them into psychopaths he says, and do I want that on my conscience? Well, of course I don't, so I'm kind of holding fire and hanging in there hoping a flash of inspiration will strike and I can see another way through. You got inspiration among your tea selection, B?'

'What about Turmeric and Ginger? That's supposed to cure everything, even awaken the dead, so they say, though I've read you'd have to eat about a kilo of turmeric a day for it to have any effect. Still the ginger might ginger you up.'

'Ha ha,' said Mel unconvincingly. 'Uncle Arthur, have you got a Christmas concert coming up like us?'

Arthur Davison was caught completely off guard. 'What? A concert?'

'Your choir?'

Beryl remembered. 'Oh yes, you sing with the Choral don't you? Mel said.'

'Oh, the choir.' Arthur came down to earth. 'Oh yes. It was last week. Not exactly Christmas. It was... it was curious. For some reason, our conductor, Bernard Pontdexter, chose an assortment of Coronation Anthems, I don't know why. Usually we do carols and that sort of thing, and well, it was... the attendance was poor, the audience... was poor. Yes. I don't know why he chose them.'

Mel laughed, a sound which would have reminded Arthur of the song of an Australian magpie if he had ever heard one. 'Silly man,' she said. 'Would I know any of these anthems?'

'I don't know. Maybe *Zadok the Priest*?' Mel shook her head. '*My heart is inditing*?'

'What? Where's that?' said Mel.

'Oh dear,' said Arthur, 'that's Rupert's little joke. He kept coming out with it. He's the Choir chairman, and he is... well, he is a bit much. "Where's Diting?" he kept saying every time Bernard said we were going to rehearse it, "why did I leave my heart there?" It got a bit boring... I don't mean you're boring, Mel. It's your first time... at it as a joke, I mean... I mean... "Inditing" means... I'm not sure what it means. It's the gerund, is it? from "to indite", but I'm not sure what it means to indite something or someone, or just to indite. Anyway it's an anthem by Purcell. And there's one by Handel, better known, which we didn't do, one of his four Coronation anthems along with Zadok, I've got them on CD, but with instruments, not just organ, which is how we did them. Instruments would have made the concert much more interesting. As it was, it was sort of undiluted jollity and all sounded rather similar.'

'Instruments are always cool,' said Mel. 'Aren't they, B? Sack the organist, Uncle Arthur. Bring us in. We'll make your Coronation anthems rock. Anyway, you never told us about your concert, or we'd of come, wouldn't we, B? Are you coming to ours?'

Arthur was nonplussed for a moment. He reckoned to keep well informed of musical goings-on in Chervil, but for the moment... 'Your concert?'

'Tomorrow, Sunday, the seventeenth, seven-thirty' said Beryl. 'At St Boni's. You know St Boniface's? Doesn't the Choral Soc rehearse there? It's where Oscar went for his audition.'

'How did he get on?' asked Mel.

Beryl turned to Arthur. 'Do you know Oscar? He's going to join your choir after Christmas. No? Oh well, you'll meet him then. Yes, Mel, he's got in. Their conductor is ecstatic at him joining, according to Oscar, but I expect he's exaggerating. Anyway, our concert, the Chervil SO, is Scandinavian. Like with you and your Coronation anthems, I don't know why. Usually Christmas Concerts are a bit light. Though our programme is at least, how would you say, Mel? Upbeat? Not exactly full of Scandi-noir gloom, anyway. Grieg and Sibelius. It should be good.'

'And *Finlandia*,' chipped in Mel. 'Who's that by?'

'That's Sibelius.'

'Oh cool. So it is just Grieg and Sibelius. With Grieg's *Piano Concerto* to bring in the crowds. With, what's his name, B? The pianist?'

'I can't remember, dear. He's famous, I know that. Clifford says so, so he must be. Or she must be. Clifford is our conductor, Mel's uncle. Clifford Hope-Evans, director of music at Chervil College.'

Arthur knew this. He had heard the orchestra before. He tried to go to all their concerts. He had simply been unable to bring the imminence of this one immediately to mind. And the soloist was... 'Dmitri Waldstein,' he said. 'I think he's your piano soloist. He's quite famous. He was born in Whitby, I think I read somewhere, something like John Brown, and changed his name to sound more, well, international.'

'Like Oscar,' said Beryl. 'So you know of the concert? Will we see you there?'

Arthur told her he already had his ticket, he'd just momentarily been confused.

'Cool,' said Mel, 'that's my Unk. Hey, we're joining forces next year, aren't we? Haydn's *Creation*. Combined effort. The cream of Chervil's musicians. We'll see you after the concert tomorrow, then? In the Hippo? You can tell us what you think. And tell us which of us watches the conductor more.'

'That's me,' said Beryl. 'Horn players think they're special.'

'Because we are.'

Arthur was not one for banter; it tired him. 'I'm coming to the concert,' he said, 'and I'll watch if I can. I may end up behind a pillar. It tends to happen.' He sighed. Perhaps if he was more assertive. Or got there earlier. But that meant time to kill, and after you'd read the programme twice and found to your dismay that someone exceedingly tall had decided to sit in front of you, what did you do? He could take a good book, he supposed. Maybe the Creation score and study it. 'I've been practising it,' he added.

Mel turned. 'What? Practising what, uncle?'

'*The Creation.*'

'What, in your flat? So that's why there's always an amazing crowd outside in the square gazing up, like, in awesome awe?'

'No, no. I sing very quietly along with the CD. Nobody could hear outside.'

'Where's your flat?' asked Beryl.

'In the Market Square. I look down on it all. It's like being a controller at an airport. Not that I've ever been to an airport, but I expect it is.'

Beryl sat up. 'Market Square? Tell me, Mel's uncle…'

'My name's Arthur. So please feel free to use it. I know Mel is my niece, but…'

'Arthur, then. Tell me, if you live in the square, do you know a man – I think it's a man – who calls himself, what is it? Jess Jerkin, the Jester? Does extraordinary tours of the Tangle, quite surreal, all fantasy, and yet… He has a three-cornered hat with bells on… I think. Or perhaps he doesn't.'

Arthur thought. 'No,' he said. 'I've seen some pretty weird-looking people down in the Square, but that doesn't ring any bells. Is he or she often there?'

'I've no idea. He was there a couple of weeks ago, I know that. At least I think I know that. Over near Stan Bun's bakery. Somehow it's all rather strange.'

'No, I've not noticed anything, I'm afraid,' said Arthur. 'Why?'

Beryl shrugged. 'Oh, it's nothing. Just sort of... odd. I just wondered, you know...'

'Of course there's Blind Bella. You don't mean her, do you?'

'No, oh no. I know her. She's quite a character, isn't she? The Jester was standing by her bench, though. She wasn't there.'

'Well, there do seem to be several pretty weird people around on market days, but I'm sure that is so wherever there are crowds. Sometimes there are these chaps who stand like statues, or sit apparently impossibly in mid-air, but I understand that there is a kind of metal framework hidden under their clothing. It's just trickery. But I've not seen a jester with a three-cornered hat. I'm sure I haven't.'

Mel had been looking at her phone and dragged herself away from it. 'Who's this Blind Bella, then? Is that the smelly old witch who sits on the bench by Stan's bakery?'

Beryl suddenly looked very prim. 'That's not very kind, Mel dear. She is said to be very wise.'

'Oh yes, she is,' said Arthur, remembering his reporter's notebook of Bella's prophesies, as he liked to think them. 'She does utter words of wisdom, allegedly, only usually they are cryptic and you can't be sure what they mean. And you do have to give her something in exchange. Money, or a doughnut, or something like that. And she is a bit odoriferous in my experience.'

'How do you know they're, like, wise if you can't understand them, Unk?' asked Mel.

Beryl replied instead. 'Trust,' she said. 'You simply have to believe some things. Like your Gnoxies, Mel dear. You believe in them, don't you? They are real to you. Or talking animals who get inside your head...' She petered out.

Why did she say that? thought Arthur. She was looking suddenly confused. He saw Beryl as a sensible, practical woman, and here she was now apparently uncertain and... and a little frightened, it seemed to him.

'No, I don't, like, believe in them,' said Mel. 'I made them up. It's just a story for children, that's all. 'Cept that Jason says they're too terrifying. I don't agree. Kids love being scared in books and films and that. I know I did. I mean, not real scared, like when Mummy really lost it. You know what she can be like, Uncle, don't you?'

He did. Constance was alternately totally bossy and totally frightening when they were growing up. 'Give me your sweeties,' Constance would demand after a visit to the shop with newly-distributed pocket-money rations, 'or I'll stick hot pins under your finger-nails.' And she would have, he was sure, except that he always gave in and never found out for certain. He felt the fear even now. No way would he willingly go and visit Constance's house nowadays. Not if Mel begged him. Strange that Mel should be so pleasant a girl with Constance as a mother. 'Oh, she could be a bit much at times,' he said tactfully. 'She has strong opinions, and I respect that, I do. And she does rather like things her way.'

'Go on, Unk, tell me what she got up to when you were children. Tell it like it is, or rather like it was. I want the juicy goss, like. Promise I won't tell her who I got it from.'

Beryl butted in. 'Mel, dear, I don't believe it. You sound like you want to use it as a weapon, like you want to blackmail your own mother. That's not fair. And not fair to ask Arthur to tell you. I speak as a mother myself.'

'You? A mother? You have children?' Mel looked astonished.

'And why should I not, Mel dear? I have a past, you know. Just the one child. Algy. Algernon. Not my choice of name, I assure you. He pops up every now and then. He's not one for keeping in touch.'

'You never talk about him. So you're married too, then?'

'Was. He passed away a few years ago. But come on, Mel, what's your game? First you try to get Arthur to give you the low-down on your mother, and now you want to know all about my past. You should be an interrogator. What are you up to?'

'I'm not up to anything. I'm just, like, interested is all. Curious, yeah? A successful writer's got to know people, yeah? Know how they tick, like. Call it research.'

'Call it nosey if you ask me. Don't tell her anything, Arthur. Keep shtum. Like suspects say in all those cop series on tele, say "No comment" to everything and they can't touch you.'

Mel looked offended. Arthur wondered if there was an ulterior motive behind her probing after all. People didn't ask questions just to pass the time, did they? There must always be a reason behind them. Or must there? He decided to play safe and keep his counsel about his and Constance's childhood. Partly he simply didn't have a stock of practised little anecdotes to tell, partly he actually didn't want to dwell on those times. They were not the happiest of his life.

The conversation drifted onto other things. If Mel took umbrage at Beryl's remarks, it soon seemed to wear off, and before long, both of them proclaimed they must go, in Beryl's case to get back to work since cafés didn't run themselves even with an Irina to help, and Mel said she was due to meet some friends somewhere else.

So they parted, and as Arthur dived into the mystery of the Tangle once more, he found himself wondering if indeed creatures he drew were simultaneously created in the real world, and if so, what would happen if Cuddles suddenly appeared round the next corner, all fluffy and endearing. Well, he would lock his drawings away when he got home. Not even a Gnoxie could escape a locked drawer, surely.

It was then that there was a kerfuffle. It was gloomy here in the Tangle, the sunlight completely failed to penetrate; the cobbles were still icy. From round the next bend, there skidded, not a

96

Gnoxie, but a rabbit, chased by a cat. A black cat. Mostly black. Like Tom and Jerry. The rabbit almost collided with Arthur, who dropped his folder in astonishment. The papers, his drawings, scattered, blown by the passing gale from the frenetic chase. As soon as the kerfuffle started, the animals were gone again. The buildings settled down once more to brood on dark secrets, the cobbles went back to sleep. Arthur picked up his drawings and stuffed them back into the folder and resumed his way with hastened tread.

Did he create that rabbit? Was it one of the ones he drew? It didn't seem like the sort of place for rabbits to live. In the centre of a city. They liked fields and woods and things didn't they? Perhaps it was an escaped pet. Whatever the explanation, it had to be better than that drawings could come to life. That was absurd, ridiculous. But this was the Tangle. It did not obey the normal laws of existence.

Arthur was making himself frankly scared. It was with great relief that he burst out into Market Square, where the crowds thronged the Saturday market stalls. Rabbits? Ridiculous. Overactive imagination. Too much caffeine. Imagine how sister Constance would scoff, were she here. She had had – she undoubtedly still had – a very choice line in scathing remarks. Nonetheless, the moment he entered his little second-floor hideaway, his first action was to put the folder in a drawer and lock it. There. Sorted, as Mel would probably say.

11 The Orchestral Concert

The moment of entering the performing space, that was when the nerves hit home. So thought Beryl as the players of the CSO walked the few yards from St Boniface's Church Hall into the church. They left behind a mess of discarded outdoor clothing and instrument cases, and a riotous cacophony of last minute practice of tricky bits. The church was a cavernous stillness in comparison, its lurking expectant audience, though in fact mostly chatting, no more than a benign atmospheric rustle, a blurred haze in that looming space.

At that moment, there was no going back. If you had managed to get away with fudging a passage in rehearsal without Il Maestro noticing, this time there were many pairs of ears who might be both expert and critical, and there was no second chance. Was it nerves? Oh yes. Every time. It was as though the world was poised, waiting, and this time, she, Beryl, first flute of the Chervil Symphony Orchestra, could be the one to screw things up spectacularly. Of course she wouldn't. But she could. Perhaps miscount an entry. So easy.

And then Evelyn, oboist in their little quintet, who had beaten Beryl to it, was already settled at her stand and was making outrageous squawking noises with her reed, a needy chick clamouring for a grub from Daddy's beak. Evelyn was clearly impervious to the hushed stillness, the holiness of the ambiance. Good for Evelyn. Her squeaks and squeals made it so much more normal.

During the milling in the church hall beforehand, Beryl at one point found herself in touching distance of Gerald, the tubaist, or tubist, or whatever the correct name for a tuba player was. She had never been physically so close to him, not outside her dreams of old that was. Now she observed that his moustache was less than fulsome, rather frayed and moth-eaten, even possibly – oh horror – even a bit nicotine stained. His musical beloved, his tuba, she could see was terribly tarnished, and boasted several war-wounds in the form of dents and scratches. There was even a bit of sticking-plaster in one place, covering who knew what blemish or injury. Gerald was, in short, shoddy goods, and she was well shot of him. He, oblivious of her presence and thoughts, carried on popping cow-patty blobs of sound into the melee. Beryl felt a weight shift from her, and relief; she had managed to avoid making a total embarrassment of herself.

In the church, a fine and lavish example of Decorated Gothic according to the Visitor's Notes, there was space to spare. If it wasn't for Chervil Cathedral, St Boniface would be Chervil's numero uno. At least its rather biased clergy and faithful congregation thought so, and were fiercely loyal. Beryl was not among their number. She found the church cold and intimidating, and architecturally dull. Not that she gave it much thought. Apart from the chill. The prudent tended to prepare with thermal underwear under their formal attire. God help the poor old pianist's flying fingers. Probably even now he was soaking them in a basin of warm water and hoping the effects would last long enough. Perhaps even fingerless mittens. Not elegant, but practical. Now, that would be a talking point. Had he taken such prophylactic measures in the rehearsal that afternoon? Beryl hadn't noticed. She plonked down into her seat, adjusted her music stand just so, and raising her flute, breathed warm air into it while surveying her surroundings. The audience seemed decently numerous, as indeed it should be. It was a pretty popular programme. The pianist was quite famous, so Clifford Hope-Evans had told them rather too often for it to be believably true, but anyway, who didn't like the Grieg?

Old Cyril arrived beside her, sat himself down. He was wheezing a bit from the exertion. She hoped he would last the concert. And also, completing the flute regiment, a young *wunderkind* from Chervil College, where El Maestro was the main music man. The girl had been drafted in to play piccolo and gain experience. There was not a lot for the picc to do, but it did have to be right. Everyone could hear a piccolo. They had had stiffeners from the college before in the orchestra and they had usually been just fine. There was a good peripatetic music teacher there, taught flute and voice apparently. Dee somebody. Beryl met her once somewhere.

Over there in the distance, she espied Gerald had lumbered in and was limbering up. Mel was there, second from the right in the formidable quartet of horns, barricaded in behind their serpentine wall of brass. Fred, first clarinet, was plonked in his chair like a sack of potatoes. Next to him in absurd contrast, the second clarinet was an austere, grey-haired beanpole of a lady, who, Beryl believed, had the name of Primrose Peach.

And of course, a little further along the line beyond Fred, she could just see the top-heavy might of Stan Bun, his torso making the bassoon look like a twig. He mimicked Evelyn's raven cries an octave or two down on his reed.

That was all familiar and comforting. But look the other way out into the haughty nave, and there were the strangers. Down the central aisle she could see a dumpy lady and a tall, stooped man being ushered with deference to their seats. Both had glittery chains round their necks. Beryl recognised them from the local paper. Madam Mayor and her Consort. Well, they might be Chervil bigwigs, but they probably knew diddly-squat about music. Why did she think that? Was she a snob? Tut tut. But it helped her to feel reasonably composed. It was remarkable, she noticed, how few faces she could actually see. If she couldn't see their eyes, they couldn't see her. That accounted for almost all the audience. A mere consequence of the orchestra area not being raked. Also there were a fair number of pillars obscuring the view. Of course there were, otherwise the roof would fall down. Oh, her mind rambled. She was not nervous. Not at all. Except that she was. But not enough for her hands to shake and her lower lip to sweat. With luck.

Then Mildred Trimble, leader of the orchestra, appeared at the front, stood, and waved her bow towards Evelyn, principal oboe. The signal. The tuning began, the orchestra became slightly disciplined as they executed the ritual. Except Gerald, Beryl noticed, who carried on uttering random poops as though he needed further practice. What an arsehole.

After that was the moment of maximum nerves. The silence that awaited the conductor, the silence that radiated out over the audience, until the church was one enormous hush of expectation. At that moment, Beryl spotted that old Cyril next to her had *Finlandia* open on his stand. She swiftly whispered 'Peer Gynt' to him just in time for him to make the swap and get the music the right way up.

As befitted a Great Maestro in the Making, Clifford Hope-Evans kept them waiting, doubtless delayed conducting Important International Business on his phone instead of getting out there to conduct the Chervil Symphony Orchestra. When he did appear, it was at a brisk trot, the briefest bow to the audience, the baton aloft... and they were off.

Beryl's gentle little solo in the first movement of Peer Gynt, *Morning*, she reckoned represented the sun rising, caressed by clarinets and bassoons creating a landscape beneath, a vista of calm that had always been there and only required a little light to twinkle into being. Beryl was steady as a rock. She generated tingles down her own spine with her playing. Wahay! Here they went!

It went swimmingly. That was not to say it was perfect. Oh no. Even the most uninformed critic would detect a lack of unanimity in the tempo – you could blame Clifford for that if you liked – and in the tuning, particularly of the strings, but nothing disastrous occurred. Aase died nicely, Anitra danced politely, and Stan Bun and his bassoon colleague set off into the *Hall of the Mountain King* with promise of an exuberant ride to come, as indeed it did, a bit ragged, but brimful of gusto with dollops of whipped cream on top.

So, first item out of the way, and the audience applause plus the relief of making a reasonable fist of things was heady. Beryl thought, *This is it. This is what it's all about. All that practising and dreaming. This is fame and glory. For now. This moment.* Okay, it was not exactly a humble assessment of the performance so far, but what the hell? The audience was happy, Madam Mayor slapped her podgy palms together enthusiastically, and Beryl was happy. So roll out the fairly famous piano virtuoso and on with the Concerto.

Dmitri Waldstein, he of moderate fame, had long locks slicked back and an arrogant stance, with head thrown back to give his beaky nose a chance, underpinned with a thin arch of a mouth. Very Lisztian. If he was her son, Beryl would tell him to wash his hair and sit up properly, but she had to admit he got round the notes pretty well. Quite famous, quite competent. At the end, he sprang to his feet, flung right arm across his chest as if about to break into the American National Anthem, and bowed suddenly and low. The audience loved it. After that, he recalled it wasn't actually just about him alone, and shook Bernard's hand, then planted a kiss either side of Mildred Trimble's outraged face, waved a hand to embrace the rest of the orchestra and repeated his bow. Several times. He then evidently seemed to remember another pressing appointment and scuttled off, head in air, only to return a few moments later and go through the whole palaver over again.

In this manner, the first half was over. The orchestra was released for the interval, and being an amateur band, splintered off into the audience to greet kith and kin and saunter over to the Church Hall for tea or coffee. Not wine nor beer, certainly not. Not for the band. Perish the thought. If Beryl spotted Gerald in a corner clutching a bottle with evidence of whitish foam on his moustache, she choose not to censure.

What surprised her was that she saw Oscar queueing. She had not thought he would think of coming to hear the concert. Also that uncle of Mel's, that unassuming little man with a fine line in drawing psychopathic ducklings with arms.

She approached them. 'What do you think?' she asked.

Before either could reply, Mel was upon them. 'Stop queue jumping, B,' she said. 'Or let me join you. Hi, uncle. It's going amazing, don't you agree? That piano dude, he looks a bit of a crazy guy, but he's pretty ace. Hey, I could murder a glass of wine, but better not, eh? Come on, Uncle Arthur, tell me what you really think of it. Did you hear my trills in *Morning*?'

Uncle Arthur looked a little bewildered, but he rallied. 'I did notice, I really did, but I wasn't sure whether it was you or one of the others. I couldn't see very well. But it sounded very... very professional.'

'Thank you, uncle. That's the right thing to say.'

Beryl wondered if he could really remember back that far. After all, it was right at the beginning of the half.

Arthur turned to her. 'I was also struck by your playing of the opening phrase. It immediately set a perfect, um, limpid tone. I've heard *Morning* so many times, but this really pushed the dark aside and let the sun shine through.'

What a lovely thing to say. *He looks as if he actually did notice*, thought Beryl. And that he remembered. 'Thank you, Mel's Uncle. You're very kind.'

'Oh, go on, B,' said Mel. 'Call him Arthur, go on. There's more to him than just being my uncle. Atta girl. Or Mister Davison, if you want to be formal.'

'Stop it, Mel. Very well, then. Arthur, thank you.'

Arthur smiled. A moment of meeting.

Beryl noticed Oscar was trying to drift away. She knew what he was doing. He wanted a glass of wine or beer and thought she would disapprove. Well, she did. But now that he was moving out of her house – or said he was – he had got to become his own conscience. She looked the other way.

The second half was rumbustious. It was as though the presence of an outsider in the first half, the pianist, made the orchestra be on its best behaviour, and now he was not there, they could take their shoes and ties off and loaf about in slippers and disgraceful old sweaters in front of the tele. So Sibelius got a fine if rough airing as they ripped through the *Karelia Suite*. They then touchingly lyricised Grieg's *Solveig's Song* from Peer Gynt as a contrast, and finished by tearing *Finlandia* to pieces.

A short second half. Before Beryl had really returned to consciousness after the rocky ride, players and audience were starting to disperse home or to their favoured places of refreshment. In Beryl's case, this was of course the good old Hippocampus. No doubt Gerald the Tuba would be joining his mates in the Duck and Grouse. Pooh pooh. Beryl floated to the pub on a wave of adrenaline in the company of Mel and Stan. Mel's Uncle – sorry, Arthur – was tagging along with them. Good, good. Not many others. Just the select few. That was good too. The Hippo was quieter than usual, but then, Beryl had hardly ever been in there of a Sunday evening. Maybe that was how it always was. Anyway, with the iron determination that she could exhibit when necessary, Beryl managed to pre-empt Stanislav Bun getting the drinks in.

'I am desolate,' he said. 'I have pride. My honour, the honour of Poland. She is insulted.'

'Oh, shut up, Stan,' said Mel. 'You talk a load of bollocks. Did the concert go well for you?'

'It is brilliant. Did you not hear? Do you listen only to yourself?'

They were standing at the bar as the drinks were poured. Beryl, in command, felt maternal. Her little brood. 'We are a team,' she pronounced. 'The CSO takes collective credit for the genius of its component parts. Don't you think, Mel's... um, Arthur?'

He started. 'Oh,' he said. 'Yes. I mean, I expect so. It was... very jolly. Very enthusiastic playing. I felt you were all enjoying yourselves. It was infectious.'

'Awesome,' said Mel. 'Hey guys, that's enough of the post mortem sort of thing. What's everyone doing for Christmas, yeah? Uncle? Why don't you come to Mummy's? It'll be a riot. We could work on Poppy and the Gnoxie, yeah? Though I don't suppose there'll be much time when we aren't completely piddled. I'm going 'cos Jason's doing a self-denial thing in a monastery or something, and I'm not staying in the flat on my own, not at Christmas, and anyway Mummy may be an Amazonian tyrant but she cooks a mega-meal.'

Beryl thought Arthur for a moment looked terrified. But he seemed to rally, and said, 'Oh. Oh. Thank you, Mel. I... I would be in the way... Constance would not... She never did. No. I'd be... No, I have my own little routine. I enjoy Christmas in my own quiet way. But thank you for asking. Yes, I must decline.'

'You sure, Uncle? She wouldn't mind. I'd tell her not to. She can't browbeat me. No, all right, she can. But she's taught me to fight for my rights. Never say die, yeah? But yes, I can see that maybe charades and Twister and that aren't your scene. Okay, I won't bully you. I don't want to be like her, not really.'

She turned to the others. 'What you doing, Stan, B?'

'Me?' said Stan. 'My wife, she work at night club, so I have the friends from Poland to come on Wigilia – that is your Christmas Eve – and we drink much Polish vodka and eat *povitica*, which is Polish holiday bread. And fish and chips. Is proper to eat carp, but the fish man do not sell him, so fish and chips for us. After vodka, everything tastes the same anyway. And Arthur Davison, in Poland, we always leave place at table for the unexpected guest, so if you would like to drop in...? We talk Polish though, so maybe you feel not at home.'

Beryl was quiet for a moment. She was thinking. 'I'm having a quiet Christmas too. It'll be a change. I suppose I might invite Oscar over, so I've somebody to cook for. And Mel's uncle, if you're not going to your sister's and if you care to drop in, well, it would be… you would be most welcome.'

Arthur looked confused. 'Oh, thank you, thank you all. But I do have my own little routine, so…'

There was silence, insofar as it is ever silent in a busy pub. Mel looked at Arthur, then at Beryl. Beryl looked at the table. Stan thumped his mighty chest and bellowed, 'Fish and chips and vodka. It becomes new tradition, no? All the best people eat him at Christmas?'

'What if the chippies are closed on Christmas Day, Stan?' said Mel.

'The offer stands,' said Beryl. 'Just drop in.'

Arthur muttered something inaudible.

The moment passed.

12 Starting the Creation

Christmas came and went. Carol concerts were played and sung, audiences clapped. Bakers baked, Chervil meandered along, like the river Cher on three sides of the centre, always different, yet always the same. Rabbits hopped around the Market Square. Or perhaps didn't. Who could say for sure?

Arthur spent the day itself alone, doing what Arthur did on Christmas Day, which involved singing along with the King's Carol Service (quietly), at least those bits that featured in OUP's *Carols for Choirs* and the congregational carols that he knew. He then progressed through a glass of Chardonnay to two of the Co-op's finest chicken Kievs (they came in twos in the packet, and yes, he ate both, with a gleeful anarchic freedom) plus oven chips and petit pois. This was topped off with a rum baba (only one, though there were two in the packet, but stomachs only have a finite capacity) and finally coffee and a glass of port. Yes, port! So far it had lasted him four years. Next year he would have to buy a new bottle. But perhaps next year, things might be different. How could he know? By the time he had finished his port, the day was in that odd period between late afternoon and early evening, so he snoozed a little, and finished off with watching a DVD of the *Railway Children*, which made him cry. Then he went to bed and dreamed he was singing in the Albert Hall in a Prom, except that it appeared to be on a cruise ship in warm sun-drenched climes.

At some point during the day itself, Mel rang him to wish him a happy Christmas, to tell him her mother Constance was driving her to drink, that they were about to play charades, and that she'd decided to give up on Poppy and Cuddles because maybe Jason was right and it was too vicious and might incite juvenile readers to a life of violence, but it was what she had wanted to write and she wasn't prepared to compromise. So to the wastepaper basket with it. Instead, she was going to write a best-selling romance which Mills and Boon would fall over themselves to publish. It would be a doddle and she'd be rich and famous.

That had left Arthur despondent. He revisited his drawings and sniffed a sorry-for-himself sniff, and put them back in the drawer, to be confined, as far as he was concerned, to oblivion.

If only.

He may have wondered whether Stan and friends did indeed eat fish and chips. He had no doubts about the vodka. He may have wondered what Mel's friend Beryl was doing. He didn't know – he couldn't have known – that Beryl and Victoria were feeling sorry for themselves too in their day *à deux*. Truth to tell, Beryl only knew of Victoria's anguish when the cat inserted an unambiguous message in Beryl's mind to the effect that she wished to gorge herself on chicken giblets, it being Christmas, instead of the poxy cat biscuits, which was all Beryl had produced. Beryl did respond with a bit of chicken skin, there being no giblets in the chicken she had cooked and barely touched, but it was not enough. Beryl had even wished her disappointing son Algernon had decided to stay over Christmas, or at least come for the day, but he'd gone to some commune or suchlike; something to do with the Winter solstice.

So Christmas passed. A week later, the New Year opened its bedroom curtains and let in the predictable chill and drizzle of January.

And now it was the first rehearsal in the year of the Chervil Choral Society, and their start on Haydn's *Creation*. The prospect of performing with the Chervil Symphony Orchestra was, for them, a big deal. Usually their concerts were more modest, accompanied by piano or sometimes organ.

Arthur Davison was in his chair in good time, second from the right in the basses, if you looked at the choir from the front. He had his legs crossed, which was a big no-no from Maestro Pontdexter's point of view, since it, as he said, stopped the chest opening properly and strangled the sound. But they were not yet singing, and Arthur thought he could take the risk. In fact most of the choir were currently chatting away loudly. After all they had the Christmas gossip to catch up on. For Arthur, it was rather tedious. There was also a new person in the choir, a bass, it seemed. He thought he might have seen him at the orchestral concert; Mel had greeted someone called Oscar. But then, why not? Lots of people were at the concert. Oscar, unusual name. It rang a bell from much earlier. Some years back. Here in Chervil. This Oscar seemed to be well in with the others already. Some people just naturally bonded.

'Ladies and gentlemen, please,' cried Bernard Pontdexter, exasperation oozing from every crease and fold of his bulk.

To reinforce his point, Iris, rehearsal pianist, played a stentorian taradiddle. The talking in the choir gradually subsided, to be overtaken by a wave of 'Ssh's' from the virtuous.

'Thank you, thank you,' said Bernard. 'Right. *The Creation*. Only three months to get it shipshape. Lots to do. Lots to do. Let's get cracking with "The Heavens Are Telling". I reckon most of you will have sung that before, so let's get it note-perfect first time, ha, ha. Oh and let me introduce our new recruit, Oscar, um…'

'Silvero,' supplied the new recruit.

'Silvero. Oscar Silvero. No stranger to singing in front of an audience, ha, ha. Some of you may have seen him strutting the boards. No strutting here, Oscar, thank you. Don't want the ladies in the audience chucking their knickers at us.'

There was a stunned silence. It seemed to Arthur that even Bernard, who was usually oblivious to criticism, realised maybe he had overstepped the bounds of good taste this time.

Rupert, choir chairman, broke the hiatus. 'Bernard,' he said. '*The Creation, Die Schöpfung*. Are we doing it in English or German?' Arthur, who sat next to him in the basses, cringed anew. Rupert always had to show off, in an eager puppy sort of way. Arthur knew that Rupert knew full well they were singing it in English. For one thing, the hire copies they were using, except for

Rupert, only had the English text. They were rather battered Novello copies. Rupert had to be different, and fielded a venerable Peters edition, bound in leather. Probably his grandfather's or something, which apart from having both German and English texts, would undoubtedly have different page numbers. And probably different underlay in places. Arthur knew from experience that Rupert would consistently and constantly feel obliged to point these out.

Bernard Pontdexter was wise to Rupert's foibles. 'Will you all use the same edition, please,' he said mildly, his momentary indiscretion in witticisms forgotten. 'It will save ages of argument. All of you. There are enough copies, aren't there? It's in English, so unless you all want to engage in real-time translation or copy all the German text in and then rub it out again after the concert, because these are Hire Copies and all marks must be rubbed out, so I hope you've all got pencils. Now page 42, if you please. The last eight bars of number thirteen, please, Iris.'

And controlling his temper admirably, he waved his conducting pencil.

Iris, on the ball as always, started off with the final eight bars of the preceding recitative. Bernard, with magnificent flourish, brought his pencil down for the start of "The Heavens Are Telling", but the response was meagre to say the least. Most had not yet found the page, or missed the page number when Bernard announced it, or didn't understand where Iris was going from. Bernard should have known better. Bad start to rehearsals. Bad start.

Arthur sighed. It was always thus. He himself was ready, right page and everything. He quietly prided himself on paying attention.

Bernard stopped them. Or rather, he stopped waving his pencil about. Most of those who were actually singing carried on because they weren't watching. They were, after all, sight-reading, thought Arthur. It was perfectly predictable.

But not to Maestro Pontdexter. 'Oh for God's sake,' he said. 'I stopped five minutes ago. Hold your copies up. Up, up, up...' he prodded his pencil towards the ceiling to illustrate his words, '... then you can see me and the music, not to mention opening the chest and improving the sound and... Oh, never mind. Page 42 for those who were asleep. Eight bars of the recit as before, Iris, please.'

And off they started again. Apart from old Walter in the tenors, who was still having trouble finding the place. His neighbour flicked Walter's score to the correct page for him, commendably while still singing. He was used to it.

Maybe some of them had sung it before, but it was hard to tell. So they belted it out without attempting to phrase or shape or pay attention to dynamics. Copies, if they were being held up, gradually slumped down, as did heads.

At the end of the first chorus section, they stopped, though Bernard's pencil had stopped earlier.

'Loud and wrong,' he said. 'Better than quiet and wrong, but it would be nice if you attempted loud and right. I know, I know, first time through and that, but some of you are half-way decent musicians allegedly.'

He rolled up his left shirt sleeve which had worked itself loose during his waving, and mopped his brow with the back of his hand.

'Okay. Let's work on it. From the top again, stopping this time.' He addressed Iris at the piano. 'Straight in, Iris. Just give them the chord.'

Naturally since most of the choir failed to hear his remark to Iris, they were caught unawares. It was a shambles. He stopped them. 'Okay, okay. Let's do it in parts. Let me hear just the Sop and Alt for starters. Ladies only,' he shouted. 'Stand, please. Thank you. At least you've got that right. The notes, Iris, please.'

Arthur allowed himself to muse. Why couldn't Bernard Pontdexter manage without sarcasm? If he only thought a bit about what he was doing. Like being clear where they were going from. It wasn't difficult, surely, and he would get much better results.

However, for this concert, Bernard wasn't going to be conducting the performance. At the helm would be the chap from the Chervil Symphony Orchestra, about whom Arthur knew very little, though he usually put in creditable performances with the orchestra. Chap with a double-barrelled name. He might prove to be worse than Bernard with a choir, of course. Now, now, be positive, he chided himself. He was likely going to be fine. And with the soloists. After all, he had been okay with that Dmitri Waldstein fellow, but solo singers were different. Divas, that sort of thing, with temper tantrums.

He surveyed the altos in front of him. The backs of their heads were a familiar sight. It was sometimes surprising when he saw them from the front, coming into or leaving rehearsal for example, or during the milling around before a concert. Familiar backs but unfamiliar faces. Just now they presented a fearful wall of bodies, because they were standing and he was sitting. Not for the first time, he reflected that singing in a choir was a lonesome business. Yes, of course he was part of a team. Well, two teams: one, the basses, two, the choir. But how many could he actually put a name to? He had been singing with the choir for about ten years and wouldn't count any of them friends. He knew the names of all the basses, but although he sometimes went to the pub after rehearsals, he was generally ignored in the banter.

The basses. Currently eight of them plus this new Oscar chap. Rupert, on his right, was chair of the choir, and was, Arthur considered, objectionable. Charles, on the further side of Rupert, was in his seventies, reliable, but tended to turn up late to rehearsals allegedly to miss warm-ups. In fact, Bernard only occasionally did warm-ups. Rupert was always nagging him to. Rupert loved them, particularly when they involved what Arthur thought of as physical jerks – stretches, shaking bits of yourself, breathing exercises. Rupert flung himself around wildly, mortally endangering those next to him. Arthur had learnt to duck.

The other five basses had names like Geoff and Simon and James and Michael. Just names. Collectively, their abilities averaged out to a reasonable sound, but individually they were various. Charles was okay, Rupert was erratic and loud. Arthur tried to assess his own prowess as a singer as objectively as he could. He considered he was precise and accurate, but rather quiet. A brick in the wall, that did its job efficiently, instead of the flamboyant render on the surface. Arthur was pleased with the analogy, though he didn't know he knew so much about masonry.

And there was this new chap. Looked vaguely familiar. Arthur glanced down the row. Oscar Silvero? He was sure he had seen the name somewhere sometime. It sounded an unlikely name. Italian? He didn't look it. He was quite short, sparse hair. Looked nervy.

The ladies reached the first solo passage. Bernard bellowed out 'sing along with the solo,' as they reached it, and they did, with gusto. Particularly the altos, judging by their heaving shoulders in front of Arthur. Where did all that breathing from the diaphragm stuff go? Another thing Bernard was keen on. Keep the shoulders down, don't tighten the neck, allow the free passage of air.

After a couple of phrases of solo, Haydn brings the chorus back in, and, predictable as night following day (which incidentally was probably what the soloists were singing about in Arthur's view; the English was a bit odd) most of them failed to notice the choir entry and carried on singing the soprano solo line.

Thus it went on. Bernard's shirt became progressively less tucked in round his straining belt, his shirtsleeves descended and were re-rolled like yo-yos. His brow perspired freely. After the ladies, the men did their bit, then they all did it together. Arthur predicted, based on years of experience, that the time had come for a little lecture.

'Okay, chaps, take a seat,' said Bernard after they achieved a more-or-less accurate run-through of the number. 'Ladies and gentlemen, *The Creation* is arguably Haydn's greatest creation.' He waited for a non-existent murmur of appreciation at his choice of words. 'Imagine that first performance, back in 1799. Imagine the audience hearing the tumult of the overture, the "Representation of Chaos". It ends in the darkness of C minor. By the end of part one, with "The Heavens Are Telling", we have reached the light of C major. By then, chaos is meant to have been put in order. Your job is, at the very least, to make sure the chaos stays well and truly in the overture. You should be ordered in your singing, accurate, at the same time enthusiastic, awestruck. It's not every day a world is created in front of the paying public. You're getting there, you're getting there, however...' Bernard was fond of pregnant "however"s in his little lectures. 'However, be aware, ladies and gentlemen, there are tricky moments in the work. Taxing. You come in and out, framing solos and orchestral bits. You will need to be *alert*. This, if I may say so, is not always your forte. When you come in for an entry, you must be bang on the ball. You can't spend pages getting the hang of it, trying to remember how this or that bit goes. No time for doziness. However...' He mopped his brow down. 'You have assistance in three ways. One, there is the orchestra. Let them do the chaos bit, you do the creating of life and light. And there are the soloists. I can't recall who they are offhand, but they're top-class, top-class. You must live up to them, not get carried away listening to their beautiful, beautiful voices. And then there is Clifford. Clifford Hope-Evans, maestro of the orchestra who is conducting the performance. Not me. That must be a great relief to you.'

Bernard clearly expected a chorus of protest, which did not occur. Undaunted, he finished his little lecture and continued the rehearsal. By the end, Rupert, choir chairman, had only three times put his hand up to enquire about differing underlay or dynamics in his Peters edition. Each time Bernard told him to get a Novello copy. Rupert wouldn't. Arthur predicted that. It was a power-play thing. Peters was his weapon.

During the rehearsal, Arthur Davison had been vaguely aware of some difference in the sound of the basses from normal, most obviously when they sang their line on their own. There could be only one reason. This Oscar chap. Everything else was unchanged from the previous line-up. He was having an effect. The name was familiar to Arthur; he was sure he had seen it somewhere a long time ago. It was the sort of name you noticed. During the tea break in rehearsal, Arthur found himself near to where Oscar was talking to Bernard, who was fitfully paying attention. Apart from Oscar having maybe been at the orchestra concert, the man's face was entirely unfamiliar, and yet he knew the name. Curious.

'You see, Bernard,' Oscar was saying, 'I actually trained as a classical singer. At the Guildhall as it happens, but then I realised the stage, touring, the light repertoire, offered more money. And as it happens, I've had a look at the bass solos in the Creation, and if you'd like – I don't want to force myself on you – but if you like, I could fill in the solos during rehearsal. Give the choir a feeling for the real thing. What say you?'

'What? Yes, perhaps. I don't... Oh, Rupert,' Bernard cried as he spied the choir chairman going by, 'can I have a word. Look, thing is...' And off he went. Oscar looked a little put out. He glanced about, presumably to see if anyone had noticed he was all on his own, spotted Arthur and smiled. Insincerely, Arthur thought. And over he came.

'Oscar,' Oscar said with outstretched hand. 'I'm Oscar Silvero. You've probably heard... But no. The past is the past. New beginnings. Whatever I was, I am now a member of the... what's this choir called?'

'The Chervil Choral...'

'Society. Of course, of course. Never forget a name. And you are?'

'Arthur Davison. I've been singing with the choir for goodness knows how many years. I also am a bass.'

'Arthur. Arthur. Good to meet you, Arthur. Little trick, that. Learnt it while touring. Repeat someone's name several times when you meet them. That way it sticks in the mind. I am always meeting new people on the road. I used to, that is. Not now. Settled here now. Ah, it all comes back to me, singing in a choir like this. I was a choirboy, you know. A chorister at Southwark Cathedral. Long time ago. Very long time. Ah... Then I was going to be a solo singer – oratorio, opera, recitals, that sort of thing. Trained at the Guildhall, would you believe. But the lure of the clubs seduced me. At least the money did, and so I became England's Frank Sinatra. Songs from yesteryear. Something to make you laugh, something to make you cry. Yes. Or you could say Sinatra was the States' Oscar Silvero, ha ha ha.'

Arthur was not really very interested. Nor was he convinced. This Oscar seemed to need to puff himself up and it didn't quite ring true. Still, so what?

'And you?' said Oscar.

'Me?' What did Oscar want to hear? Arthur was not given to advertising himself. 'Oh, I'm just a...'

But Oscar saw Mike, one of the other basses, walking past. 'Hello there,' he called out. 'Just wanted to check. The pub afterwards. Okay if I come along? The name's Oscar...'

Mike said he knew he was Oscar and it was no problem, everyone was welcome. It was a public place, after all; it was a pub. Mike thought he was a bit of a wag. Arthur had noticed that before. But at least it took the onus off Arthur having to explain who or what he was to Oscar. He wondered what answer he would have come up with if Mike had not walked past. As it was, Iris was signalling the Call to Return to Seats in her traditional way on the piano, which for reasons known only to herself was to bash out the beginning of the Grand March from *Tannhaüser*.

The rehearsal continued. Up and down. Like Bernard's shirt sleeves. Like the choir as they alternately stood and sat, which was Bernard's strategy for keeping them awake.

While Arthur walked alone to the Hippocampus afterwards, he searched for words to describe the difference in sound from the bass line as a result of Oscar. It was richer, yes, perhaps more together. No, not quite that. More focused, that was it. Almost as though the various voices, instead of being a shot gun firing pellets in a halo around the bullseye, were turning into a laser beam zeroing in on target. Arthur felt this was probably mixing several metaphors, but it seemed to sum it up. But why was Oscar's name familiar to him? Then he remembered. He'd seen it on a poster outside the theatre a while back. Last year, was it?

He arrived at the Hippocampus somewhat ahead of the small but noisy contingent of others from the choir who imbibed there post-rehearsal. His early arrival was partly because they tended to yatter before they set off and partly because he wanted to choose his own seat, usually in a bay window. If they chose to sit with him, all well and good. If they didn't... well, they didn't. And they usually didn't.

However, on this occasion, he arrived at the pub at the same time as a small group arriving from the other direction. They carried cases of odd shapes and sizes. One of them yelled across to him. 'Uncle,' she cried. It was Mel, the case she carried possibly containing a very large snail. Or a French horn. With her was, yes, Stanislav Bun the baker and seer of the Dwelf and invisible rabbits. And Beryl, Mel's chum from the Motley Brew. Friendly faces, the three of them. They greeted him as long-lost friend or customer or uncle, and wouldn't he join them? Well, why not? It would make a change from the rather tedious choir chat.

Inside Stan insisted on buying drinks for all of them. 'No, no,' he protested in the face of objections, 'you are my friends. I am saying thank you, is all.'

'He always does this,' Mel told Arthur. 'But hey, if it makes him happy, I'm cool with it.'

They sat in a cosy area just around a corner, out of sight of where the choir group usually went, which was presumably why Arthur had never spotted Mel there before, assuming they always came there, assuming their rehearsals were also on Thursdays, assuming, well, anything you like. The fact was he hadn't.

As they settled, Beryl asked Arthur, 'How did Oscar get on, Mel's uncle?'

Arthur was momentarily confused. 'Oscar?' he said, trying to work out, first, whether he should know why she should know Oscar and second, why she should know Oscar was at the choir practice, since it was his first appearance, and thirdly whether

Oscar was the Oscar who had been at the rehearsal or perhaps some other Oscar, which would make even less sense. Oscar was not a common name. 'Oscar? The new man? In the choir?' he said.

She smiled. 'Oscar Silvero. Yes, it's his first time. He auditioned before Christmas. You met him at the orchestra concert. At least, he was there?'

'Yes, oh yes,' said Arthur. 'Yes, I remember. Tell me, I'm sure I've seen his name before. Outside the Lyric Theatre, advertising something, some show.'

'That's him. He's what they call a crooner, I think, or he used to be. He's retired from the stage now. He lodges with me. He used to look after my mother, who has Alzheimers. When he sings to her, she's a young girl again. It's marvellous.' She wondered why she was going on and on so. 'Anyway, did he seem to fit in with the choir all right?'

Arthur was about to answer when there was a wave of laughter from round the corner in the bar, topped by a mellifluous baritone.

'Oh,' said Beryl. 'That's him. I hear him. He seems to be in his element. Ah, well, I can't stop him.'

Mel put a hand on her arm. 'He'll be okay, B. It'll be cool, you'll see.'

So, Arthur thought, how could he describe Oscar's contribution to the Chervil Choral? 'He was good, I believe,' Arthur said. 'He has an effect on the bass-line. I was trying to think in what way as I walked here, and I think he helps us to be more focused. Yes. Like a laser...' He decided his metaphor, no, it must be a simile if there was the word like in it, was too complicated to venture, and petered out.

Stanislav appeared brandishing a tray with four glasses on it on one hand like some professional waiter, the other hand behind his back. He distributed the largesse. 'Is the singing people,' he said. 'They are noisy, yes? And your Oscar person, Madame Flautist, he is there too.' He turned to Arthur Davison, giving him his small dry sherry. 'Oscar, he is real person, yes? Flesh and blood. Not like that small man in the bakery. But is true, he is not very big, this Oscar. Big voice, small body. Sorry, sorry,' he said to Beryl. 'That is rude. I apologise. Normal body, nice body.'

Beryl laughed. 'It's okay, Stan. If that's the worst you can do in insults, you're a very polite person, which you are, of course.'

'No, no,' cried Stan. 'I can be very, very rude. I am Slav. We have the hot blood. We are passionate. And sensitive,' he added for Arthur's benefit. All of which seemed to exhaust him, so he thumped down onto his chair and downed half his pint of beer in one swallow.

Oh dear, thought Arthur. How noisy everyone was, when you came down to it. And yet, when they strove together towards a common purpose, what wonderful music they could make. All they needed was a conductor. And a creator, of course.

13 Beryl Demoted

It was a month or so later, a Thursday evening. In Castle Street Comprehensive School Hall, the Chervil Symphony Orchestra was assembling for its rehearsal.

Beryl wove around a knot of cellists to her place. She put down her bag and opened the plastic container of experimental flapjacks so they could cool off; she had only just taken them out of the oven before she left home. They were her interval reward, and she wanted to try them out on Stan and Mel afterwards. Beryl's flapjacks at the Motley Brew were famous the length and breadth of Chervil, or so she liked to believe. It was the touch of molasses and a little balsamic vinegar that made them totally toothsome. The current experiment involved a little cayenne and ground sumac instead. They might be ghastly. She unfurled her music stand while looking around. It was strange, but the cellists seemed to be the only gregarious group. A few violins were diligently practising. The second oboe slouched in his chair, alternately grinning vacuously and sucking his reed with squeaky noises; the first oboe was of course Evelyn, who was primly and properly bolt upright. Next to them, Fred, first clarinet, was reading a magazine. As well as those in her quintet, Beryl knew who most of the players were, she knew their names, recognised their faces, but they all seemed to belong to separate worlds, coming together only to make music. Except for the cellos, lucky bastards. And the brass, of course, but they only came in for the last couple of rehearsals. Apart from the French horns, which for reasons Beryl had never understood were regarded as woodwind and turned up all the time. Well, most of the time. They were a funny breed. She must talk to Mel about it sometime, why they had to play from treble clef parts without any key signature, how a horn made it into the regular wind quintet, why sometimes they stuck their hands up the bell; it was all very esoteric.

The second flute, old Cyril, was pleasant enough, but he and she were different generations and she had no respect for his playing. How could you play for so many years and still be so awful? Not to mention his little problem counting rests. Beryl assembled her flute and squinted along the barrel to ensure alignment, then breathed down it to warm it up a bit. As she did, she spotted a new face entering the hall, a young man, more a boy really, with an insolent quiff. The case he was carrying—too thin for a clarinet, too wide for a flute. Must be an oboe. There wasn't a third oboe part, was there?

The young man came over to her, said 'Hi,' sat and opened the case. It contained both flute and piccolo, which was why it was wider than her case. A serious player.

'Where's Cyril?' she asked. It sounded abrupt. Why should he know? If something was up with the old guy and this boy had been drafted in to take over, he wouldn't know.

'Who's Cyril?'

'He's second flute.'

'I was told one of the flutes has had a heart attack. I was asked to play first.'

This was appalling. If a tornado had suddenly removed the roof, Beryl could not have been more shocked. Not because of Cyril, poor old Cyril. He had never looked well. She found herself forgiving his ineptitude. No, it was this young man, this smooth-faced quiff, announcing he was playing first. She was first flute. She was proud of it. The little shit.

Before she had decided how to retaliate, he raised his flute to his lips and played a limpid flourish. The tone took her breath away. Nevertheless, it was an outrage. To be ousted by a mere child and made to sound incompetent by comparison was too much. This was the Chervil Symphony Orchestra. This was meant to be fun. This was meant to be Beryl starring in her own small way, particularly in the showy solo bits in the "Representation of

Chaos", as the overture to the *Creation* was called. It should be renamed the Representation of Beryl's Prowess. Not of Some Little Shit's Prowess.

Without a word, she stormed off to confront Marcus, second desk, second violins, no great shakes as a fiddler, but the chief organiser and stirrer of the CSO.

'Well?' she demanded.

'What?' he said. Then he saw the new flautist twiddling away.

'Cyril,' he said. 'Poor Cyril. Last Monday. A stroke. It'll be weeks, probably months, if ever, before he'll be able to play again, apparently. Luckily, this young chap, Lucien, has just taken a post at Castle Street Comp. We're lucky to have him. Ex-NYO, principle flute. Very keen.'

'NYO? Don't fob me off with initials.' Beryl seethed. 'And what's this about him playing first? I'm first. I've been first for three years, no, nearly four. And I've been practising the solo bits,' she finished weakly.

'NYO is the National Youth Orchestra, Beryl. He's really up-and-coming. We're incredibly lucky to have him. I couldn't say "Oh, by the way, you'll be playing second," could I? If we play our cards right, he might do a concerto with us.'

This was the last straw. 'Lucky!' screamed Beryl. 'It's not bloody lucky. Not for me it isn't. This is a community orchestra.'

She became aware of a tapping sound. Maestro Clifford Hope-Evans was signalling a desire to get going.

'Here's the second flute part,' whispered Marcus. 'I got it back from Cyril's wife.' Beryl grabbed it from him and retreated to her place, where she saw this Lucien person had swapped his music stand for hers and had sequestered the first flute part. She sat in Cyril's place and glowered. As a result, she managed to make a dog's breakfast of everything she played, while Lucien tootled away like an infallible angel.

At the break, she went off to the Ladies to slap cold water over her face and try to compose herself.

When she came back, Beryl bent to her flapjack container for reassurance. There was one missing. She was sure. The abhorrent Lucien was deep in some conversation on his phone. She looked at him. There were definite crumbs on his trousers. That was the last straw. If he had shown any decency, she might have given him one as a peace offering, but now he had completely blown it.

As she trudged off to the Hippocampus after the rehearsal, it started raining, which was definitely Lucien's fault. She dripped, she seethed. And she planned. Beware the flautist flouted, Lucien. Trample over Beryl at your peril. She was vaguely aware that Mel was saying something to her, but her peevement made her deaf.

Inside, as Stan, as usual, was buying drinks, she overflowed with it to Mel. 'The little shit. I'm first. The upstart, the snotty-nosed whatsit, the… the bastard. Is he too high and mighty for second? Am I supposed to kiss his feet and be grateful? Well, I'm not. I am a hundred and twenty percent not.'

Mel said she hadn't a clue what Beryl was talking about.

'Oh, I am sorry, Mel dear. It's that boy they've brought in who has to play first because he's so bloody brilliant. I ask you! Anyway, let's forget it. I'm big enough to be magnaniwhatsit. Deep breaths, that's the thing. There'll be other times, other concerts, and there's the quintet. What did you call us? The Famous Five? That miserable boy is nothing to me, nothing. The little shit.'

'Well, B. He's certainly got you motoring? Forget it, yeah? Not worth the aggro. Nobody is. To me, you're the great flautissimo.'

'Thank you, dear. I know I'm over-reacting. But just let him screw up once and… Do you know what he did? He stole one of my flapjacks while I was in the toilet. Can you credit it?'

'The rat-bag. Unspeakable, B. Cut his bollocks off, that's what I say.'

'No, I'll tell you what, Mel dear. They are a trial, these flapjacks, I brought them in for a snack during the break and to try them out on you and Stan. There's a bit of… No I'm not going to tell you. Wait till Stan's back and you can try them blind, as it were.'

As if by command, there was the man himself, two pints and a glass of white wine in his huge hands.

'We've got to try B's flapjacks, Stan,' said Mel.

They did.

'What's in them?' asked Beryl.

'Oats,' said Mel. 'Easy-peasy.'

Stan chewed with enormous concentration. 'I have something with the bite. I chew, and then this thing chews me back. I like. Is chilli, that is what I say.'

Beryl felt a warm glow. 'I knew I couldn't pull the wool over your eyes, Stan. And there's something else...'

Neither of them identified the sumac. It was subtle, a trace of acidity. But the two of them declared the result a triumph.

And Beryl decided, she'd make some more next week, and she'd put more chilli in the top ones. A lot more. And maybe some garlic. Or Epsom salts. No, no, just the chilli. That should be enough. That would teach the little shit. With luck his lips would be tingling so much it would ruin his embouchure. Revenge! She attacked her wine with gusto, and thought of having another, and then remembered she had the car because she hadn't wanted to carry the flapjack tin all the way from Beech Grove, and as proprietress of the Brew, a responsible citizen, she'd better not.

Later she confessed all to Hattie. It felt wonderfully naughty to see her plan for retribution written down in pen and ink there in front of her. Liberation. All she needed to do was to go through with it.

14 Choir Discord

Meanwhile, at the same time as the orchestra was rehearsing, the Chervil Choral Society had also been having its regular session over in St Boniface's Church Hall.

Architecturally, the hall was an insult to the church. There was a tinge of pre-fab about it. But it was a good space for a choir to practise in, with a serviceable piano, enough chairs, adequate if rather dodgy heating, and a slightly flattering acoustic.

Braving the ever-vigilant lurking caretaker and his jangling keys, Arthur Davison entered the hall, his music case (leather, rather pricey, from Notes4U) equipped with score of the Creation, pencil and eraser.

It felt like entering a haven of rest and tranquillity. Over there, Iris was quietly strumming away on the piano. Maestro Bernard Pontdexter was talking to his wife, whose name Arthur didn't know. A few singers were there, chatting. And of course, Rupert, chairman. He looked as if he was mentally deranged, thought Arthur, his shock of red hair apparently trying to escape in all directions. Arthur did not want to talk to Rupert, but alas, Rupert thought otherwise.

'Arthur,' he cried. 'Just the man. What do you think of warm-up exercises?'

In his mind's eye, Arthur had a vision of Rupert doing star jumps and push-ups, limbering up ready for a marathon singathon.

'Well...' he began.

'I agree, Arthur. Vital. Get you breathing properly. Deeep... in... out...' He demonstrated, flinging his arms wide as he did. 'Mi mi mi mi,' he intoned. Suddenly he lunged at Arthur, jabbed a finger in his chest and dropping his voice to a terrible whisper, said, 'Thing is, he's fickle, Arthur, fickle. Sometimes he does, sometimes he doesn't. We need consistency. Warm-ups shouldn't be an option; we should do them whether we feel like it or not. But thing is, Arthur, Charles... You know Charles? Ever asked why he's always late? To avoid the warm-ups, that's why. It's not on, Arthur. I'm right, you know I am.'

Arthur was actually ambivalent about warm-ups. Yes, they could help get frogs out of throats and maybe help to focus the mind, but the physical bits, stretching and so on, he found embarrassing and, since Rupert sat next to him in the choir, there was a real danger of being hit by his uninhibited arm-waving. Arthur would rather they just did the vocal exercises. But Rupert was undoubtedly right about Charles, and it was galling. His late arrivals disrupted the rehearsal when they'd hardly got started.

At that moment several others came into the hall, and Rupert started doing exercises of his own, little running steps on the spot, shaking bits of himself, wagging his head, making various animal-like noises. It was all to demonstrate how keen he was to the others. Possibly he hoped it would encourage them to do likewise, but they ignored him, engrossed in chatting as they were. They took to their chairs and firmly sat.

So did Arthur. He felt alone. There was nobody on either side, nor in front. There would be, not least Rupert when he'd finished his physical jerks, but at the moment, he felt he stuck out like a sore thumb. Not that anybody paid any attention to him. 'Shoo, shoo, shoo,' he heard Rupert intoning. 'Buddle, biddle, boddle, buddle, biddle, boddle...' Arthur opened his score of the Creation, and idly flicked through. What a lot there was. How much had they achieved in the last month? It didn't seem much. But then, an awful lot of the Creation was soloists, Raphael and Gabriel and Uriel and company. And he did trust Bernard Pontdexter. They would get there; it wouldn't necessarily be a smooth ride. For himself, he considered he was well prepared, after all that singing along with the CD back in his flat. That was more use to him than Rupert's beloved leaping about.

The time ticked round to seven-thirty, the seats filled up, Bernard called them to attention, Iris played her taradiddle; the rehearsal began. No warm-up today. Instead, Bernard said, 'We're going to start really quiet today. That'll get you concentrating. None of your usual belting – and a lot of the chorus bits are pretty upbeat and loud, I know, I know. So page three, number two, bottom of the page. Dead quiet, folks. Get those tummy muscles working. I want control and precision, a tight focused sound. And then on the last note, "light", "And there was light." Open the gates, let the King of Glory in – quote there, Messiah, yeah? But I still want control. It's not a football cry. Right folks, up, up, on your feet. Playtime's over. Iris, top of the page, please.'

First mistake, thought Arthur; "page three, number two," Bernard had said. Half the choir would be vainly trying to find number three on page two. He could see people looking over at their neighbour's copy to see what page they were on. Second mistake, don't mention football. It was bound to set Rupert off. He'd belt that last note like the last trumpet (quote, Messiah). *Oh, he chided himself, do stop being so critical. Could I do it better? Could I do it at all?* Arthur reckoned if he was to stand in front of the choir, his pencil aloft, they would continue chattering away until the cows came home. But there it was, some folk are born to conduct, others to sing. Now *quietly*, as Bernard had exhorted them to do, that was right up his street. A lifetime of not disturbing the neighbouring flats' occupants had its rewards.

Meanwhile, Bernard was doing a pathetic rendition of the opening recitative in which Raphael introduced the initial creation of the world, without form and void, and cloaked in darkness. Raphael was a bass, preferably sonorous – later on, when God got round to creating the humble worm, he was expected ideally to go down to a bottom D – and Bernard, Arthur happened to know, was an alto. Or counter-tenor, whatever the difference was. And quite a fine one, he was led to believe. Quite how he knew this, he couldn't now remember. Anyway, as a sonorous bass, Bernard was pants, as they said these days.

Then the pencil dropped and they were in. "And the spirit of God mov'd upon the face of the waters..." 'Good, good,' encouraged Bernard over the choir, because they were actually keeping down to a rare pianissimo... " ...and God said,..."

At which point, the hall doors swung open, and in marched Charles, the always-late-because-I-hate-warm-ups Charles, and his long-suffering wife, Ann.

'Oh, for heaven's sake...' cried Bernard. The mood was lost just as God was on the point of creating Light.

'Sorry, got held up,' said Charles.

Rupert swung round on them. 'Look, are you in this bloody choir or aren't you? Everyone else can get here on time, but you, just because you don't care about nurturing your voice and that, you think you're above all that and can swing in here whenever you please...'

Bernard was trying to stop him. 'Rupert, thank you, that's quite enough. Please...'

But Rupert went on and on. Arthur thought Rupert had been so keyed up to explode on the word "light" in the chorus, that his pent-up energy all went into exploding at Charles and poor meek Ann instead.

Charles, still hatted and coated, turned and marched back towards the doors. Rupert's invective stopped mid-stream.

'Charles, stop! Calm down!' said Ann.

Charles turned on his wife savagely. 'Nobody speaks to me like that. Nobody.' He marched away. 'You stay if you want. I'll be in the Duck.'

He banged out through the door to the great wide world. Maestro Bernard Pontdexter, his shirt already making its own bid for freedom from his trousers' top, started to follow, then turned to Ann.

'Ann,' he said, 'for God's sake, can't you get him back? He's one of the only basses who know what they're doing.'

'And I suppose I don't matter,' she said. 'So I'm going too.'

'No, I don't mean that. Of course we need you.'

'Listen, Bernard. I suggest you find a new chairman. He's poisoning the whole thing. There is a limit...' Ann, Mrs Charles, wheeled off out through the doors, head high. The Maestro stood, one hand scratching his scraggy locks, the other his corpulence through the soggy shirt. His mouth worked like a beached bloater. Then he returned to his stand before the choir, who were various astounded or puritanically fascinated. 'Once again,' he barked at his flock. 'From the top, Iris, please.'

Arthur sneaked a look at Rupert next to him. His red hair seemed to be standing on end with steam rising from it. His face was even redder. Whether it was triumph or rage, Arthur couldn't tell.

Just as Bernard reached the end of the recitative for the second time, pencil poised to bring the choir in, the doors burst open once again.

'Who the hell has parked their bloody car across my space? Red Polo.'

This time it was a man in what looked like workman's clothes, and he was very clearly furious, no mistaking it. Behind him lurked the key-jangling caretaker.

There was total silence, then Bernard yapped, 'Look you can't just waltz in here...'

'I've got to see to the bloody electrics, mate, and if you wants the bloody urn to work for your bloody refreshments and that, you'll sort it quick-smart.'

Again a pause, then Mrs Maestro, Bernard's wife, chirped up. 'I think it's ours, dear. I'll go and move it.' She went out followed by the triumphant man.

Before the inevitable talking could begin, Bernard cut in with, 'Right, that's quite enough. Simmer down, forget all that. From the top again, and this time we're going to go on. We damn well will create Light even if they fuse.' There was an expectant moment, as if he was challenging the poor electrics to live up to the challenge. Rather naughtily, Arthur thought that it would be fitting if it was the other way round; that they started in darkness and suddenly the lights came on when they reached the dreaded word.

They achieved the impossible. God created Light, though everyone was so on edge that the abrupt *fortissimo* was more a *mezzo-piano*, even from Rupert. Nevertheless, the soft bits were excellently quiet and focused and controlled, so Bernard told them, clutching at sounding optimistic. He was not a bad man, Arthur mused. It was not an easy job, when you had Ruperts and Charleses and electrics people and all.

From then until the break, everything went remarkably smoothly. Mrs Maestro returned very discretely to her seat after, presumably, shifting the offending car, Rupert looked rather shell-shocked. As Chairman, a role he took very seriously, it seemed he felt he was losing control, Arthur reckoned. Ah well, it was not his problem. He had no intention of ever being anything more in the choir than a steady if soft-voiced stalwart of the bass department. Others could move and shake. Let them. However, the loss of Charles, assuming he never returned, was significant, for he was confident and reliable. Without him, the bass-line would be seriously depleted. But then, there was this new chap, this Oscar. Arthur could hear him from further along the row. How would he describe what he heard? Robust, accurate, on the ball. Altogether very commendable. The man might look a bit like a razzled weasel, but he clearly knew his onions in the singing department.

Come the break in the rehearsal, roller shutters spooled up at the end of the hall to reveal two of the lady choir members who had slipped out earlier to prepare the libations in the adjoining kitchen area. Arthur did not ask why it was always ladies, nor enquire how they were selected. None of his business. It would appear that the chap who demanded the moving of Bernard's car had worked his magic on the urn, because there was no hitch there. It dispensed faultlessly, and tea and coffee were on offer.

Arthur queued obediently. The choir members were reasonably well disciplined at this. In front of him, Oscar was being idolised by Moira, who looked oddly star-struck for a matronly lady. Standing uncertainly beside the queue was old Walter, octogenarian, nebulously wobbly tenor and Rupert's uncle. He looked as if he couldn't quite fathom where the end of the queue was, so Arthur indicated for him to stand in front of him. 'Thank you, thank you,' bleated Walter. 'So kind. So very kind.'

'How are you keeping, Walter?' asked Arthur.

'Oh, thank you for asking. I'm well, thank you, quite well.'

'Have you sung the Creation before?'

'Oh yes, thank you. Several...'

'Walter, is that right?' Oscar turned round and addressed the old man. 'I'm Oscar. Oscar Silvero. You may have heard of me. How do you do?' He stretched out a hand.

Walter shook the hand. 'Oh thank you, no, I'm afraid, I haven't...'

'Never mind. Different worlds. I used to be quite a name, but things change, do you find?'

'Change. Yes, oh yes.'

'How long have you been singing, Walter?' Oscar seemed really interested in him. Arthur found this surprising. Moira, who was left talking to the back of Oscar' head, looked like a spurned bride jilted at the altar.

'Oh, how long...' quavered Walter, 'how long indeed. I was a boy chorister at Salisbury, I suppose that was when it all started, thank you. A long time ago, a long, long time. But I remember singing *Oh for the wings of a dove* as if it was yesterday. Ah, me.'

'Really?' said Oscar. 'There's a coincidence. So did I. Sang *Oh for the wings* as a boy. At Southwark, not as grand as Salisbury, but I did a good job, thinking back. That was what took me into singing as a career, I suppose. That particular solo. It is rather special, touches peoples' hearts, maybe because of Ernest Lough's recording. That touching of hearts, I took that into the world I slid into. Crooning ballads; England's Frank Sinatra.' Oscar laughed. 'I did it my way,' he sang. Several choir members in the queue turned to look. He had a charisma when he turned it on. But the looks were not all appreciative. There were frowns among them. There were those for whom anything later than Haydn was outrageously modern. Even Haydn was a bit avant-garde at times. 'Those were the days, eh, Walter?' went on Oscar. 'Little tousled-haired angels in surplices and gowns in the choir stalls, singing as though butter... But outside the cathedral or church, oh we were tear-aways, eh? I bet you were, Walter. Naughty rascals.'

'Well, I don't know...' Walter began. Arthur thought he looked more like a startled rabbit than a rascal.

'Ah yes. "Oh, for the wings, for the wings..."' Oscar trying to sing it at treble pitch was a frail falsetto at odds with the rich confidence of his full voice, and he ended up in a fit of coughing.

Walter tried in turn. Surprisingly, given his wavering tenor voice, he produced a remarkably pure sound, almost ephemeral, a thin thread winding through the air. It vanished in the general morass of chatter.

They were by now at the receiving end of the queue, and as they left equipped with cups of tea and coffee, their ways diverged and Arthur found himself alone again. He saw old Walt and Oscar over there, but made no move to join them. They looked rather private. Then he saw Walter perch his cup precariously on a nearby ledge and, what was he doing? Fumbling in his jacket pocket. Oscar was looking around as if there was some clandestine conspiracy afoot. What could it be? Arthur was transfixed. Walter produced an object and did something to it. And then he was... No! He was pouring some liquid into Oscar's cup, and then his own. Arthur woke up to the reality. The object was a hip-flask, that's what it was. Dear, oh dear. He glanced about to see where Rupert was. There would be an almighty fuss if he saw. Or perhaps worse, if one of the more morally righteous of the choristers, of whom there were several, noticed; censorious and sniffy. But the only person nearby was Mrs Bernard Pontdexter. She and Arthur acknowledged each other with a nod, and that was that on the communication front. He really ought to know her name by now. He had been in the choir goodness knows how many years. But there they were. He didn't, and didn't like to ask. Not now. It would be embarrassing. Then it occurred to him that he could look on one of their concert programmes – he had kept copies since he first joined. They had a list of personnel. Tut. Showed how interested he was.

It was reasonably quiet where Arthur was, quiet enough to hear rain on the roof above. It helped to dampen his spirits. He was not enjoying this rehearsal.

The second half of the rehearsal was up and down. There were no interruptions from outside. The good news was that Bernard suddenly announced that they had at least made a start on all the chorus bits in the Creation. That was good. There were, what, still a couple of months to get them into really tip-top form. It would make a change from their usual concerts, which tended to be touch and go. The low points of the rehearsal were that Rupert recovered his form after his bout with Charles, bounced back like Tigger and managed to pose some particularly abstruse questions about the differences in underlay between his Peters edition and the Novello ones everyone else was using. Arthur wondered if Rupert did this deliberately to rile Bernard. Because it most certainly did. Rupert had been told repeatedly to use the Novello and persisted in not doing so. But Bernard was more-or-less in control of himself, and his standard riposte now was to point at Rupert, say calmly 'Wrong score,' hold up his Novello and jab it with his finger. Then he carried on. This, of course, riled Rupert in turn. Probably, thought Arthur, hell would freeze over before Rupert gave up and gave in. Pity Haydn didn't also write an oratorio on Armageddon. He could have called it *The Destruction*.

After the rehearsal, they filed out past the caretaker who was jangling his monster bunch of keys, ostentatious badge of office. Arthur happened to go out at the same time as Oscar, who had taken old Walter by the arm. As some of them walked down Conduit Street, where just over the bridge lurked the Hippocampus, Oscar took Arthur's arm too, thus making himself the filling in a person sandwich. Arthur was acutely embarrassed.

'Fine night,' said Oscar. It wasn't. It was cold, but the rain had mercifully stopped. 'Do you know my pal Walter? Walt, old fellow, this is… Sorry, don't know your name.'

Arthur mumbled, but Oscar had good hearing. 'Arthur, eh? Excellent. I'm Oscar. Oscar Silvero at your service. I used to be quite a name, you know.'

And on they marched, though in Walter's case it was more of a totter. It would seem he was unused to such a pace.

'I have persuaded my pal Walter to come to the pub. Do him good. Wind down after the exertions. Singing is hard work, you know. Not just something you do in the bath. I remember when I was performing at the Borough Theatre in Abersomething in Wales, I think it was… Did you ever see one of my shows? I've been here several times. Here in Chervil. At the theatre, what's it called? Anyway, hard work, that's what it is. You feel drained afterwards. It's giving so much to your public, you know. It takes it out of you. Giving emotion, giving hope and uplift and, yes, pathos and heart-rending sorrow too… Oh yes. It's no ride in the park, believe me, Arthur. You need a little something afterwards to pick you up. Eh, Walt old man?'

At which, to Arthur's mortification, Oscar let rip his weedy falsetto again. "Oh for the wings, for the wings of a dove…" And Walter joined in, shaky but with more body. "Far away," they warbled, "far away. Far away would I roam."

By this time they were on the bridge, the river Zed snaking off into blackness on either side, and there before them lurked the Hippocampus. As the three of them crossed the bridge, Arthur thought all it needed to complete his utter embarrassment being in their company in public was for a Gnoxie to come and join the party and wreak havoc. Not that any passers by were paying any attention to them.

Once inside the Hippocampus, Oscar lost no time in buying double scotches for himself and Walter. Belatedly, he asked Arthur what he would like, and added a small dry sherry to his order. They sat in the usual place that members of the CCS occupied on a

Thursday evening. Arthur felt obliged to sit with them, though he'd have preferred to be further away on the window seat. Oscar was reliving his choirboy years, and drawing Walter in. They started warbling Fauré's *Pie Jesu* when a bunch of the other choir members came in.

'Oh Oscar,' cried Moira, 'give us *My Way* won't you?'

No, no, no, chorused the others. Enough of singing. Time for drinking. As they settled themselves, Arthur found he was forced to move his chair further and further out, until effectively he was excluded. *Suits me*, he thought. Oscar very quickly responded to the audience as raconteur. He had many tales to tell, well forged and polished from his years of touring the stages of Britain and regaling locals in the hostelries.

It suddenly occurred to Arthur that maybe Mel and those people from the Orchestra might be here, hiding round the corner. He muttered 'Just going to the... um...' not that anyone was listening, and went off to see. He happened to take his sherry and the brief case containing his music and pencil with him.

They were there. Mel, Beryl and Stanislav Bun. Mr Bun the bassoonist. They welcomed Arthur. There was a seat. It became his seat. He wondered if he should take up an instrument, because the orchestral players seemed much more friendly than his fellow singers. At least these three did. But an instrument – it would take years to reach the required standard, and what would the neighbours say to him practising? And he might have no aptitude. And what would he choose? Which instrument? He had had a few piano lessons when a boy; got to grade five, with Merit he proudly remembered. But that was a long time ago, and there were not many pianos in orchestras.

'Mr Arthur, my friend,' said Stan. 'Tell me, you are singer. Which is most like human voice – flute, or horn. Or bassoon, eh? Tell truth, now. Think carefully. Remember bacon rolls...'

'Stop it, Stan,' said Mel. 'Stop trying to influence him. Uncle Arthur, hey, we're family, yeah? Just thought I'd remind you.'

Beryl smiled. 'Remember who makes the best coffee and walnut cake? And too many others to mention.'

Suitably bribed and threatened, Arthur searched for a diplomatic answer. Ah yes... 'The oboe,' he said.

After that, it went splendidly, but not for long. For round the corner came Oscar.

'Ah, there you are,' he said. 'Arthur, isn't it? Arthur, Walter, we need to get him... Oh hello, Beryl, and you two. No time to chat. Another time, eh? Now Walter is feeling a bit wobbly and we need to get him home. Can you help me? The others all have important reasons why they can't. Story of my life.'

'Of course, yes.' Arthur stood. 'Will you excuse me... Excellent to see you all. Better go.'

15 Seeing Walter Home

Arthur and Oscar returned to the group of CCS choristers round the corner, who were back to criticising Bernard, a seemingly inexhaustibly interesting exercise.

Slightly outside their circle, sat Walter. He had wilted, almost shrivelled. Arthur and Oscar took an arm each and escorted him outside. The clash of cold air seemed to stir the old man a bit. 'Oh, thank you, thank you,' he bleated. 'So sorry. Thank you. It's very near. Bishop's Court, yes.'

That was indeed convenient. 'I know it,' said Arthur. 'It's just behind the cathedral. Very handy.' He could hear singing, oh so quietly. It was Oscar, he realised. He was crooning something into Walter's ear. It sounded familiar. Then he caught the words: "Blue moon." Ah yes. Not the sort of music that Arthur would choose to be quizzed upon if he was a contestant on Mastermind, not at all, but he did know *Blue Moon*. Why, they had to sing an arrangement of it in the Choral Society some years back in a light informal Summer concert. He could feel Walter weigh less heavily on his arm as they went. Oscar seemed to be weaving a little web of magic around the three of them. "Blue moon"... And there was a moon now. Normal looking. Not blue at all.

Bishop's Court contained a small terrace of elderly cottages originally built for clergy members of the cathedral, so Arthur understood, and it was one of these that Walter indicated with a feeble hand. A lovely peaceful place to live, thought Arthur, looked over by the cathedral itself, which spread its solidity and certainty upon the row of houses.

Walter unearthed a key and they went into the cottage. Directly into the living room. Surprisingly large inside. Oscar sat the old man in an armchair with remarkable tenderness, and went to light an anachronistic gas fire plastered into the lovely old stone hearth. 'I wonder, can you see if you can make him a cup of something, cocoa maybe, old pal,' he said to Arthur. 'Something hot and sweet. That'll see you all right, won't it, Walter, old pal?'

Arthur went out of the only door he could see other than the front door into a musty passage from which stairs rose to the left. At the end he emerged into a room that had vaguely food-like aromas lingering. He fumbled around and found a light switch. It was, he saw, as the kitchen emerged rather dimly to his eyes, a porcelain switch with a tarnished brass dome. The switch lever had a little brass ball on the end. Arthur rather suspected that the electrics in the house should have been condemned as a fire hazard years ago. The whole room felt like a small museum. Under the faint fragrance of kippers, if Arthur was to believe his nose, was a clammy smell of damp.

While he was in no way technically minded, Arthur was quite competent in dealing with kitchens. He had lived in several different places before coming to roost in his singular garret in the Market Square. So he managed to find, not cocoa, but a jar of Horlicks, some milk in a fridge, a battered but reasonably clean saucepan, and a mug and spoon. He even managed to light a gas ring on the stove, which involved first finding a box of matches and puzzling out how to initiate gas flow. The little hairs on the knuckle joint of a couple of his fingers permed into frizziness by the sudden eruption of fire as he achieved lift-off, but, well, the casualties of war…

He took the mug of Horlicks in to Walter. Oscar was tucking a rug around the old man's legs. Walter clutched the mug with both hands as if he could draw nourishment from the feel and the heat. Arthur perched on the edge of another armchair and watched the two of them, frail old Walt in his nest and Oscar the clucking mother hen looking out for her chick. This was not the Oscar that Arthur saw in the choir, resonant and confident in voice, nor in the Hippocampus, loud and raconteuring life-and-soul. And yet, given his slight stature, his sparse locks and tired eyes, the man before him now seemed a much more genuine Oscar. An Oscar with heart and soul.

'Walter,' said the man himself, his voice a comforting purr, 'would you like me to come and look after you? I need to move from... from where I am now. Would you like that? I would pay a generous rent. I have money. Thanks to my adoring public over the years.' He sighed.

Walter turned from tentatively testing the heat of the Horlicks with his protruding lips to look at him, to gaze up at him, his eyes very tired, gazing gratefully out from beneath unruly eyebrows. 'Oh, thank you, thank you. So kind of you to offer. Oh, thank you. I couldn't ask...' His voice waned to inaudibility.

Oscar turned to Arthur. 'Thank you for your help, old pal. I'll stay with Walter for a while. See him to bed. Don't feel you have to stay. You'll be wanting to get off. If you see Beryl, you know Beryl, don't you? Could you tell her I'll be back later, old pal. I... I lodge in her house, you know. She might worry.'

Beryl, Mel's friend, of the café, the flautist – that Beryl, presumably. Well, he could, if she was still there at the pub. Or he could head straight home, rather than go back that way. No, of course he would go back to the Hippocampus. It was the least he could do to help. Poor old Walter. He felt remorseful that he had ever even momentarily thought the old man past it in the singing department. Heavens, the time would come when he should resign from the choir himself, through a wayward voice, maybe. When he could no longer stay reliably in tune. There were a couple of sopranos who always seemed to him to sing a tiny bit flat; presumably they thought they were in tune. Perhaps for some people, the ears, or the brain, could hear what you yourself sang as being in tune when it wasn't. Perhaps it could develop with age. He hoped he would have the sense to quit before that happened and Bernard took him on one side and... It would be mortifying. In Walter's case, his vocal uncertainty was more a quaver, an uncontrollable querulousness that wobbled either side of the correct pitch to provide a sort of halo round the note.

Looking up at the cathedral as he left, Arthur saw something flitting about the tower. For one dreadful moment he thought it was a Gnoxie. Sweet innocent little duckling with melting eyes and grasping arms and an evil beak. No, of course not. It must be a bat. It went so fast. But didn't bats hibernate? It was February after all, and pretty cold. Not a night for dawdling.

An appalling thought crossed his mind: could the flying something, could it just possibly have been a little dragon, one of those he had drawn so many times in the past? Could they be at large? He tried to replay what he had just seen, but it was too elusive. No it wasn't a dragon, cute or otherwise, he told himself. He was sure. Wasn't he? It was a bat. Just a bat.

He didn't like bats.

He made himself stride out, trying to generate a little heat, and was back at the Hippocampus in the twinkling of a Gnoxie's eye.

The choir contingent were still busily yapping away and naturally failed to notice him flit by. Round the corner he was relieved to see that niece Mel and Beryl from the café were still there.

He saw Mel pat Beryl on the arm in a motherly sort of way, which seemed odd given their respective ages. She stopped when she saw him standing there. 'Hiya, Unk. What was all that about? Oscar dragging you off like that?'

Arthur explained about Walter. 'Oh yes,' he added, turning to Beryl, 'Oscar asked me to tell you that... what was it? Yes, that he'll be back later. He's staying on a bit to help Walter get to bed safely, I think. The old chap is dreadfully shaky.'

Beryl nodded. She looked tired and drawn. 'That would be like him. He seems to work wonders with the old and frail. Was he singing to this Walter? That's what he does with my mother.'

'Yes, oh yes. Well, actually they were both singing. *Oh for the wings of a dove*. Apparently they both sang it as a solo when they were in church choirs as boys. I'm afraid it sounded awful. And Oscar sang something else. You're right, it seemed... very calming, I suppose. Soothing.'

'Oh, he has a knack. I believe he had a vast and adoring public in his prime. Well, relatively vast. For places like Chervil at least. His visits to the Lyric were very popular years ago. Then they tailed off. As so did he.'

'He asked old Walter if he'd like him to come and look after him… Oh, I don't know if I should repeat that. But Walter seemed to brighten at the idea. But I don't know. It was probably just talk. Please take no notice.'

And yet Beryl too seemed to brighten. Mel said, 'There you are, B! Could be the answer to your prayers, yeah?'

'We'll see,' replied Beryl. 'I'm not getting my hopes up. Thank you, er, Arthur. Thank you for telling me that. Where does this Walter live?'

'Just over the road in Bishop's Court. He has a house in that little terrace overlooked by the cathedral. I must say, it's rather primitive. I don't suppose it's had any modernisation for, oh, I don't know how long. Could Oscar cope with that, do you think?'

'I've no idea. He's never volunteered to do anything useful in my house, except to look after Mum. Of course, there's no way I would let him loose in the kitchen. He might find where I hide the wine. Oh dear, I'm being indiscreet now.'

'Hey hey,' said Mel. 'High fives, B. This might be the beginning of a big change. Next thing, perhaps this Lucien will get himself run over by a bus and you'll be, like, Queen B again in the famous flute department of the CSO. See, it's like Stan said.'

'What did he say? He says lots of things.'

'It was in Polish, yeah? "Blubbedy blubbedy blubbedy blub" or something. Anyway, he said it meant, "See everything in bright colours," didn't he? Like, "Always look on the bright side of life," like we might say.'

Arthur, who was still standing, said he must go, he only popped in to pass on Oscar's message.

'See you next week, Uncle, yeah?' said Mel.

'Still no further with your book?'

'No, not really. Like I said, I've gone off it after Jason... I mean, I look at it every now and then, and I reckon he's right, Unk. It ain't got legs. It ain't gonna fly. Nor is the Gnoxie. But I've got ideas for a really cool romance. Should be a doddle. Then I can start making a fortune with Mills and Boon or mags like Woman's Own and that. They're always printing romantic stories. But, like, you never know, Unk darling, Poppy and Cuddles may rise from the dead again sometime. Don't throw away those sketches, yeah?'

Arthur wandered back to his flat. He unlocked the drawer and brought out the folder containing his drawings for Mel's rejected masterpiece. There was Cuddles on the table looking as if butter wouldn't melt in his beak. There he was grabbing the chocolate from the fridge. Here he was spilling the cereal as he came in the window. And... Shouldn't there be a fourth one? Yes, Cuddles swinging from the light shade. Where was it? Not in the folder, not in the drawer.

He thought back. It was after showing them to Beryl at the Motley Brew; he shut them away then and hadn't opened the drawer since. So where... Then he remembered; on the way home, he had dropped the folder in the Tangle. There was a rabbit, yes, chased by a cat and he dropped the folder, startled, and the drawings flew out. He must have missed one. A drawing of a Gnoxie. Swinging from a lampshade. At loose in the Tangle.

He shivered involuntarily. Somehow he felt that this was not good. A bad omen. Immediately his thoughts went back to the Dwelf incident and Stan Bun. And the rabbits. It was all ridiculous. And yet...

16 The Sun Comes Out

The next Thursday, Beryl woke for the third morning of lightness of spirit. A quiet house. Her house. All on her own.

'*Well, if you think that...*' said a voice in her head, the voice of Victoria, who stretched with exquisite ecstacy and in the process managed to apply a little acupuncture to Beryl's left foot which was only covered by a sheet. The claws were a warning.

Beryl adjusted her thoughts. *Our house*, she thought. *Me and Victoria. Victoria and me. Just us. No Oscar.*

Yes, on Monday he had decamped to this Walter person, to care for him, as Oscar put it. Beryl had not met Walter. Beryl did not know that Walter was very fond of his hip-flask, but she suspected there was more to Oscar's desire to move than simply to care for an old man, which even so he would probably do very well. Look at Mum. And Oscar was happy to carry on visiting Restawee regularly. She understood that he more or less gave an entertainment there when he went. His crooning of songs delighted many of the residents, not to mention the staff, and of course Mum. So he was Mr Popular. And if now he could drink to his heart's content (and detriment), he was clearly a happier bunny.

Meanwhile, Beryl immediately set to work to restore the spare room to her practice room, where she could tootle away day-dreaming without causing too much distress to Victoria. Now that Victoria has decided to start communicating directly, she had made it clear that to one finely attuned to the nuances of purring and an assortment of chirrups and prrmeows, the sound of a flute was intolerable. Beryl was too polite to mention caterwauling and was only too happy to return to the spare room.

And so, on this Thursday morning, Beryl cheered the customers in the Motley Brew with her good humour. Even Irina was showered with murmurs of appreciation at her work. Until lunchtime.

While Beryl slaved over lunchtime orders, churning out toasties and soup and fish finger sandwiches as usual, she found time to run over what she would do this evening. Which was, to go to orchestra rehearsal. That normally would raise her humour even more. But today there was the unsupportable prospect of the infant upstart, the malicious, flapjack-stealing demon in human form that was Lucien playing first flute. And again and again, week after week, until the concert. First flute: Lucien (snake in the grass, spawn of Satan). Second flute: Beryl Carson (abused virtuoso reduced to mere also-ran). It smarted. The child in her pouted and sulked. Some people were happy to spend their lives being seconds, but not her. She had served her time being second to old Cyril. It had been a way of getting her foot in the door of the orchestra. She had earned her promotion and…

It was with reluctant step that Beryl arrived at the rehearsal. In the hall, she ran straight into Marcus, chairman of the orchestra, second violin. He had evidently been waiting for her.

'I'm so sorry, Beryl,' said Marcus, 'that chap from the Comp, Lucien, he's had to back out. I gather he discovered the date of our Creation performance clashes with the day he's due to play with the NYO. He has been invited by them, get this, only invited to play a concerto with them. Can you credit it? If it was me, I'd have the date engraved in my heart, not that anyone would want me to play a concerto, and nor would I, come to that. I know my limitations. Yup. I'm Mr Second Violins, me.'

No Lucien! Wow, wow, wow. Suddenly the sun came out from the clouds. 'Oh dear. What a shame,' said Beryl, insincere to a fault. 'What a blow.' And it would be a blow, for her. A fine and glorious blow once more as she shone in her rightful place. They could easily find a replacement second flute for Cyril. The world was full of flute players who'd jump at the chance, just like she did, years ago. Reasonably competent players, not liabilities. What about that girl from Chervil College who played piccolo in the last concert, for example?

'Lucien's posted the part back,' said Marcus. 'Here you are. I know Sheila is looking for another flute, but I don't think she's had any joy as yet. Can you manage on your own this week?' Sheila was secretary of the orchestra, on whose shoulders the brunt of trying to find any extra players tended to fall.

Could she, Beryl, manage? She was first flute again, that was what mattered. Who cared about second? Bet nobody could tell there wasn't one tonight. Well, maybe Clifford could – he should, if he was any cop as a conductor – but the first flute was the one with all the best bits, the one to crown the piece, the orchestra, with a halo of brilliance.

She settled down, arranged her stand to her satisfaction, and was about to place the first flute part on it, when a voice said, 'Are you Beryl?' It was a severe-looking woman, not one to trifle with. 'Clifford twisted my arm,' the woman went on, waving an arm in his direction, 'and asked if I could take over the first flute, so you don't have to worry. I gather that Lucien de Fêbre let you down. Tch, typical. I've met him. Cocky little chap. Unreliable. Oops, smacked hand, talking out of school again. Well, hello. I don't think we've met. I'm Dee; I teach flute, oboe and voice at Chervil College.'

'Oh,' said Beryl.

The clouds veiled the sun again. The sky turned grey.

As Dee assembled her flute, she said, 'You had one of my girls on picc at your last concert. But Sophie's got a lot of work to do for her A-levels this term, so I thought this time I'd do the gig myself, since it's a big occasion for the band, so Cliff tells me. Keep in practice as it were, ha ha ha. Was Sophie okay, by the way? My pupil? On picc? Smart girl. Ah, I see you have the part.'

Beryl was indeed still clutching the first flute part. Her first flute part. What could she do? Should she hand it over? Her first instinct was to fight her corner, but a voice of caution sounded in her head. Clearly this woman considered she was doing them a big favour, not trusting the "gig" to one of her "girls." Dee did not look like someone who would consider for a moment playing second flute. Besides, if Beryl tried to make a thing out of it, this Dee was a colleague of Clifford, and he could be a right bastard if riled. She had seen a couple of players thrown out of the orchestra in mid-rehearsal over the years for repeated screwing up of a passage or miscounting. She could find herself surplus to requirements just like that. So what could she do? What choice had she?

She handed over the first flute part.

Oh, why couldn't Cyril have kept going a few months longer?

As had happened with Lucien, she managed an appalling standard of playing during the rehearsal. Playing the boring, unvirtuosic second. And to make matters worse, Clifford decided to start the rehearsal with number 3 *"Now vanish before the holy beams,"* the bastard. Second flute part, the one word: *tacet*. First flute had oodles to do. Beryl simply had to sit there and fume. Of course she had plenty to play later on in the rehearsal, but she hated and loathed every note of it. Dee breezed through everything, all those tricky bits that Beryl had practised at home. Her tone was limpid, expressive, her technique effortless and bloody faultless. Even Dante could not have dreamed up tortures in Hell to match those that Beryl wished upon the great Dee.

As it happened, Dee was actually polite, friendly and, an unbiased observer might say, a very pleasant person. That made it worse. Why couldn't she be a supercilious Medusa with snakes for locks? Or was that the Gorgon? And on this occasion, Beryl had brought no flapjacks nor refreshment of any sort to consume in the break, in order to teach the ghastly Lucien a lesson. And who suffered as a result? Why, she did. Poor put-upon Beryl.

It was in a spirit of self-pity and anger that she went to the Hippocampus afterwards. She only went there because that was what she always did. Mel and Stan nattered away, their words sawdust in her ears.

As Stan attended the bar, Mel said, 'What's up, B, yeah? You know what, you look like thunder. Like you'd like to kill someone.'

Indeed she would, but she didn't want to dump her feelings on little Mel, nor on the generous and comforting Stan. She had made herself seem pretty petty and foolish last week with that Lucien. She had a bit of pride left. To say she was... she was what? Yes, she was jealous, that was the long and the short of it. To admit that would be childish. After all, after the Creation, next concert, the orchestra would recruit a new second flute, she would insist on it, coolly, rationally. Or maybe Cyril would recover enough to come back, but she doubted that. He was shaky enough before this stroke. Fate had seen fit to deal her this hand. She must bear it with dignity. She was Beryl, proprietress of the Motley Brew, and bloody lucky to be in the Chervil Symphony Orchestra at all, when it came to it. Not to mention the quintet. Suddenly in her head, she thought she could hear the voice of Victoria the cat saying, '*That's it, keep your whiskers stiff and your tail up. Don't let the fleas get you down.*' Quite right.

She smiled at Mel. It might have been a little forced, but hell... And she managed that spontaneous ability that the human brain is so good at, inventing spurious reasons to justify things. 'Oh, I'm sorry, Mel dear. No, I'm fine, I'm fine, really I am. It must be the shock of Oscar moving out. That must be it. It hasn't really sunk in.'

'But I thought you wanted him to go, yeah?'

'Oh, I did, I did. He was... Let's face it, he was in the way since Mum went into Restawee. Not that I don't appreciate what he did, and him visiting her and that, but...' She tailed off. She didn't really want to talk about him, she was free now he had gone. If it wasn't for this bloody first flute business, life would be good. But there they were; she had brought the subject of Oscar up as a spurious excuse. Her own fault.

'Right,' said Mel. 'Right. But I wondered... Hey, who was that dame playing first flute today? What's happened to that young guy who came last week, that little shit I remember you calling him. You done away with him, yeah, B? Like, murder? You were proper fuming last week. I'll come and visit you in prison, promise. Won't we Stan?'

'Prison?' he cried placing the drinks carefully down before liberating a bag of crisps he had trapped under his arm. 'Is not me. Is my twin brother. He's the bad one. I am not guilty, me. What is it they say I have done? They lie.'

'Not you, Beryl here. She's murdered a fellow flautist who had the cheek to take over as first.'

By the time Beryl had explained, the whole thing didn't seem quite so bad to her. After all, there were other things in life, there would be other concerts. And besides the second flute part, if she was honest, was in its own way interesting to play, and a brilliant flautist like herself should be able to make it sound every bit as important as the first. But her pride remained insulted. Acknowledge it and move on.

A little later, she, who had her back to the main body of the bar, saw the other two look up and past her. She turned to see Mel's uncle coming towards them. Mel leapt up to get a chair from another table. Uncle Arthur looked forlorn, like a small boy hoping for a kind word, a nod of recognition. An Oliver Twist wanting not some more, but something in the first place. Her heart went out to him. Well, he got a right royal welcome from the three of them. He settled into the chair and seemed to light up. Stan, irrepressible as always, a Fezziwig to Arthur's Oliver, to mix the Dickens, insisted on furnishing him with a small sherry and a jolly time was had by all.

At the end, Beryl found herself walking down Southgate with Arthur. It simply happened. They were both going that way.

'What a good man Stan is,' she said. 'I was really fuming when I reached the Hippo and somehow he simply made my anger evaporate.'

'Yes,' said Arthur. 'Yes, he is. Yes. I was feeling a little low after choir. They're all so... so... I don't know what exactly. But I suppose that's what choirs are. Oscar seems really to fit in. One of them.'

'Oh, Oscar. He has a knack of charm. Did you ever see one of his endless farewell tour shows? He switches it on. I've seen him... Well, I shouldn't talk out of school, but underneath he is like a lost little boy.' She lapsed into silence, thinking back, remembering the sad creature in the Royal hotel a couple of years before.

Arthur said, 'Lost... Yes. I wouldn't have thought... Of Oscar. He's so...' And Arthur too fell silent in his personal thoughts.

They reached the Cross. For Beryl, she only needed to go straight over and along Northgate and then turn left into The Trees, the anachronistic nineteen-fifties housing estate in which she lived. For Arthur, he usually turned right, along Eastgate, into the High Street and nip through by the Clement Cow into Market Square, thus avoiding the worst of the horrors of the Tangle at night. And these days, with the ridiculous notion that spectral rabbits and Gnoxies might be lurking ready to pounce, who would do otherwise?

Even so, he ended up going along Northgate too, even though it meant negotiating Hot Pie Alley and Here Today Squeeze to reach the Market Square, both alleged hot-beds of dreadful deeds of yore, back when footpads would cheerfully cut your throat to relieve you of your linen handkerchief.

The two walked side by side, not speaking. As Beech Grove, gateway to the little Trees estate and devoid of beech trees of any kind, branched off left and Hot Pie Alley sneaked darkly away off to the right, the two separated.

'Good night, Mel's uncle,' said Beryl.

'Arthur. Yes,' muttered Arthur, and scuttled rapidly off into Hot Pie clutching his coat around him as though rabbits might nibble his shins.

Back at home, Beryl poured herself a G&T. She deserved it. She sat herself in her second favourite armchair with Hattie and a pen and drank deep. Her favourite chair was occupied by a Victoria, one paw curled around her nose, deeply asleep. The gin rasped in Beryl's throat. She wrote:

Good evening, Hattie,

>*Good evening, Beryl. How are things?*

>*Well, up and down, I would say. At the moment, I feel sort of tremulously good. I don't really understand it. Get rid of a little shit named Lucien (there! Name names, Beryl. I'll say what I please, thank you, world.), only for him to be replaced by this Dee, who is actually probably a very nice person, but not one to argue with. I mean, she's yonks better than me, I know. She's a professional.*

>*What would I do without Mel and Stan? And now Mel's uncle Arthur. He's gentle and unassuming. How different from the Selfish Shit. All three are all so, how can I put it, embracing. Like you, dear Hattie, they are interested in me. At least, I think so, I feel so. I matter, and not just because I'm an unrecognised virtuoso flautist, but because I'm me. Selfish Shit never... He only married me because of Algy, and then found me a useful housekeeper, to feed him and look after the boy. And then...*

>*Scumbag.*

>*No, this is not a time to feel sorry for myself. There is optimism in the air. I feel it.*

>*So, good-night, Hattie dear. Sleep well.*

>*And you, Beryl.*

Beryl restored Hattie to its hiding place. As she got up, Victoria opened one eye from her queenly position on the best chair in the sitting room. '*You have been quite mature. For you. Well done,*' she purred and inserted the message into Beryl's mind. Beryl went to bed feeling rather proud of herself. Victoria turned into a fluffy little kitten and joined her on the bed, and both slept sound.

17 Problems

A month later, with three weeks to go before the performance, the choir were supposedly familiar with all the choruses in Haydn's masterpiece. By the break there had been four interventions by Rupert. Hand up – always the eager schoolboy – 'In the Peters edition, the underlay...' 'When Haydn has marked *piano*, do you really want *piano*?' and so on.

Bernard Pontdexter, it seemed to Arthur, had reached a plateau beyond irritation, a plateau of resignation, of 'Never mind for now. Let's just get the notes right. Right notes in the right places...' A plateau that was not endless, but which at any moment could give way to the final sprint to the summit of Bernard losing his temper entirely. And that, as Arthur had witnessed a few times in the past, would produce a thoroughly embarrassed and jittery choir, one that was suddenly hyper-alert and obedient. For a while anyway.

Maestro Pontdexter would also be embarrassed by his failure of self-control. If he could keep his meagre but serviceable charisma going at such times, he could capitalise on the moment and achieve great things, but in losing his temper, he also lost his impetus and had to resort to auto-pilot. Altogether counter-productive.

On this occasion, Rupert's assaults on his patience failed to reach the tipping point by the break in rehearsal. It was then it became apparent that Bernard had something on his mind. He addressed his flock.

'Chaps, before you get your whatever, we have a problem. Well, two problems. By we, I suppose I mean me and Clifford, you know, the chappie who conducts the orchestra, who's waving the baton at the concert. But I just wonder if any of you might have some ideas? Something to mull over while you drink your whatever.

'Thing is soloists. Thing is, they're from the Foster Academy of Voice. Star singers of tomorrow. Big solo in Chervil, next stop international fame. Covent Garden, the Met, La Scala...'

'Cheap students, he means,' muttered Rupert in Arthur's right ear.

'Thing is,' Bernard went on, hoicking up the wayward belt, 'sometimes another, er, opportunity arises at short notice, and they can, in a word, let us down. You know, I understand their dilemma. We're small time, relatively speaking. If something bigger crops up – professional opera house, broadcasting gig, whatever – they would be fools to turn it down. I see that. It is understandable, chaps, but it leaves us with a problem. Two problems. Not to mince words, chaps, at this moment of time, we haven't got a soprano soloist. Nor, so I learnt today, a bass soloist. They're big parts, big parts. The tenor chappie, fine fellow, very promising I'm told, is still definitely on, thank God, so he says, so that's good, that's good.'

'Probably he's rubbish and nobody else wants him,' confided Rupert. 'This is what comes of doing things on the cheap.'

Bernard glared at him, though Arthur doubted he could hear what Rupert said. He went on. 'Thing is, chaps, it's not your problem, it's Cliff's really. I mean it was his idea to get them from the Academy. Probably. Anyway, Cliff and me, let's be fair, it's our problem, not yours. But I thought you might have ideas, or leads. Have a think and have a word with me during the break. No promises. But you're chaps of the world, wide experience, different contacts and so on, so...'

At which point he petered out, and a wave of talking swelled up amongst the ranks as they began to form a disorderly queue in front of the serving hatch.

In due course, cup of tea in his hand, Arthur inadvertently found himself standing near to Bernard, with whom Moira was having a private word. Private it might be, but Moira's voice was penetrating. Arthur eavesdropped.

'Bernard,' she was saying, 'I can't help with the main thrust of your problem, but it may have escaped your attention that there is a brief – brief but crucial – alto solo in the last number.'

Escaped Bernard's attention? Arthur was incredulous at Moira's naïvety. Of course he would know that. As a conductor he might have faults, who didn't? But he knew the score. Moira was… Well, frankly, Arthur admitted to himself that she was the epitome of irritating and generally unspeakable, and if he was Bernard he would tell her to go and boil her head in a vat of sulphuric acid. Or just ask her to go away, or something. The arrogant cheek.

'At least that's no problem,' Bernard was saying. 'I'm doing those bits. No, it's the sop and bass, they're the poser. It's all Cliff's fault. If I'd had my way…'

He droned on. Moira had her mouth open. It dawned on Arthur that she had been on the point of offering herself as alto soloist, with all due modesty of course – 'I am not worthy, but…' and not to worry if he didn't think her suitable, even though she would feel deeply hurt if rejected. And then he floored her before she could begin. Perhaps she didn't know of Bernard's fine countertenor voice. She should. He showed it off often enough in rehearsals demonstrating how this or that bit should go.

Moira stuck nose in air and flounced off while Bernard was still wittering on. Arthur could guess what the talk would be in the pub after the rehearsal. 'There am I,' Moira would say, 'offering my services, and he grabs all the glory for himself. Typical…'

The tea was stewed, in Arthur's opinion. It tasted pretty awful. It was probably Bernard's fault. If he hadn't wasted so much time with his little appeal to the troops at the start of the break. Arthur sipped daintily, as if forcing down medicine. 'Must keep hydrated, keep the voice tip-top,' preached Bernard often, while himself oozing perspiration from every pore.

But another voice was addressing Bernard now. Arthur ought to feel guilty listening in, but he didn't. This time it was Oscar. He had his back to Arthur, so it was difficult to make out what he was saying. He could hear Bernard's replies though:

'Yes, yes, I remember, but... Well of course... Yes, I know... Now look, er, Oscar, it's not up to me, not me alone, Clifford must... Yes, I – we, that is – would need to hear you, yes... Look, Oscar, an audition, right? No promises. I know you're an old hand in front of an audience and – come to think of it, you could be quite an attraction – your name and that. But got to think of the effect of losing you on the bass line... No, no, doing both, definitely not on... Look, an audition, right? I'll talk to Cliff, see what he says. Give me your number, okay, and... Yes, yes, no promises. If someone else...'

From which, Arthur thought, *Well well, Oscar has lost no time.* But then Oscar hadn't had the career he had by being a shrinking violet. Don't hide your voice under a bushel. Well, well. He wondered if Oscar could manage a bottom D on the worm, when it was created and crept with sinuous trace. An audible bottom D. Even he, Arthur could manage one in his mind. It was just that he didn't actually produce any sound. In fairness, Haydn didn't write a bottom D, but what bass who had one could resist it? Well, well.

He also wondered about the tea. Either there was something wrong with it, or with his sense of taste. Others seemed to be swilling it down happily enough. In the past, he had noticed that when he was beginning to develop a cold it could affect his taste. No, please not. As they cracked on with the second half of the rehearsal, his fears grew. By the end he was feeling weak, a bit wobbly. No Hippocampus tonight. Straight home, perhaps a hot shower and bed with a cup of tea. No perhaps not, if it tasted as bad as the one earlier. Just water. It was a mild night, but he found he was shivering. The way home seemed endless, though it was only less than quarter of an hour's walk. Today, those on the streets, not many even in Northgate, seemed woozy phantoms, remote, far away. Why was he going along Northgate? It was shorter, but he had to traverse more of the Tangle than if he went via Eastgate and the High Street. He was not thinking clearly. The Tangle was not his friend.

As he turned into Hot Pie Alley, the beginning of the Tangle where the street lights barely penetrated, his shivering got worse. Something with a whirring flitted past his head. He stumbled and managed to regain his feet just in time to see... What? He had a woolly impression of a little body flapping off round the corner. A body with a beak that was laughing, a sardonic cackle. 'Pissed again,' came the echo bouncing off the cranky walls. No, no, no, he was not, he was ill. *Be kind to me,* he called out in his head.

At the end of the passage was a minute square, more the meeting of three alleys. Small it might be, but as he turned into it, the ground was a heaving mass of fluffy bodies, rabbits in ranks and rows, gazing up at him with eager eyes. Pink rabbits, pea-green rabbits, all the pastel colours of a washed-out rainbow, all with big eyes, fluttering their lashes. Again he stumbled, trying not to step on them. They were singing in appalling harmony. "Unnumber'd as the sands, in swarms arose the hosts of rabbits," they warbled. Arthur was singing that bit of Haydn's *Creation* only that afternoon along with the CD, but the word wasn't "rabbits". It was... It was... something else.

Then he zigzagged into Morrow Passage, staggering now, shambling his way, heading for the Market Square ahead, bathed in the meagre glow of street lamps. Again he heard the laughing, the cackle, saw the beak. 'I know you,' he cried. 'You are...' and the name flew from his mind. He had drawn it, his pen had caressed the outline into life, and now it jeered and snided at him, who was ill, who only wanted his bed. Who only had a few yards to go as he wobbled out into the Square. The space lay there, a peaceful oasis, the sea of tranquillity. Only a little man sitting on a bollard, twiddling his moustache. *How quickly that has grown,* thought Arthur, as he fumbled for his key, and then as the door closed behind him, he was in that other haven of calm, the stairs up to his flat. Stairs that were now far, far longer than ever. Far, far steeper. He reached the top on hands and knees, clutched at the door to his flat and fell into the safe space.

There he lay, for minutes, maybe longer. The shivering subsided; he breathed deeply, trying to achieve equilibrium and normality. Instead it made him cough and cough, curling into a ball so that bits didn't fall off. The shivering started again. It was some time before he could raise himself up, to stagger to his bedroom and collapse fully clothed, and drag the duvet over himself. Gradually, imperceptibly, the warmth oozed into his body, the shivering quietened, drowsiness crept down and the earth was without form and void, and darkness was upon the face of the deep. The phone rang in vain, unheard, unanswered.

When he woke later, he was shivering again and sweating at the same time. The pillow case was damp. He was damp; he was burning. He opened his eyes into the darkness, and a luminous duckling – Cuddles, that was his name – was quacking round the room throwing burning snowballs at him. At the bottom of the bed was a group of other Gnoxies, squabbling and disembowelling rabbits, pecking off the flesh and spitting it at Arthur. It scalded and froze him.

'Will you stop that? Arthur croaked. 'Stop it this instant. I feel dreadful.' It was a cry of pathos, a call from a wretched person who feels terribly sorry for himself. But it worked. The Gnoxies, including Cuddles, stopped.

'You wanna parley, cowboy?' said Cuddles. 'We're having fun, fun, fun, here.'

Arthur tried to focus. He wanted to die, or at least go back to sleep and wake to find a clear head and a cloudless sky. 'I'll rub you out,' he whimpered.

Cuddles let rip a peal of sardonic laughter. 'You inked us in, chum. Silly boy. And I've multiplied since then. We're here to stay and we're going to be such good friends.' He waddled onto Arthur's chest and jumped up and down, which brought on a paroxysm of coughing. Everything swam, a maelstrom of aches.

When Arthur eventually managed to breathe again and opened his eyes, the fitful light of dawn was oozing round the curtains and there were no Gnoxies in sight. All was quiet, bar early morning market sounds from the square outside.

He felt exhausted, but a bit relieved. In order of blessedness, the boons were, that he could draw breath, that he felt marginally better, his headache only a muted throb; it was almost day, and the Gnoxies were gone. On the basis of all this slim evidence, he deduced – he earnestly hoped – that the fever had passed, or at least the lights were amber for its departure. It would be foolish to think the same might be true of the Gnoxies, he feared. Whatever reality they existed in he couldn't fathom and didn't really dare to think. It was a bit like his computer. It would suddenly decide to select a bright red, bold, san serif font for his emails by itself, or to play an irritating jingle at frequent intervals for no apparent reason. At least he could suppress the latter by muting the beast, but why? Why? What sins had he committed that he deserved these things? And Gnoxies. And rabbits.

It was probably all his fault. He had, unwittingly, created or caused them, and he must suffer. He blew his nose despondently and his head throbbed the more. Your sins will find you out. Well, he was sorry. Really sorry. But he didn't know they were sins, whatever they were. How should he? Where was the rule book?

He resolved, at least as far as the Gnoxies were concerned, to go and talk to Stan Bun about them. When he felt up to it. Which wasn't yet. For now, it was bad enough rising out of bed and going for a pee. When his head stopped swimming, he changed from his sweat-clammy clothes into his wonderfully dry pyjamas and curled back up in bed, where the familiar morning chorus of the emerging market below lulled him into a restorative and mercifully dreamless sleep. Until, that is, the phone rang. And rang. And rang.

Arthur dragged himself out of bed and picked it up.

18 Feeling Chipper

While Arthur was staggering home after the choir rehearsal, Beryl was walking to the Hippocampus from orchestra. Mel and Stan had gone ahead by car, but Beryl wanted to walk because she was feeling chipper and wanted to savour the moment.

Her humour was because Evelyn, first oboe, who sat next to the flute department, told her that Marcus had told her that Dee, the latest first flute, was not coming to the rehearsal and to let Beryl know. Beryl's heart had leapt. It meant she could at least play first flute for that rehearsal, and if she played it brilliantly, everyone would really regret that she wasn't to be first at the performance. Except there was one small problem. She hadn't got the first flute part. Of course not. Presumably Dee still had it. So when there was a prominent flute solo, people would look at her expecting her to fill the gap and she wouldn't be able to. What mortification!

Conflicted and grisly, she had sat herself down and assembled her flute when she saw Marcus threading his way over to her, desolation on his face. He was so sorry, he said, it was terrible messing Beryl around like this, but what could he do? If Clifford decreed, he could but obey.

And he had pressed a piece of music into her hands.

The first flute part.

Well!

'I knew there'd be problems working with a choir,' Marcus said. 'Honestly, singers. They are not like proper musicians, if you ask me. So she's promised to try to persuade her star pupil, Sophie – do you remember her? – to play, but she'll have to do second, which means you're on first. It's really throwing you into the deep end, but what can I do? That Lucien chap and now Dee, it's bonkers.'

Beryl had been flabbergasted. Marcus wasn't making a lot of sense, but whatever was going on, if she was back on first permanently, suns were shining, blue-birds singing, there were crocks of gold at the end of rainbows. 'Dee? She's out? Why?' she had blustered.

'Long saga,' Marcus said. In brief, it seemed that the soprano they had signed up to do the soprano solos in the Creation, a student at the Foster Academy of Voice, had been offered a chance of taking part in a recital in London at short notice, prestigious venue, okay, okay, possibility of important people hearing her, etcetera, etcetera, couldn't turn it down when after all, what did a measly concert in a godforsaken hole like Chervil matter to the up-and-coming diva of tomorrow? So the girl had left them in the lurch, and guess what, the only really competent soprano they could find in Chervil who was free that day, was Dee Carriero, their first flute. 'Oh yeah,' Marcus had gone on. 'She just happens to be on the peripatetic staff at the place where Cliff just happens to be head of music. So they have really searched high and low, haven't they? Anyway, upshot is Cliff says you can probably manage the first flute, and Sophie should be okay on second.'

And Marcus had handed her the first flute music.

Manage? Probably manage? Before the Lucien fiasco, wasn't Beryl managing just fine – no, more than fine, bloody brilliantly? Well, never mind. If the outcome was that the first flute part was hers once more, that was what mattered. Let them try to take it away from her again! She was Queen B of the Flute Department.

She had played with modest élan all rehearsal. At the end, just to exert her dominance, she had gone up to Marcus, as Queen B, and said, had he actually noticed that there actually were, in just one number, three flutes needed? Oh that was all sorted, he had said, didn't she know? Fred was going to do it. No clarinets in that number. Fred? On the clarinet? No, said Marcus, on the flute. Oh, said Beryl.

So now, re-elected first flute fantastico, she was metaphorically skipping to the Hippocampus along Conduit Street outside Chervil Castle when her phone rang. It was Algernon, her fair-weather son, or more accurately, her rough-weather son, for he tended to turn up when things weren't going well for him and he needed something, usually money. The rest of the time he led a largely mysterious existence elsewhere.

'Algy, love,' Beryl said, glowing with bonhomie.

'Mum. Okay if I doss down chez you for a couple of nights? No probs if its not, but nice to catch up, yeah? I thought, being in the district as it were, drop in, see how the old biddy's coping with Gran.' Algy always managed to rile her, even now when she was in a good mood. *Old biddy*, indeed!

'Gran's in a home. She's in Restawee. I emailed you.'

'Did you? I use Twitter and Instagram most off. Don't look at emails much.'

'Clearly. I live in the Dark Ages, obviously.'

'So if Gran's sorted, there's plenty of room in the old house, then?'

Beryl sighed. 'I suppose so. Where are you now?'

'Just passing the Finden services.'

'You're not phoning while driving?'

'Course not. Fay's driving.'

'Who's Fay?'

'My girlfriend. She'll be staying too. Just a couple of nights.'

Beryl sighed. So much for being able at last to forge an independent life, away from caring for the sick and the demented, to make her own decisions and do what she pleased, when she pleased, to exult in the return to first flute. She could say no, but Algy was her son, flesh and blood and all that.

'I see,' she said. 'Well, two nights then, okay? I'm not a free B&B. Have you still got the key to the house?'

'Sure thing, Mum. Aren't you there?'

'It's rehearsal night. I'll be back about ten thirty.'

'Wow, wild, Mum. Savouring the night-life.'

'There's most of a quiche in the fridge. You can have that. And some salad.'

'Champion, Mum. So see you later, yeah?'

Pooh. Well, she could cope. Beryl can cope. Beryl always copes. With good grace. Meanwhile, the Hippo awaited and a celebratory glass.

'Got a carrot?' said a voice.

Beryl looked about. The voice seemed to come from the grassy sward in front of the castle. Castle? Chervil Castle was little more than jagged piles of stones these days, had been since the fourteenth century as townsfolk plundered the walls for material to build their houses, but it provided a dramatic silhouette against the sky. In the meagre light of street-lamps, the grass patch in front seemed to be just that, grass. Then she detected a movement. It was, surely it was, a rabbit.

Rabbits didn't talk.

Nevertheless, 'Hello,' Beryl said, 'are you talking to me?'

'Or a lettuce?' the voice said.

Beryl couldn't think what sensibly to say. So she said, 'No, I don't.'

'Pah,' said the rabbit and hopped off behind the castle ruins.

Whatever next? Talking rabbits. Reinstatement to first flute must have gone to her head. Or she was going a bit doolally. After all, she had heard Victoria the Cat talking a couple of times, or thought she had. Enough of such thoughts; on to the imbibing! Celebration time.

Nevertheless, 'You're frowning,' said Mel as Beryl arrived at their table in the Hippocampus. 'Trouble?'

'No, no,' said Beryl. She wasn't going to mention the rabbit. 'Just my son inviting himself and girl-friend, who I didn't know he had – I'm sure he told me he was gay last time I saw him, perhaps he's bi or trans or whatever – anyway, he wants to stay a couple of nights. It had better be a couple, meaning two, no more. And two *nights*, not weeks. After that he's out, and knowing him, I'll probably be a few hundred pounds poorer. Oh, Mel, the trials of parenthood.'

'Is same the world over,' said Stan emerging from the throng around the bar with libations. 'A joy and a curse.' He lifted his glass in a toast and drank deep. Beryl and Mel reciprocated.

'Oh, that's better,' said Beryl. 'Hey, chaps, I'm back on first. Back to stay! Hallelujah!'

'Yeah, noticed,' said Mel. 'That's great. It's definite, then? Permanent, like? No what's her name, Dee is it?'

'Definite, Mel. Dee – listen to this – she's going to be doing the soprano solos. Apparently she's a fine singer as well. So it's win-win all round, as they say. And you'll never guess what they're doing for third flute.'

'Are there three flute parts?'

'Only right at the beginning of Part Three, in one number. Anyway, apparently Fred is going to do it. There's no clarinets in that piece.'

'On the clarinet?'

'No, on the flute. He used to play in a cruise ship band, remember. He can play almost anything that you blow, apparently.'

'Not the horn though, I bet.'

'Nor the bassoon,' said Stan. 'That is job of great skill.'

'Yeah, yeah. Fred. Gosh.' said Mel. 'And there are the brass to come to rehearsal next week. There are three trombones. Evelyn told me – she's on the committee – two are coming from the Chervil Silver band, and they're going to ask that chap who sometimes plays tuba to do the bass trombone, 'cos there's no tuba part. He's playing bass trombone and contra-bassoon too.'

There was a stunned silence. Beryl was thinking, 'That's Gerald the Moustache. Tickling. Huh. At least he will hear me shine and feel sorry at what he's missed.' Not that he had any idea of her little embarrassing episode.

Stan was frozen in wide-eyed astonishment. 'Bassoon on tuba? Is mockery. I resign. I am mortally offended.'

'No you're not, Stan,' said Mel. 'Don't be silly. You're the bassoon boss.' A wave of laughter crept round into the alcove in which they sat. 'That's those choir people. Bet it's your Oscar setting them off.'

Beryl bridled. 'He's not my Oscar. But talking of them, where's your uncle Arthur? He usually joins us.'

Mel leapt up and said she would go and ask because she wasn't frightened of a few jumped-up singers. After all, they weren't proper musicians – where were their instruments?

'That's an awful thing to say,' said Beryl. 'Go on with you, I know you don't mean it. But I'm worried about your uncle. Where is he?'

Mel went round the corner into the opposing camp – and returned very quickly, unscathed. 'They say he was at rehearsal and now they don't know,' she announced. 'Unhelpful peasants. Tell you what, I'll give him a ring.'

She did. Stan and Beryl watched, frozen. After a while, Mel realised there was going to be no answer. 'I'll try again in the morning. Just to check, yeah? I mean, I don't know his habits or anything. You know what, he might be anywhere, visiting a friend or something. Yeah.'

'Yes,' said Beryl. But it was concerning. 'Let me know when you get through, Mel dear. Set my mind at rest.'

Stan waved his hands dismissively. 'Is okay, for sure. Mr Arthur, he is big boy. What bad thing could happen?'

Exactly.

19 The Worlds

At half-past nine the next morning, Mel rang her uncle. She let it ring and ring and ring, and eventually a groggy voice answered. Arthur said he wasn't okay. 'Fever,' he croaked. 'Nightmares. Feel rotten.'

'I'm coming round,' said Mel. 'Be there in twenty mins.'

She arrived to find him in pyjamas and dressing gown looking distinctly frazzled.

'Sit down, Unk, Have you had breakfast? Can you manage anything? Or something to drink? Feed a fever, starve a cold – or is it the other way round? Is the kitchen through here?'

Arthur fumbled. 'Yes, no, I don't know. Oh, it's been terrible. Gnoxies.'

'Gnoxies? Like Cuddles?'

'They were here. They frightened me. They're vicious, Mel. They're monsters.'

'This was your nightmare, right?'

'I suppose so. It must have been. Oh dear, I felt awful. Sweating. Too hot, too cold. Head throbbing. Aching all over. I'm a little better this morning. Perhaps I could manage a bit of toast. Perhaps an egg? Have I got any eggs?'

'I don't know. Have you? Poor Uncle. I'll have a look.'

'In the fridge, in the door.'

He had eggs. Mel toasted bread and, as Arthur refined his order, scrambled two of them, buttered the toast and spread on a little Marmite at his request and plonked the eggs on top.

Arthur demolished them with no problem, plus another piece of toast with marmalade and two cups of tea. He must be getting over the fever. Can't be very serious. A day of hell and Gnoxies, that was all. Mel drank tea too, and watched the invalid recovering.

'So Cuddles is bugging you, yeah?'

'Yes, and several other Gnoxies too.'

'He's been breeding?'

'It seems so.'

'Randy little bugger. What have I created, Unk? I won't have them terrorising you.'

'And there are the rabbits.' Arthur told her how he'd seen rabbits all over the market and nobody else seemed to notice them.

'Stan,' said Mel, abruptly leaping to her feet. 'Stan's the man. He's used to all this spooky stuff, like, he can help you deal with it if anyone can. Come on, go and get dressed.'

'I'm not sure I can...' began Arthur.

'Yes you can, come on, chop chop. Oh my God, I'm beginning to sound like Mummy. I'm bullying you, Unk. I'm so sorry. I don't want to be like her.'

Arthur said it was all right, he'd got used to sister Constance's strong-arm ways as a child. He had learnt to cope with them.

'But it's disrespectful, yeah? I mean well, honest I do, Unk. I really do think Stan's the man. Don't you think it's a good idea?'

Arthur sighed. 'Yes, I suppose so. I expect you're right. But I'm so tired now. I think I'd like a little rest first. Perhaps this afternoon.'

'Okay, okay, fair dos. Look, you have a bit of a lie-down, and I'll go and see Stan and see if he can get away for half-an-hour or so sometime after lunch, and then I'll text you and come and pick you up when he says and... OMG, I'm Mummy again. Anyway, have a rest and then look at my text.'

'I don't know how to text,' said Arthur, looking small and wretched.

'But it's easy-peasy... Sorry, sorry. Look, you do email, right? I'll mail you a message, yeah? That okay?'

'Yes, yes. Email. Yes.'

'And I said I'd ring B and tell her if you're okay. Hang on...'

'Bee? Who's Bee?'

'Beryl, yeah? She's worried.'

'Beryl? Oh yes. Beryl. She's worried?'

'She is, Unk. She's a caring sort of guy... Hi, B... Yeah, I'm at his place. He's had a bit of a bad night, but he's living, like. Do you want a word?'

'No, no,' said Arthur. 'I'm not...'

'Here he is.'

Arthur's face went through various contortions as he listened to the phone. Eventually he got a word in. 'I'm all right. Really I am. Just a bit... No, Mel's here. We're going to talk to Stanislav... Why? Because he might be able to explain... After lunch. Mel says I'm to have a rest, and then... So... Yes, really... Thank you, thank you, ah... Yes. Um. Goodnight. I mean goodbye, Beryl, and thank you for...'

'That was Beryl,' he said to Mel.

'I know, Unk. Now go and have a good rest and then look at your email, yeah?'

So Mel went, and Arthur found a blanket, and folded himself up in it on his little sofa. Nature was kind, and he slept until one o'clock, when Nature woke him to answer a call of nature. He looked at himself in the bathroom mirror, and thought, *This can't go on. I don't understand any of it.* It was for certain sure beyond his rational comprehension. Short of a priest, who could you turn to who had dealings with such glimpses of other worlds, or whatever it was, where one person can see what others cannot? Where is plain honest-to-goodness reality?

As Mel had said, maybe Stan could help. He found an email from her. 'Stan say ☺. B at Motley Brew half 3. Ill B round 10 2.' Arthur puzzled for a while, when the missing apostrophe in "I'll" and conversion of some letters and numbers into homophones made it make sense.

Motley Brew? Ah yes, Beryl's café. Why there? Oh, leave it to Mel.

• • •

'I tell the truth, the whole truth and nothing like the truth,' said Mr Stanislav Bun, with more accuracy than he intended. He stood in the upper room of the Motley Brew like Poirot unveiling the murderer. Arthur and Mel sat at one of the tables.

'There are two worlds. Is you, me, trees, houses, bakery, bassoons, is one world. Call this World A. And there is world which sensitive people see, with little men and rabbits and what you call him? Gnoxies. And goblins and demons. And fairies. This is World B. And dragons. No, not dragons, they are different kettle of pickled herrings. Perhaps they are World C. So there are three worlds…'

He was interrupted by a backside pushing the door open, that of Beryl bearing a tray of drinks and cake. 'Here we are,' she gaily announced, plonking it down on the table. It pleased her having the upper room used. It was, she thought, ideal for meetings of such things as reading groups, knitters, soroptomists, anarchists – a place to discuss in peaceful quiet amid tea and cake. Only as yet, Chervil had not woken up to its bookable availability. 'Mel, cappuccino, Stan, strawberry milkshake, Arthur, breakfast tea, and me, redbush. I'm joining you. Is that all right? You're my friends. If one of you is troubled, maybe I can help too.'

You don't turn away the provider of cake, so of course she stayed, and Stan Bun continued his lecture.

In tortured English, he told them of parallel worlds which coexisted and yet were usually ignorant of each other. Where occasionally one would rip through into the other, producing inexplicable effects. Ghosts, he said, poltergeists, the Loch Ness monster (which had slipped from World B, he said, into World A and become trapped). Or something like that.

Some people, he said, were sensitive to the other world and could feel and sometimes see the parallel movements. 'People like me and most Polska, and Mr Arthur Davison here a little bit. But Miss Mel and Beryl, I think not?'

The two women looked at each other and shook their heads. And then Beryl said, 'There's Victoria. I think she talks to me, but I'm not a hundred percent sure. Does that count?'

'Victoria?' said Stan.

'My cat. Are cats from your World B?'

'I say yes and I say no. But is sign of sensitiveness. If your cat speaks, listen to her. Like Loch Ness monster, cats are both worlds.'

It all sounded complicated. To Arthur, it made some sort of sense that he could draw a creature that then took corporeal existence, in that what he was actually doing was drawing things which he thought were pure imagination but actually already existed in World B. So he wasn't actually creating but more releasing. It was all a bit vague. But that would mean that Mel too must have sensed Cuddles the Gnoxie in order to write about him, which meant Mel must be sensitive, as Stan called it. Arthur put this to the others.

'What? Me?' Mel said. 'You saying I didn't make Cuddles up? He's my baby. Created by me, all mine. It's like accusing me of plagiarism. How can I copy something I don't know anything about?'

'Now now, Mel dear,' said Beryl, 'I'm sure it's not like that and nobody's accusing you of anything.'

Stan sat down and took a mouthful of highly chocolate cake. 'Is so,' he said indistinctly. 'Imagination, dreams, nightmares, all leaking from one world to another. Fairies and gnomes in World B have nightmares about cows and small boys on scooters. Me? I hate scooters, but I do not have nightmares about them. I shout at them and they leave my bakery quick smart. But Gnoxies, they probably have such nightmares, just as you have nightmares about Gnoxies.'

'You know that, Stan? For certain sure? Fairies dream of cows and scooters?' said Mel.

'Well, maybe not exactly those things, and not all fairies, not all the time. Do you have nightmares all the time? But that sort of thing. It must be so. Is sense.'

There was a silence. Arthur had a feeling that Stan was just waffling because he was supposed to understand these things. Even so, talking about it made his experience of Gnoxies flinging burning lumps of rabbit flesh at him seem just that – a nightmare. And after all, he wasn't physically injured. Just traumatised. Talk about things, bring them out into the open. That was the lesson. Talking is good. He'd been alone too long; his entire life really.

The door burst open. 'Oh, there you are, Ma. Girl downstairs said you were up here.' It was Algy, Beryl's fickle son. Behind him drifted a wafty looking young woman, presumably his girl-friend Fay.

'Ssh,' said Beryl. 'Private meeting. Find a table downstairs and tell Irina what you want. I'll be down in a moment.'

'Full up down there, Ma. You're too popular.'

'Well, go and order from Irina anyway, and Fay, sit over there and please don't interrupt us. Sorry chaps, my son and his girlfriend. If they just sit quietly…'

'Okay, okay, Ma. We'll be quiet as mice. You won't know we're there. You be long?'

'Ssh.'

Algy went off. Fay tried to be mouse-like, which was difficult with lurid purple hair.

Arthur meanwhile was thinking. His drawings coming to life. First that vulture on the clock tower, then the little man on the bollard, then rabbits, and finally Cuddles the Obnoxious Gnoxie. Rabbits weren't other-worldly. Very much of this world, World A in Stan's terms. Also vultures, not that he'd ever seen one, except on the television. So it was just the little man – the ex-little man – and Gnoxies that belonged to World B, then. But before all this, over the years he had drawn loads of little chubby dragons, which Stan seemed to be saying belonged to a World C and were somehow different. As far as he knew, the ones he had drawn hadn't manifested themselves in physical form and flown from the page. And if they had, what then?

'Stan,' he said. 'Dragons. I've drawn dozens in the past and I don't have nightmares about them and they aren't flying about terrorising people.'

Stan rose to his lecturing feet again. 'Dragons, yes.' He wagged a finger. 'Dragons. World C. No parallel. Think: here is World A...' he drew a horizontal line through the air with his finger, '...and here is World C.' His other index finger executed an elaborate curlicue in the air. 'At times, he cross World A. Other times he poof... somewhere else. Yes. Maybe one day, you meet your dragons. Maybe not. Mostly not a nuisance. Not like little men and Gnoxies.'

'They were only little dragons.'

Mel said yes, they were cute and loveable.

'Dragons,' Stanislav pronounced portentously, 'are dragons. Beyond our knowings.'

Arthur asked if he should stop drawing them.

'Mr Arthur Davison, my friend, I say it makes no difference. How do you know what dragons look like? You have met one, yes?'

'No, but...'

'You don't know, then. Perhaps it was not dragons you draw. Perhaps dragons look like this.' He picked up a bowl with lumps of sugar in it.

'Oh come off it, Stan,' said Mel. 'You're just being silly, yeah?'

'No, no, no.' Stan sat and thumped the table on each word. 'I... Am... Not. No. Gnoxies, goblins, fairies, phantoms, yes, I see them. No problem. And your pestilential rabbits, Arthur, my friend. But dragons. Dragons different.'

Beryl sat up. 'Rabbits, Stan? Are you saying they're sort of supernatural, from the World B? And my cat?'

'No, no. Only the ones Arthur draws in the Market Square, which I see and he sees and you probably do not because for most people they do not exist. But they are there even so.'

Beryl said she was confused. Mel said she thought that Stan meant they seemed real to some people, like dreams and nightmares seem real but aren't really real, they just felt that way, yeah? And Stan said that wasn't quite what he meant.

…when a voice came from the other table. 'Excuse me,' said Fay. 'You mentioned your cat, Beryl. Perhaps I can help. I am an Animal Intuitive, I talk to animals and they talk to me.'

'That's right, Ma,' said Algy, appearing in the doorway with two cups. 'She's a Pet Psychic, and wow! You wouldn't believe what people's pets tell her. She was talking to your cat before we came out. Did you know that what he really wants is tinned salmon – it was salmon wasn't it, Babe?'

'Pilchards,' said Fay. 'What he *needs* to be whole is pilchards. He told me. Cats know, you see.'

Beryl said, 'My cat is Victoria. A female.'

'Of course,' said Fay, 'Algy got it wrong. Of course, she/he is marginal transgender through being spayed. But pilchards, tinned, that's right. Victoria was very clear about them.'

'Well, that's not surprising,' said Beryl. 'She's a greedy little pig. She even stole some icing from a cake I was making once.' No way was she going to tell Fay that Victoria spoke to her, down-to-earth Beryl. She hoped nobody else would mention it.

Mel had had enough. 'Look, guys, we're here to help Uncle Arthur because he's been having a really dreadful time with his demons, Gnoxies and that, yeah? And I feel sort of responsible, because I came up with Cuddles and persuaded Unk to do the drawings and honestly, I wish I hadn't because then all this wouldn't have happened or seemed to happen or whatever. Unk, has what Stan has said helped at all, do you think, yeah?'

Arthur said, yes, strangely it had. 'I don't pretend to understand, Stan. It's as though it's something just outside my experience that I can't quite grasp. As soon as I try to find the words, it floats off, round the corner, and when I look round the corner it's gone. What helps, I realise, is being able to talk about it and not to feel completely stupid.'

Stan's beefy hand landed on his shoulder. 'Arthur, my friend, you say it very well. Enough. I must go now, clean the bakery. Remember, you can talk to me, I try to help, and if I cannot, I give you bacon bun, which cures all known disease of the head. You are not alone, my friend.'

'That's right,' said Beryl. 'And if his bacon butty doesn't help, I've always got Devil's Food Cake, which must come a close second.'

'There you are, Unk. Told you you needed to talk to Stan. Come on, let's get you home. B, how much do we…'

'Don't be silly, Mel. It's the least I can do.'

• • •

At home that evening, Beryl started preparing herself a light supper (after feeding Victoria, of course), when the phone rang.

'Hello,' she said, cautious as always. You never knew.

It was Oscar. Oscar was loud. Oscar was clearly at least three sheets to the wind. She managed to extract meaning from his somewhat incoherent ramblings.

'You're doing the bass solos?' she said. 'It that what you're telling me?'

'Yes, oh yes. Little old me, big bass man. They were unanimous… umani… unaminous, Bernard and Clifford, fine chaps they are. I'm to be a star again. Can't keep an old dog down.'

'Oscar, Oscar…'

'Beryl, old pal, are you pleased for me?'

'Oscar, listen. Listen carefully. It's a great honour for you. I am pleased for you, yes. But you've got to take it seriously. There's very little time before the concert. You must stop drinking, you must.'

'Me? Drinking? No, no. I only drink water, me. From now on. Serious. Yes. They can trust me. Old hand, I am. Beer, wine, spirits, no, no, no. No do. Only medicinal...'

'No, Oscar, not even medicinal. You know what you're like.'

There was a silence.

'Yes. Beryl, old pal, I know... But I'm a new me now. A new creation. Upright, sober citizen, me. You'll see. Big star. Big time. New direction. New life. Sober life, yes sir. Oh yes.'

'Oscar do be quiet. Go to bed now. Sleep it off. Tomorrow you must focus on learning the part, doing us all proud. Doing Walter proud. You're his lifeline now. You've got responsibilities to him, to us, to the choir, to the orchestra. Take it seriously, I beg you.'

'Yes, thank you, thank you, Mary. I will. Going to beddibyes now. Good boy, me. Good night, Mary. Thank you. Thank you.'

Mary again. Would she ever discover who Mary was or had been? Someone from his past, clearly. Well, she'd probably never know. Did she actually care?

No, she decided, writing in Hattie later, she did not really care. It was none of her business. But that Oscar should manage to bring off the bass solos, that affected them all. What could she do there other than exhort him to give up drink? Nothing, when it came down to it. Just hope he transcended the inevitable transgressions as he had, no doubt, throughout his crooning career, at least in more recent years. He was, she was certain, an old soak and would carry on that way. Just let him manage this one occasion. Please.

'*Huh,*' said Victoria in her mind.

And then the front door opened, and noise entered her sanctuary, accompanied by son Algy and Fay, the alleged Pet Psychic. They had been wining and dining somewhere, that was evident, and had more wine with them.

'*Huh,*' said Beryl in her mind. As soon as was decent, she left them to it, and went to bed. Victoria was already there. A cat knows all about self-preservation.

20 Szarlotka

A couple of weeks later, in the Motley Brew, things were slack. It always seemed to be that way on Tuesday mornings. Beryl had toyed with dispensing with the services of Irina on Tuesdays, but it seemed churlish, for although Beryl knew little of Irina's circumstances, the poor girl seemed to be in need of every penny she could earn. So on Tuesdays, while Irina kicked her heels in front of a simmering coffee machine, Beryl did a bit of experimenting in the kitchen. It was important to provide variety and novelty in the cake line.

Today she was trawling the internet for inspiration, and, for some reason, Stanislav Bun came into her mind and she searched for Polish goodies. She had no idea what motivated people to put recipes, photos, even videos on the web when there appeared to be no financial incentive, but there they were. What was judged superb, it seemed, was *szarlotka*, a sort of apple pie from the Tatra Mountains, of which total perfection could be found at something called the Hala Ornak Mountain Hut. Thinly-sliced eating apples sandwiched between shortcrust layers, plus a bit of this and that. What made it different from an English apple pie eaten cold? Hard to say. She would try it and see.

Or perhaps she would take a break and go and see Stan the man himself. If simply hearing the name *szarlotka* started him drooling with ecstasy, then it was definitely worth trying to make one. Anyway, the wisdom of the web told her that *krupczatka* was the flour to use for the pastry, a Polish hard flour. Stan would know about that. He might even have some which she could buy.

Off she went to the bakery, and it being a clement day, braved the Tangle as her route. She passed the Houses of Parliament that weren't, and the Gallows Tree, which was actually a buddleia growing in a crack in a wall, at least in Stan's World A, and emerged into the relative brilliance of the Market Square. There were few folk about, though plenty of parked cars. No Jess Jerkin, jester extraordinaire, today. The bench under the rowan tree had but one occupant, Blind Bella, who may have looked at Beryl or may not, depending on your choice of eye.

Heedless, Beryl entered Mr Bun's domain. It seemed quiet, like the Motley Brew. Merrylin was perched round-shouldered on a stool gazing at her phone.

'Yeah?' she said.

'A bacon roll, if you please, and a cappuccino,' said Beryl. Why not? Once in a while. 'Is Stan in the bakery?'

'Yeah.' Merrylin sighed, slipped inelegantly off her stool and started pushing some rashers around on the hot plate. 'You want butter?'

Oh, temptress. 'Please,' said Beryl. 'And Stan, can I have a word with him?'

'Dunno.' Merrylin slouched over to the bakery doorway and vanished within. Moments later she re-emerged and resumed the alchemy of assembling the best bacon roll in Chervil.

'So, is Stan coming?'

Merrylin said, 'Yeah, prob'ly.'

And as if conjured up, Stan was there.

'Beryl,' he cried. 'Is honour. On house,' he said to Merrylin. She sighed again.

'*Szarlotka*,' said Beryl.

'Is good, but put stress on first bit. "*Szarlotka*." You are learning Polish?'

'No, no. I want to make one.' Stan was not drooling at the word, as she hoped; instead he was being picky about pronunciation.

'That is good. *Szarlotka* is a fine, fine thing.'

'How do you make it, Stan? Do you have any tips?'

'Me? I don't make it, Beryl. I am baker, not pastry chef. But there are recipes online, I bet. Look it up.'

'I have. They say you should use… um… ***krupczatka***. Do you know where I can buy some?'

Stan wagged a finger. '*Krupczatka*. I know I say everything Polish is finest in world, but maybe I exaggerate a tiny bit. Use ordinary strong flour, that is what I say. Who's to know? I have eaten *szarlotka* in Kraków, but it was long time ago, and all I remember is it was very good. So is your English apple pie, I admit it. I hold my hands up.'

'Stan Bun, I am disappointed in you. I hoped you might have some of this special flour you could sell me. Instead I find you have feet of clay.'

'Of clay? What does this mean?'

Beryl explained. Stan said he was mortified, and admitted that not everything he said about Poland was strictly true, but if he didn't champion that fine, fine land, who would around here? And look, here was Merrylin proffering the bacon roll of rapturous aroma, and look outside there, wasn't that Arthur Davison settling onto Blind Bella's bench, possibly to eat his lunchtime sandwiches, and maybe benefit from Bella's wisdom as a side dish, though he, Stanislav Bun, personally would not care to eat anything in the proximity of Bella because a baker, Polish or otherwise, needed to look after his olfactory senses. 'Baking is in the nose,' he proclaimed. 'Now to excuse me, Madam Beryl, I must into the bakery. Bread and buns wait for no man, as you English say. Again my apologies for the not knowing about *szarlotka*. Feets of clay, as you say.'

● ● ●

Out in the square, Arthur had indeed seated himself on Blind Bella's bench as far away from her as he could, though perhaps the wind was blowing offshore, because the atmosphere, if not that of attar of roses and the perfumes of Arabia, was perfectly bearable.

'Do I know you?' said Bella, half looking at him.

'We have spoken before,' Arthur said, 'a few times. I have written down your prophecies.'

'Have you so, young man? Well I'll have you know, sometimes I don't tell the gospel truth. Or maybe I does. Something will come of nothing, that's what I says, and I speaks what knows what's what, but beware of quackery.'

'Quackery?'

'You deaf or something? You what sings and suchlike? Quackery is what I says. Something will come of nothing, and beware of quackery. What's in your sandwiches?'

'Fish paste and cheese.'

'Nobody eats fish paste, not in these modern times. No jam?'

'I'm afraid not. I've got a slice of cherry Madeira for afters, though.'

'Go halfsies? I'm a fair woman. The half with the most cherries, mind.'

'Very well.' Arthur opened his lunch box, unwrapped the cake from its greaseproof paper, and broke it in two. Bella snatched the larger half, thus scotching any residual belief that she was actually blind. As a gull with a stolen chip, she rose with surprising speed and headed off for the alley behind at an efficient shuffle.

'And this quackery,' Arthur called after her, 'how do I...'

'Fire,' came the croak on the breeze. 'Remember the Blitz.'

'I'm too young,' said Arthur to himself. Though now empty, Bella's seat on the bench still felt occupied. If he was to reach out a hand, he was sure it would meet solid layers of unidentifiable clothing. Instead, he unwrapped his sandwiches, two with fish paste – comfort food – two with aged Gouda, which he currently favoured. Perhaps Bella thought he'd mixed the fish and cheese together. That would have been gross.

As he sank his teeth into a fish paste one, a voice spoke. 'Hello, Mel's uncle, may I join you?'

It was Beryl, bearing a roll and a cup of something.

'Of course, ' he said, and without thinking, slid sideways into Bella's space. He encountered no resistance, though maybe some of Bella's cussedness seeped into him. 'That smells like one of Mr Bun's bacon buns.'

She smiled. 'Oh yes. I'm indulging myself. I was hoping to get some Polish cookery secrets out of him, but he's not the fountain of knowledge he makes out to be. However, I have got a famous bacon bun for free, so something's come out of nothing.'

Arthur started. 'What? That's what Blind Bella said.' He looked at Beryl.

She saw fear in his eyes. 'Are you okay?' she said. 'Is something wrong?'

'No, no. It's just... I brought my sandwiches out here because I wanted... I know it's silly, but sometimes I ask Blind Bella's advice. They say she is like the Oracle, you know, in Greek myths, that she tells the future. Only it's very cryptic. So I write what she says down and hope it makes sense later. And today she said "Something comes out of nothing." Just like you did. And that I should beware of quackery. And something about fire and the Blitz.'

'Gosh. That's spooky. I just meant my trip wasn't wholly in vain. You know, I've tried offering bacon rolls in the Motley Brew, but they weren't a patch on Stan's – or maybe Merrylin's got a magic touch. And I wasn't prepared to offer inferior goods, so I stopped. I do a mighty fine quiche, though I say it myself. Come and try it one day.'

'I wonder if she meant...' Arthur stopped.

'What?'

'Bella... Quackery. Gnoxies. They're sort of little ducklings, which quack. Could she mean Gnoxies? How could she know about them?' Arthur felt a shiver of terror.

'Oh Arthur, they're not real. Don't you think you're taking Stan's theories too literally? He does exaggerate. He likes, you know, to make an effect. And all this World A and World B stuff. It's double Dutch to me. Or double Polish.

'And Arthur,' she went on, 'I didn't want to mention it in front of that Fay, my son Algy's current girl-friend, the other day, but sometimes I think Victoria – she's my cat – sometimes I think she talks to me. Of course, she doesn't really, but it feels that way.'

She smiled at him. Was she just being patronising, thinking he, Arthur, was a nut-case?

'I do see rabbits, though' said Arthur. 'Look, over there.'

'I don't see anything.'

'Look, by that vegetable stall. Oh, it's just gone behind a box. I'm not making it up, really I'm not. Stan sees them. There are lots.'

'I believe you, Arthur. It's just that... Well, if I can't... or don't... that's my problem, perhaps. But there was a rabbit by the castle... or so I thought... but no. No, no, of course not. Sometimes the imagination... No. It's silly. Stan is fanciful. You know that.'

Arthur did. He wanted to think that rabbits and Gnoxies were all products of his imagination. Or did he? Wouldn't that mean he was going mad? Either he'd created an infestation, or he was going mad. Which was preferable? As far as the world was concerned, compared with being faced with a plague of Gnoxies, his going mad was a trivial matter.

Oh, to be Stanislav Bun, where experiencing strange goings on could be simply explained by the statement "I am Pole." As far as he knew, he, Arthur Davison, was simply a good old British mongrel, bits of this and that from whoever invaded the island through the ages. That included the Celts, though, and they were rather superstitious, so he had read. He understood that they had plenty of supernatural beings to contend with – pixies and leprechauns and so on – and took them in their stride. He probably had bits of Celt swimming around in his DNA. Hence rabbits and little men. And that vulture. And talking cats and drawings coming to life. Maybe.

He fell silent, trying not to think about the possibility of dragons escaping from his pictures. Beryl too was quiet. They sat and watched rabbits scooting about the veg stall, or not, as the case was.

And then, as if through some unseen influence, they both turned and looked at each other. In the eye. And like with Blind

Bella's true gaze, it was disconcerting, and both turned back. Arthur felt altered in some way he couldn't quite fathom.

After a long little moment, Beryl said, 'I must be getting back to see how Irina's coping. Thanks for the chat, Arthur. Keep your chins up, as Stan would probably say. Will you be in the Hippo after rehearsal on Thursday? Oh, goodness me, the performance is next week. It's going to be intense.'

'Yes, yes, I will try to come along. Is the orchestra ready? I feel reasonably well in command of the bass line in the choir, but there's going to be the getting used to the orchestra instead of Iris. She plays the piano at rehearsals. And a different conductor. Oh yes, and Oscar Silvero taking on the bass solos. At such short notice. Is he up to it, I wonder? He didn't come to the rehearsal last Thursday. Bernard told us he'd been working with Oscar all week, and your conductor too, drumming it all into him, I suppose. It's worrying. It's awfully important.'

'Oscar. Yes. He has his weaknesses, Arthur. But he has had a long career of putting on a good show whatever condition he is in. The last concert he did – on his Golden Farewell Tour, I think he called it – he was pretty pickled by lunchtime, and the show still went on like clockwork. The old trooper. We have to believe he can pull it off. But as for the orchestra, are we ever ready? Never knowingly over-rehearsed, I would say. But we'll put our all into it and with luck, pure animal spirit will carry the day. And Cliff, you'll find him very clear. He can be – how shall I put it? – brusque, but he is always clear in his beat. Ah well, until Thursday, Arthur. Must be off.'

'Goodbye, Beryl. And... thank you.'

'You too. Bye.'

He watched her go, and a tiny twinge of desolation swept through him.

• • •

Dear Hattie,
   How are things, Beryl?

181

Thank you for asking, Hattie. Yes, I feel rather
inspirited, if that's a word. Buoyed up. Must be the
excitement of the Creation looming over the horizon.
It's always a bit invigorating when everything comes
together and you're first flute with some pretty smart
showy bits, not that I want the limelight, of course, I
mean, I just want to do Mr Papa Haydn justice, not to
mention the wonder of the creation of the world in
seven days and all that. Seven days! It's taking us
about three months!

I'm rambling, Hattie. Oh and yes, I'm well
chuffed too that Irina managed without me like a
trooper. She's all right. I made a good choice there,
though I say it myself. Goodness, I am in a funny
mood! After cooking Szarlotka today (and rather
well, no thanks to you, Stan – we'll see what the
clientele think of it tomorrow), I shall simply have a
pilchard pasta bake this evening, and Victoria shall
have a small portion of the pilchards and not because
that Fay said it was her heart's desire. Fancy her
thinking Vicki was a boy. Some animal psychic or
whatever she is! And maybe a glass of wine. Just me,
that is, not the cat. And that's not a precedent. Either
for me or Victoria. Wine and tinned pilchards are
luxuries.

Oh Hattie, I ate my lunch with Arthur, Mel's
uncle today. On that awful woman's bench outside
Stan's bakery. With, I confess, one of Stan's bacon
buns. Poor old Arthur. He's really worried by Stan's
theories about worlds and weird creatures coming to
life. But then, I thought, what about Victoria talking
to me? If she does. But she couldn't, could she,
because cats' vocal chords aren't capable of doing

human speech, surely? Except, perhaps it's some sort of telepathy or something. And then there was that rabbit outside the castle a couple of weeks ago. I thought that spoke. Perhaps I'm going loopy. Well, I'm in good company!

At least Victoria and that rabbit don't frighten me, not like these Gnoxies seem to be doing to Arthur. Poor man. It's as though he has created his own demons. He and Mel, since it was she who dreamed them up.

And then there's Jess the Jester's Tortuous Tour, how the buildings seemed to move, to react to our passing. How the windows seemed to be drawings, cross-hatched. Should I tell Arthur? What is there to tell, really? I'm not sure I can describe the experience. And that was in the Tangle, where you can imagine all sorts of strange things! But you could argue that the Market Square is part of the Tangle.

Oh, I don't know. When I see Arthur again, on Thursday I expect, after rehearsal, I'll try to be sensible and reassuring. Anyway, have a good evening and night, Hattie, and maybe I'll write again tomorrow. And tomorrow and tomorrow...

21 Misgivings

The Thursday after Beryl and Arthur's little chat on Blind Bella's bench, the respective choir and orchestra rehearsals were prosaic. Looking at all those little corners where trouble skulked. In both camps was a sense of grim determination that awkward passages and transitions could no longer be shirked.

In St Boniface's hall, the choir seemed subdued. Even Rupert. Arthur thought he might be saving up a few choice discrepancies between his score and everyone else for the final joint rehearsal the following Thursday. Bernard failed to give any little lecture, he simply got on with it. His belt was no better behaved at holding trousers up and shirt in than usual, but he himself was a model of clarity for once in the where-they-were-going-from and the beating departments. Of course, Arthur realised, if the choir screwed up next Thursday, in the final plenary rehearsal, when Clifford Hope-Evans took over the baton, blame would rest on Bernard's shoulders for not having prepared the choir properly, so he was highly motivated to get his forces in shape.

After the rehearsal, Arthur wended his solitary way to the Hippocampus, leaving much of the choir faffing around. As he walked towards the ancient bridge over the river Cher, in the fitful illumination of the street lights, he thought he could see a shadowy shape hunkering on the balustrade. For a moment, the memory of what might have been a vulture on the clock tower back in the Market Square when he'd just drawn one on his Square-scape haunted him. Silly, idiotic; a vulture in England indeed! Anyway, he'd only drawn it in pencil and then rubbed it out.

The shape spoke. 'Let's play pooh-sticks, Pavarotti. Fun, fun, fun!' With a terrible dread, Arthur thought he recognised Cuddles, who was waving something. It looked like a conductor's baton. 'Get yourself a stick, bonzo,' Cuddles quacked.

Arthur looked about vaguely, but there were no trees or bushes near anyway to provide something serviceable.

'No, no,' he said. 'There's nothing. I haven't got a...'

'What's that in your icky music-case, buster?'

Despite all sense, Arthur opened the case. As he knew perfectly well, it contained his score of Haydn's *Creation*, a pencil sharpener, an eraser, his diary... and a pencil.

'There you are,' cried Cuddles. 'Pencil. Not like what you drew me in. I'm in ink. Indianipoodle ink. Ineradicabibble. I'm here for keeps, me. Whacko! Pick up your pencil pooh-stick, dude, and get yourself ready.'

'But...'

'After three. One... Two...'

'No,' bellowed Arthur, 'Enough. Begone. Go and drown yourself.'

There was a terrible hush; only the gentle susurration of the river below in the blackness.

At length, the shadowy figure that seemed to be Cuddles spoke with spine-freezing clarity. 'I'm a duckling, chum,' he said. 'We don't drown. We swim. But you will regret threatening me. Till the end of your pathetic days. Don't forget...' he added as he flew off, '...I have friends. Lots of them. Legion.'

Cuddles soared off, and as Arthur watched, it seemed a skein of other shapes joined with him, forming a letter C flying silhouetted against the almost black of the Chervil sky. C for chaos. The Representation of Chaos. The start of Haydn's Creation.

The trouble had begun. Unthinkable things had started. And again, it appeared it was Arthur who had precipitated it. By refusing to chuck his pencil into the waters of the Cher, of all things.

As Arthur stood and stared, so he became aware of the sound of the chariots of destiny fracturing the quiet. It rapidly crescendoed to ear-splitting volume when three of the boy racers of Chervil tore across the bridge beside him, their sawn-off exhausts, or whatever it was, producing a cavernous, rasping roar, flaying his eardrums skinless. The racers were a scourge in Chervil, much like human Gnoxies. There were outraged letters in the Chervil Gazette demanding that "they" did something about them, but "they" never did. For Arthur, it all mangled his brain into a gibbering mush, they, the three racers of the Apocalypse, and Cuddles plus the battalion of avenging Gnoxies.

In spite of all this, the unconscious majority of his brain managed to propel him unsteadily over the bridge to the solidity of the Hippocampus.

He entered, and the atmosphere poured over him like soothing balm to a tortured person. For a moment he stood, bereft of thought, of purpose, of feeling. And then, his legs took him to the table, their table. And Mel was saying, 'Blime, Unk, you look like you've seen a ghost. You need a snifter.'

'Yes,' he managed. 'Yes.'

'Sit down, Arthur, dear,' said Beryl. 'A cup of tea, perhaps, that's the best thing.'

'Or a brandy, yeah? I'm buying.'

Arthur tried to think. 'Thank you. A small, dry sherry, perhaps. Yes.' Stick to what you know. Too many unknowns zooming about. He needed… What did he need? Stan. He needed Stan to tell him what to do. 'Stan? Is Stan here?'

Beryl told him that Stan had had to go home.

'The sister of my wife,' he had said to her at the end of the rehearsal, 'she arrive today. She stay for how long? I do not know. Nobody tells me anything. My wife and Alice, together they are unspeaking.' By which, Beryl had taken him to mean unspeakable. 'They do not hold back the words. They are rude about the bassoon, the kind of music we make. They cast the aspersions on bread-baking as a profession for a grown man, do you believe? And my legs, they are… what is it? Spindly. They are not. They are good legs. And that I am not hairy on the head. That is mark of high intellect. I do not join you in the Hippo tonight. I must return to my house to the fight for my honour and that of my profession and homeland.'

'Poor you,' Beryl had said.

So round their table at the pub tonight were just her and Mel. And now Arthur.

'Oh dear,' Arthur said. 'That's a pity. I wanted to see Stan...'

'Won't we do? Was it something at the choir rehearsal?'

'No. The rehearsal wasn't too bad. It was on the way here. Coming over the bridge... Oh, never mind. It's not important.' But it was. He didn't think he could talk about it to Beryl. Nor to Mel. It was Stanislav Bun he needed.

Mel returned, proudly bearing a small sherry. 'There you go, Unk. The demon drink. So what's up? I hope those pesky Gnoxies haven't been causing you trouble again. I wish I'd never dreamed them up.'

'I'm sure it's not your fault, Mel. No, I think... Oh, I need to talk to Stan.' He sipped the sherry. It soothed his tormented soul. Beryl reached out and patted his arm. She was a comforting person.

'Thank you,' he said. 'I feel much better now. It was nothing. Really. Yes.' How could he explain the manifestation of Cuddles and the demonic hordes to them without sounding like a complete nut-case? For heaven's sake, he was a grown man. An accountant, at that. Accountants were factual, evidence-based, down-to-earth mortals, without imagination, without flights of fancy. Perhaps he wasn't really an accountant. He had just been pretending all these years. 'Oh, dear,' he said. 'It's just that I have a sense of foreboding. I don't know why.' He did know why. He sipped the sherry again, drawing normality from its complexity.

'But tell me,' he went on, 'how was your orchestra rehearsal?' Anything to get away from Gnoxies. Forget about them.

'It was okay, dear. I had a girl called Sophie, star pupil of Dee – you know, the teacher at Chervil College who's taking over the soprano solos. Like Oscar and the bass. Honestly! It's real last-minute stuff. Anyway, Sophie is playing second flute and she is perfectly competent. And for once, Cliff conducted with his baton.'

'That means business,' said Mel. 'He usually waves a pencil around. When he picks up the baton, you've got to concentrate big time.' Arthur shivered. It reminded him of Cuddles' stick of choice for Pooh-sticks back on the bridge.

'So he did his stuff,' went on Beryl. 'He stuck to being efficient, leaving out his usual sarcasm and keeping his temper. Oh, dear! I'm hard on him. But that's conductors for you. They appear, they do their stuff, they disappear again. And on the way, they are criticised by all we mere players. And then in the performance, they take all the credit. And what do they actually do, when it comes down to it? Wave their hands around, and mop their brows. I think they forget who it is who play the notes. And who wrote the notes, come to that. Surely we are the stars?'

Mel interrupted. 'That's not really fair, B. Without Cliff, we'd be, like, a total rabble. And he does give us our little moments during the clapping. And anyway, someone has to represent the band in the audience's eyes.'

Arthur agreed. It was the same with choirs. And those singers who were knocking it back just around the corner were doubtless at this moment slagging off Bernard Pontdexter as usual.

They all agreed on that.

'Oh, but...' Beryl still had some grousing left in her. 'Next Thursday. The dress rehearsal, it's going to be a mess. Did Bernard tell you?'

'Yeah,' said Mel, 'we're going to have to leave the tenor bits until the Saturday afternoon, which is meant to be just topping and tailing and that sort of thing.'

'Bernard told us the tenor soloist couldn't be there on Thursday, yes,' said Arthur. 'I suppose it makes more difference to you, because you have to play in the solo numbers.'

'The poxy little rat-bag,' Mel said. 'Why? That's what I want to know. Why can't he be there?'

Neither Beryl nor Arthur knew. But because of it, they would have to omit solo tenor numbers next Thursday, and only touch on those that had all three soloists in, and that meant they would have to do all solos and the concerted numbers that involved the tenor in full on the Saturday afternoon before the performance, in a final rehearsal that was supposed to be a brief logistical exercise to make sure seating and sight lines and so on, were all right, and just to top and tail the numbers. A sort of tech rehearsal. To make it worse, on Thursday they couldn't rehearse in the cathedral, because it was unavailable, or too expensive or whatever. Instead, they would have to be in Castle Street Comprehensive School's sports hall, which was apparently big enough for both orchestra and choir.

'I mean, we're used to playing in the school hall,' said Beryl, 'but you aren't, and this is in the school *sports* hall... Why, it'll be all echoey and yucky. It'll all sound completely different in the cathedral. '

'It's a cock-up,' said Mel. 'Great artists like us need to be able to concentrate on being totally wow, not have all this aggro. I know, maybe it's a test. Maybe we really need to be up against it, yeah? So that at the performance, a mega adrenalin rush will zoom in and inspire us. I mean, we've got the notes and that; now we need the stimulus of performance.'

Beryl tried to be a bit more positive about things, remembering belatedly she'd told Hattie she would try to reassure poor Arthur. 'And it means we'll have no time to worry what other obstacles there are waiting to upset things. Believe me,' she said, not really believing herself, 'nothing terrible's going to happen, nothing's going to go wrong. It's going to be memorable.'

'I'm sure you're right. Oh, I do hope so,' said Arthur. But he really fervently hoped it would be *un*memorable, that Cuddles and his cohorts wouldn't make it unforgettable, that the performance would be... well, boringly competent. That would do. Like accounting. Like his life.

In truth, there was a great big dark cloud hanging over all of them, he felt, in the form of an arrow pointing to Saturday week, when an audience would assemble ready to see and hear a New World being created in front of their very eyes. They had only one proper rehearsal to go before then, plus the afternoon job on the day. He could almost see the penetrating gaze of an avenging angel trained upon them, bent on rooting out all their sins of omission. And, in the case of Gnoxies, sins of creation.

Beryl said they should list all the things that were worrying them. 'I always find I can cope better if I've got a list,' she said. 'It makes me feel I'm in control of my life. It's probably a false impression, but it makes me feel better.'

So they did. It went:

• The tenor only appearing on Saturday. He might not know his part, he might be rubbish.

• Oscar might not be up to the bass solos. It was really different from singing with a mic after all. (*And he might be drunk,* thought Beryl, not mincing words.)

• Was Dee up to the soprano solos? She was out of Beryl's hair, leaving her with the glory of first flute, but would Dee, as Mel put it, wow them?

• The Saturday tech rehearsal, which was supposed to be short and prosaic, would be the first time of doing things with the full forces. Anything could go wrong. And they'd likely be tired out come the evening and the performance.

And there was a fifth worry, only Arthur did not voice it. It went, "Destruction may rain down, chaos may reign, war break out." It felt apocalyptic. Once again he wished he'd never drawn a Gnoxie, and yearned for the insight of Stan Bun and his wisdom.

The three of them looked at the list, not that they'd written it down, and agreed that there was absolutely nothing they could do about anything on it except to concentrate seriously at the dress on Thursday, and pace themselves on the Saturday afternoon. And in between, to practice, practice, practice. Poor Victoria. Poor Jason. Poor non-existent neighbours in Arthur's case.

As a result, everything would be okay, yeah?

22 Final Rehearsal

It was the final rehearsal that wasn't the final rehearsal because the tenor soloist couldn't be there. And it was in Castle Street Comprehensive School's sports hall, Clifford Hope-Evans at the helm, Dee and Oscar as soloists, plus a yawning, tenor-sized gap.

It was not a primrose path of an occasion. In the choir, Rupert interrupted several times with nit-picking differences in his score. Bernard Pontdexter sang along with the altos with considerable force. *It's not good,* thought Arthur. *The altos are used to doing their part unaided; they're perfectly capable on their own. Bernard's hooting contribution will really annoy them.*

The rehearsal soldiered on, leaving out most of the tenor bits until just before they reached the end of Part the Second. At that point, Clifford Hope-Evans, estimable conductor of the Chervil Symphony Orchestra, lost it.

'It won't do,' Clifford shouted. 'We might as well be in a flaming swimming pool. I can't hear. I can't hear. I want detail. I want precision. I don't want to hear one of the altos in the choir drowning... Like a flaming owl. There is subtlety; Haydn knew his stuff. Oh, I give up. What's the point? Find yourselves another conductor.' And he stormed out.

There was silence. Eighty odd people in shock. Arthur felt the chill of perspiration clammify his body, born of feelings of guilt, even though in no way was the source of Clifford's exasperation his fault. Gradually, voices emerged from the silence.

'What did we do wrong?' 'What's eating him?' 'Is he always like that?' 'Is he serious?'

And five minutes later, back came Clifford, mounted his little rostrum, tapped baton on stand and announced, 'Part Three please, ladies and gentlemen. We'll leave out the tenor recit at number 28 for now and start at number 29. Number 29. "By Thee with bliss." Then we'll run to the end. No stopping. There's another small tenor recit at number 32 before the final chorus. We'll just skip over that for now. It's only continuo anyway. So, number 29...'

'Excuse me.' Rupert had his hand up. 'The numbering's different in the Bärenreiter...'

'You,' cried Clifford. 'Shut up. If you interrupt once more, I shall murder you. Number 29, everyone. Choir, you stand at the beginning of this number, don't you? So why aren't you standing? Didn't Bernard go through all that with you?'

The choir rose with wonderful accord. Everyone was extremely alert for once. Clifford started off, and Part the Third proceeded on its way, Adam and Eve enjoying their first happy hours in the Garden of Eden. Apart from Oscar's lacklustre efforts in the bass solos, it ran pretty smoothly. Dee was a solid if uninspiring Eve. From his place in the basses, Arthur considered it reasonably creditable considering. He even personally managed an impressive *forte* at times. Rupert and the others might venture into the lands of *fortissimo* and *forte-fortissimo*. Let them. They might burn their voices out by the time they were his age, if they weren't already, which some of them undoubtedly were.

They arrived at the end without serious mishap. 'Thank you,' said Clifford. 'Pretty much the right notes at the right time. That's the basics in place. On Saturday, we'll add the emotion, the fizz, the magic, and Bob's your uncle.'

Arthur had a suspicion that Rupert was on the point of raising his hand to inform Clifford that his uncle or uncles weren't called Bob, but that even Rupert perceived this might not be wise. Better let an inaccuracy pass than be murdered. Thank goodness.

But magic... Clifford said they'd add the magic on Saturday. That might mean Gnoxies. They were magic, weren't they, whether real or imaginary? He hadn't felt any presence of them here, in this school sports hall, but then it was all modern – well, at least, less than a hundred years old. Not like the antiquity and devious history of the Tangle and Market Square. Perhaps

Gnoxies, as well as extraneous rabbits and little men on bollards could only exist in such places. But in the cathedral... That was even more ancient. Doubtless before it was built there were other religious buildings there predating whenever is was the Tangle grew up, or evolved, or spontaneously created itself from the primaeval ooze, or however it came to be. Was it possible that the performance in the cathedral could be affected by the little blighters?

In the Hippo after the not-quite-final rehearsal, Beryl, Mel and Stan were quiet, as if they'd been punished for a crime that wasn't their fault. From their point of view, the problems had basically been with the choir. And a certain red-haired chap who kept sticking a hand up and making pedantic observations about what it said in the copy he was singing from. Cliff had been very rude to him.

Poor Arthur Davison, as the sole representative of the choir in their little group in the pub, tried to explain that the chap in question was Rupert who was the chair of the choir and he was always like that.

'He gets over-enthusiastic,' said Arthur. 'I'm sure he'll be fine in the performance. Bernard Pontdexter, our conductor, is used to him. I suppose your man found him a bit trying.'

'Cliff is short-tempered and has a fine line in sarcasm,' said Beryl.

Stan nodded his big head. 'Is passionate. Like me. It is necessary to have the thick skin with him, so the water runs away from the duck.'

'Stan dear, you do mangle our English idioms awfully,' said Beryl, 'but I love it.'

'I am your Johnny Foreigner, me. Your language is madness. No logic. "If you knead your dough with your nose, the bread will be flat." I made that up. Is good, no?' Stan beamed upon them.

'Brill, Stan,' said Mel. 'But what about Cliff's other tantrum. The first one. When he stormed out. What was that all about?'

'I think,' said Arthur... and then fell silent as they all looked at him. 'I think he was annoyed because it seemed to me that Bernard – that's Bernard Pontdexter, our conductor – was singing along with the alto line. I think your chap, Clifford, thought he was too loud. From where I was sitting it sounded so. Bernard's more of a soloist really. He doesn't usually sing with the choir, after all, he's usually conducting us. It's just that he's doing the little alto solo bit in the last movement, you may have noticed. And Clifford couldn't tell Bernard off in front of everybody, so he lost his temper. That's what I thought it was all about. I might have got it wrong.'

But he was right. He was sure he was. Anyway, whether that was it or not, the mood in the pub was restrained. No dancing on the tables or yodelling. Arthur really wanted to ask Stan Bun if he thought Gnoxies might be troublesome during the performance, but didn't like to broach the subject in the presence of the Mel and Beryl. He felt they might laugh at him taking these supernatural goings-on seriously. Perhaps he was being over-cautious, but the memory of that dreadful night of the fever, those Gnoxies... Beryl had mentioned her cat talking to her, he seemed to remember, but that was rather different. Perhaps women weren't "sensitive" as Stan called it, or not very. Even so, he'd rather ask Stan when they weren't around.

'This tenor soloist,' said Mel. 'Honestly, it's beyond a joke. He's from the Foster Academy of Voice, isn't he? Just a poxy student. How to screw up your career before you've even started.'

'Mel, dear, you were a student until last year,' said Beryl.

'Yeah, yeah. But I didn't let people down. Not, like, intentionally, anyway. What's this guy's excuse? He'd better be effing good on Saturday, know the notes, right, and sound like Pavarotti, yeah? I mean, of course today's rehearsal was rubbish when we couldn't do a proper run-through. Continuity and that. And Saturday afternoon. Cliff said yonks ago it was going to be quick top and tailing to get used to the acoustic, and now, it'll go on and on doing all the bits this snotty little toe-rag of a tenor is in,

195

which seems to be half the numbers, yeah? And by the evening, for the concert, we'll all be knackered, yeah?'

Beryl held a hand up. 'Wow, Mel. It's really bugging you. I'm sure it'll be fine, dear.' It better had be. Perhaps these tribulations would hone Oscar's performance skills and put some fire in his belly.

It occurred to Arthur that as a result of not being able to run many of the numbers in sequence, the choir hadn't practised their standings up and sittings down, at which they were generally awful, even though Bernard had gone through them several times. Not to mention the filing into their seats at the start of the concert. They usually resembled a centipede which has forgotten in what order to move its legs.

'Now, this Rupert,' he said to the others, 'the one who annoys your conductor, he is singing from his grandfather's copy. Not only is it a different edition from those the rest of us are using, but it has his grandfather's annotations of where to stand and sit, which are, of course, not always the same as those that Bernard Pontdexter and your chap have decided on. He's likely to argue on Saturday, I'm afraid. Not in the performance, of course, but in the afternoon. He means well, I'm sure. Over-enthusiastic, as I say.' And, though he did not say, what with the possibility of interference by hooligans of Gnoxies, the result was they could be in for disaster. And then there was Oscar, who was frankly not up to scratch as bass soloist.

Stan, meanwhile, looked stern, glowering even. He had his own preoccupations, which, unbeknowst to the others, centred around, firstly, his current bassoon reeds, which were old and unreliable and he had been meaning to buy some new ones but hadn't got around to it, and secondly, the presence at home of his wife's sister staying with them. Wife and sister together were appalling, and uninhibited in being rude about him, being a baker, playing the bassoon, and so on.

All in all, it was little wonder that the four of them in the Hippocampus were subdued.

So too was the group of choristers around the corner. Oscar was notable by his absence. It might be because he was embarrassed by his efforts during the rehearsal and had gone home to soberly study the score of the Creation and do some silent practice while resolving to give it a hefty dose of wow-factor and pizazz on Saturday. Or, more likely, he had repaired to some other drinking establishment where he could get blotto and maudlin unobserved. Perhaps he was even now back in the Royal Hotel, from which Beryl had, so to speak, liberated him a couple of years before.

• • •

Back home, Beryl unleashed the bottle of gin and took up Hattie.

> *Dear Hattie,*
>
> *How are things, Beryl?*
>
> *I'm a tad anxious, truth be told. Of course you don't expect final rehearsals to be perfect. A bit of stopping and starting. Getting used to the space. Except we were in the school sports hall instead of the cathedral, and we'll only get into the cathedral on Saturday afternoon, and then only for a couple of hours, and it'll be topping and tailing, mostly because we've got to do all the bits the bloody tenor soloist is in because he wasn't there today. Sorry about the language, Hattie dear. I'm that mithered. Who does this tenor think he is? Is he that important that he, a mere boy I understand, can inconvenience a whole symphony orchestra and choral society? I ask you.*
>
> *And as for Oscar, Hattie, I only hope he pulls his socks up on Saturday. He was pathetic today. Like a timid rabbit. I'm embarrassed. After all, it was me suggested he join the choir. But it's not my fault that one thing led to another and here he is doing the*

bass solos. And it's such a big solo part! I just pray, or I would if I was a praying person, that he turns on the charisma when the time comes, the old trooper, the pro. I remember what he was like before that last concert he did here in the Lyric theatre a couple of years back when I took him leafleting, how pathetic he was then and how he changed when on stage. Let's hope, Hattie, let's hope.

I reckon we were pretty good in the band this evening, considering. We need more rehearsal time, but isn't it always so? But really, Cliff losing it twice during the rehearsal...

23 The Creation

Saturday afternoon's rehearsal happened. It went passably well; that was the best that could be said of it.

The tenor did actually turn up. Clifford introduced him to the choir and orchestra. Cuthbert Thwaites, his name was, said Cliff. Beryl felt the lad would be well advised to take a stage name if he was to hit the big time. However, he seemed to know his part and made a passable sound, if a bit weedy. That was a relief.

They practised the bits they were supposed to. Oscar seemed as so-so as he had been on Thursday. It did not make for an inspiriting prelude to the evening performance. At least it *was* in the cathedral. They could acclimatise to the ambience of that mighty space.

Arthur tried to concentrate and not think about Gnoxies. He was reasonably successful. But then, if you considered the ghastly ducklings a potential hooligan gang, they would surely wait for the optimum moment to cause maximum confusion. And that would be during the performance.

The time slowly ticked away until it became the hour for the call to arms for the performance. This was it.

For Beryl, entering the cathedral, the sensation felt much like it did in their regular performing space of St Boniface, except that the cathedral was that much more vast, more still, more ancient. She could hear a distant whispering sound, the only evidence of the admirably large audience all chatting away. But then, you could fill the cathedral with an army of chimpanzees all screaming war-cries and it would still sound like the mere rustling of dry leaves. Music was another matter in that space; it rolled and reverberated, but the chatter of an expectant audience was as nothing.

Mind you, it was exciting. They always were, these moments before the off; a mixture of fear and elation. Anything could happen, but wouldn't, because they had practised, rehearsed, hadn't they? All those hours would pay dividends. It was all an immense fusion, a coming together, each individual subordinate to the whole, the vision of a man who died over two hundred years before. Any one performer could screw up. But they wouldn't, Beryl was fairly sure. And if they did, the cathedral's reverberation would iron it out and the audience would be none the wiser. Probably.

Her optimism was not entirely shared by Arthur Davison, sat up there at the top of the raked seating for the choir. He was uneasy. Looking behind him, he could see, perched at the end of the choir stalls down in the gloom below, what looked like a carved grotesque. But Arthur was pretty sure it was actually a Gnoxie masquerading, and its presence on this earth was almost certainly his fault. The way Mel had written about them and he had drawn them (only following orders), the main purpose in a Gnoxie's life was to cause mayhem. If there was one Gnoxie present in the cathedral, surely there would be others? Lurking. Waiting for the best moment. Waiting to create havoc.

However, perhaps there was a chance that somewhere up there in the vaulted roof would be a watching dragon or two. They might be able to deal with the diabolical Gnoxies, mightn't they? But according to Stan, dragons were inscrutable alien creatures, and so who knew? With luck, what he thought might be a Gnoxie in the choir stalls, was indeed a mediaeval carving, and there were no mischievous creatures lurking, neither mythical, imaginary nor actual, and nothing would happen to upset the happy progress of Haydn's *Creation* from chaos through to light, order and concord. With luck. Lots of luck. But Arthur was by no means confident.

He looked over at Stan Bun, in the orchestra in front of him, whose bald head shone like a beacon under the lights. Stan didn't appear to be bothered. He was fiddling around with his bassoon. The sight did not appease Arthur's qualms.

Oh dear! Think positive, Arthur. Think of the wonders you are about to create. Think of filling this glorious building with something that will lift the audience off their seats and transport them to a brave new world, fresh, sparkling, created before their eyes and ears. Even down to the humble worm. And he, Arthur, must strive to sing out a bit, like the adjudicators always exhorted him in the Chervil Competitive Music Festival as they awarded him seventy-two marks out of a hundred, which he knew and they knew was meant to encourage him but actually signified a hopeless case. Today, however, he must help compensate for the absence of Oscar in the choir's bass ranks, while that man himself assumed the mantle of bass soloist. If Oscar brought his starring role off a bit better than in the afternoon and last Thursday's rehearsals, and Arthur really hoped he would, they wouldn't be seeing him in the choir any more. He would surely be too grand and mighty and sought after. Like he was as a crooner, so Arthur was given to understand. But look what happened to that career. Dwindled into drink. At least, he gleaned that that was what happened from conversation in the Hippocampus. Beryl seemed to fear that Oscar's moving in to care for old Walter would lead to a descent back into the bottle. Probably even now, Oscar was fortifying himself for the performance.

Of course, they were missing Walter too, in the tenor department. But that was maybe for the best if you valued precision. Poor old Walter.

He looked over across the orchestra at what he could make out of the audience. There was a reasonable showing. Every chorister and instrumentalist had issued three-line whips and called in favours to get family, friends, acquaintances, next-door neighbours, even the postman, anyone they could to come along. St Edith's, Chervil Cathedral, could absorb extraordinary numbers and still appear only vaguely occupied.

In their midst, if Arthur had a telescope and could see around pillars, he might spy Stan Bun's morose assistant Merrylin, together with an older, moroser woman who was probably her mother. Similarly, Irina, Beryl's assistant, was there. And even old Walter, in a wheel-chair, with what was presumably a paid carer, or possibly Rupert's wife, since, after all, Walter was Rupert's uncle. There too was a young man in the audience, who was, if Arthur but knew it, Jason, Mel's partner. And over there, wasn't that Jess the Jester, in his top-hatted, silver-headed cane guise, looking insouciant and generally cool?

At the appointed hour for the start, from the North aisle appeared a figure, violin tucked under one arm. It was Mildred Trimble, the leader. She swanned along, head in air, a picture of calm and authority. That was more apparent than real. She was Mildred all-atremble underneath, but she would die rather than admit it. As she reached her place at the first desk and waved her bow at Evelyn to play the oboe-definitive A, the audience began to quiet. The hush spread out over the nave, just as the A spread out over the orchestra. Even Rupert in the choir tried out his own A, then glanced sideways to see if Arthur next to him had heard his naughtiness. *The A is for the instrumentalists*, thought Arthur, *not you, you bad person.*

By the time everyone had caught and tuned to the A and Mildred had sat, and with the audience in the nave holding their peace if not their breaths, the Grand Procession began. It emerged from out of a door in the North Aisle, and progressed across in front of the orchestra. All of them marched formally, upright in their bearing, scores clutched in their hands across their chests: Dee Carriero (Gabriel/Eve, stolid and forthright), Cuthbert Thwaites the tenor (Uriel, terribly young, cocky), Oscar Silvero (Raphael/Adam, his suit too big, his meagre hair carefully combed over, but glowing with pride and determination), and finally, after the soloists had received their due applause, Clifford Hope-Evans (maestro, quick trot, dressed in tails, would you believe? No half-measures for our Clifford. He was magnificent; the mane of hair leonine. Alpha male.)

And they were off, straight into *The Representation of Chaos*, as penned by the great Joseph Haydn and realised by the enthusiastic but not so great Chervil Symphony Orchestra. The audience listened, rapt. If there were indeed Gnoxies lurking, their beaks were twisted in scorn and derision. What did human beings know of chaos, they might think, they, who were disseminators of trouble throughout their cuddly feathered beings?

The first bassoon part had some natty little arpeggiated passages straight off, which Stan Bun performed with brio and a frown of concentration on his forehead. Later on in the Representation of Chaos, Beryl executed her two-octave scale passage better than she ever had in practice – and practise it she had, oh yes, over and over – and then performed the little flute solo at the end of the movement with, in her opinion, limpid clarity; a heart-breaking falling phrase.

At which, Oscar arose, and, as the angel Raphael, began the narrative. Unrecognisable from his efforts at the rehearsal two days before, his voice was firm and resonant, as if this was the moment he had been waiting for all his life, the summation of his singing career. If one was to carp, his sibilants were a bit strident, hissing like angry Gnoxies in his effort to get the words over, conscious that, unlike his crooning stage shows, there was no handy microphone held a couple of inches from his mouth to do the job for him. No, here and now he had to rely on projecting his own diction, and project it he did. His lips worked overtime, now shooting out, now snarling against his teeth, now stretching wide in a toothpaste leer.

Then the chorus was on its feet, and, convincingly pianissimo, they murmured that the Spirit of God was moving upon the face of the earth, and that the net result was the creation of... LIGHT!!!! Rupert added the fourth exclamation mark all by himself by jumping up and down, causing the raked staging to shake alarmingly.

It was terrific stuff. Everyone was giving their all. The audience were witnessing a world being created in front of their ears, even though their eyes told them that it had already happened countless millions of years ago.

Oscar created the land and seas; Dee, in a forceful and shrill soprano, created plants; the far too youthful tenor chipped in with the moon and stars; and lo, all too soon, the choir was singing that the heavens were telling the glory of God, the wonder of his work displayed the firmament, and they were at the end of Part the First, as it was so elegantly labelled in the score. All was going well. Any lurking disruptors, real or imagined, were keeping out of sight and mind. If there really were Gnoxies present, surely they would have seized the Chaos overture as their cue, wouldn't they? So Arthur reasoned. But no sign of them. He relaxed a tiny bit, for he still felt very uneasy in an ill-defined way.

There was a short break before Part the Second, the orchestra retuning, everyone having a bit of a shuffle. The seats, as the audience appreciated now that they were not distracted by the music, were unnaturally hard. Some experienced attendees had brought cushions to soften the experience.

Arthur saw Stan Bun, down in the band, looking up into the vaulted heights as though he sensed something. He too was worried, thought Arthur. Luckily, everybody else, choir, players, audience, seemed to think it was proving to be a jolly good show all round.

Maestro Clifford finished mopping his brow with a polka-dotted handkerchief, resumed his podium, lifted his baton, smiled benevolently at the forces in front of him, checked Dee was on her feet and ready to go with the opening recitative and aria, and Part the Second set sail, to create fish and fowl and beast, and after that, man.

Arthur's qualms became lost in the moment. He awaited Oscar's telling of the creation of cattle and creeping things, including the cheerful lion, flexible tiger and nimble stag, and after adding insects, the final flourish: "in long dimension creeps, with sinuous trace, the worm." Would Oscar attempt, and manage to reach, the bottom D for the worm that Haydn didn't write?

Later, after everything that was destined to occur during Part the Third, Arthur could truthfully say he hadn't a clue what note Oscar gave the worm, because it was inaudible. His lips visibly stretched out in a prehensile manner and formed the round contours of the word "worm", but which octave it was was lost in the sound of the strings, playing down low, warbling lugubriously in the resonance.

What impressed Arthur was Oscar's seemingly total mastery of the part. It was a wonderful recitative, in which, as the animals were created, Haydn characterised them in his orchestration, almost cartoon-like, and Oscar seemed to respond to it like a seasoned oratorio singer. Of course, he was an experienced singer, but here, today, he was transported. He was seven foot tall, he was young, debonair, handsome. Clifford, the maestro, he of leonine head and proud demeanour, must have felt a tawdry specimen of humanity next to the great Oscar. Nevertheless, undaunted, Clifford led the band to brilliance.

Then God got around to creating man, and the up-and-coming young tenor man/boy acquitted himself creditably. He extolled Adam – "And in his eyes with brightness shines the soul, the breath and image of his God" – and God deigned to add a woman to provide Adam with love and bliss. Jolly good, cried the chorus, glory, glory, glory, and it was time for the interval.

Some of the performers mingled with the audience. For anyone up in the vaults of the roof, if any person or thing was indeed up there, the floor of the cathedral resembled a disturbed ants' nest, figures moving hither and thither, seemingly randomly, spotting an acquaintance here, heading for the refreshment tables there, questing for the toilets.

There was an atmosphere of quiet ecstasy. People seemed to find it difficult to know what to say. Normally at such a time, Mrs A would be telling Miss B about what Ms C had allegedly done with Mr D – something outrageous such as having coffee together in the Motley Brew – and Mr E would be wondering aloud to Mr F whether it was going to rain on the morrow because he wanted to pick some dandelions to begin his annual couple of gallons of wine and it did require a dry day, didn't it, and Mr F said he didn't know, he bought his wine from Tesco. But today, the world having just been created, none of that seemed important. So folk stood around and said things like, 'Gosh,' 'Wow,' and 'Phew.' And others answered, 'Yes,' 'You're so right,' and sipped their wine or orange juice, purchased from tables in the South aisle at £3 and £1 respectively.

Arthur made his way through the music stands to where Stan Bun was fiddling with the keywork on his bassoon with an air of somebody trying to avoid doing something else. 'Hello, Stan,' said Arthur. 'It's going jolly...' He petered out because what he really wanted to say was that he felt something dreadful was going to happen, and Stan was the man to tell him if it was so, if he felt it too, and what it might be.

'Yes,' said Stan. 'Is good, yes.' And carried on fiddling.

'Um, Stan...'

Stan slowly lifted his head and looked at Arthur. 'No, is not good, Arthur Davison. I do not want to look up. I advise you, keep your head down. It is not our world, what happens up there. Is foreign. Is alien. Is not for us.'

So of course, Arthur did look up. It was not certain, but it looked to him as if that great vaulted ceiling, the arched bays and fans, were slightly diffuse, ethereal, and he thought maybe he imagined he could almost make out stars shining through. There seemed to be things flying about, zigzagging, like bats catching flies on the wing. Suddenly, he didn't want to know what they might be. The thoughts on the edge of his mind were too awful. Nothing must spoil this performance of the Creation, a performance, which, while by no means accurate, had a certain something about it that was extraordinary.

He shook his head and said to Stan Bun, 'Yes, you're right. I won't look up.'

But he would.

Gradually, and then in an increasing flood, singers and instrumentalists returned to their seats, and drifting in their wake, the audience took their places once more. The last act.

The little procession of soloists began again from the North transept, this time not Gabriel, Uriel and Raphael, but Eve, Uriel and Adam. Not that they looked different, except perhaps more radiant. Adam and Eve, aka Oscar and Dee, were still in evening garb, still clothed, though the Garden of Eden was as yet uncorrupted by the serpent and temptation, and nakedness was allegedly the costume *de mode*. But then, this performance made no pretension of being a staged production. Good heavens, what would Parts I and II have been like staged? An interesting idea, but wildly beyond the abilities of Chervil Choral and Symphony Orchestra. Why, even getting the choir to file on in some degree of order was bad enough.

Here was Clifford, and they were off again. Uriel rose. 'From heaven's angelic choir pure harmony descends on ravish'd earth,' he sang in limpid tones, but before the choir could oblige with the pure harmony, Adam and Eve embarked on their duet. Even so, the Chervil Choral Society, unable to contain themselves, underlined the entwining of the voices of the first man and first woman with reminders that this was all God's doing, don't you forget it.

Arthur concentrated as never before in being accurate in pitch and time, heeding blend and the chorus's subordinate role. Even Rupert, in his right ear, was relatively restrained; undoubtedly the veins in his temples were throbbing with the restraint of it all. Arthur was tempted to look up into the heights of the cathedral nave, but that he should not do. He must not.

But he did look up. Just the once. In that single terrible glance, he saw Gnoxies. He glimpsed chubby dragons. It scared him terribly. From then until the end, he focussed only on the music he shakily held in front of him.

So he did not see the roof entirely dissolved away, revealing the stars and galaxies blotted out by waves of the small chubby dragons swooping in to mop up the diabolic Gnoxies hiding in crevices and behind curlicues. Wave after wave. *'Gnoxie on the starboard wing, skipper!'* *'Roger, Charlie Three.'*

He did not see the squadrons of dragons shoot forth jets of flame, scorching all in front of them, then wheel and swoop off into the vastnesses of the sky, dwindling and twinkling out, leaving only the stars.

But he could imagine it.

'And thou,' sang Eve, 'that rul'st the silent night and all ye starry hosts, spread wide his praise in choral songs about.'

No, Arthur kept his eyes down – or rather, up far enough to see the conductor of course, but not *up* up. And now the choir was given its head. 'We praise Thee now and evermore,' they sang, free from restraint at last. Rupert was like Tigger, bouncing and very loud, but the orchestra too was in full voice, trio of two trombones plus surrogate tuba, and Rupert's effervescence was effectively lost in the tumult. Arthur was aware that his own small contribution was as nothing, but he did not care. It was glorious, it was triumphant. As were the dragons perhaps, if he did but know. But maybe he felt and sensed that it was so.

And yet perhaps it was *not* so, for was there not a movement up there within the organ case over the South transept? Could that be a chubby little beaked face peeping out from between two pipes, an evilly mischievous gleam in its eyes? Who could say? Who was looking? Certainly not Arthur. Once had been enough for him.

Meanwhile, the choir members had resumed their seats, while Adam and Eve wandered figuratively around their Eden marvelling at its wonderfulness and the genius of the creator; they were still untouched by sin. Only briefly did Uriel hint that there could be trouble ahead if they desired more than was good for them. It was the one blot on the horizon of Paradise; the one Gnoxie among the organ pipes.

For now, though, ignoring Uriel's little warning, the chorus rose and embarked on the final paean of praise for Jehovah; a double fugue, including, for a few bars only, the Alto Soloist, sung today by Maestro Bernard Pontdexter, falsettist extraordinaire. Normally, Arthur would ponder on the unreasonableness of Haydn in writing those few bars. If he felt it essential to have an alto soloist there, why not use her (or him) in other places? But today, now in the headiness of the moment, Arthur had no thoughts at all; he was simply consumed by the music, the building, the occasion.

In similar vein, Beryl, there in the ranks of the band, at other times might have reflected: given that at the beginning of Part the Third, while Uriel introduced Adam and Eve, Haydn suddenly demanded a third flute, did he expect the player to sit doing nothing for the whole of the rest of the work? But at this moment, it didn't cross her mind. She was playing for her life. She was not Beryl, Queen of Flutes, she was a part of a Creation.

Stan also was playing in the moment and was beyond thought, unconscious of what might be happening in the roof and the world above him.

And whatever did happen, happened.

If nearly everyone was oblivious to it, and heard and saw only the performance, that was a remarkable thing. But it did not alter the fact, whatever that fact might be.

At the end, as the final echoes chased about and buried themselves in the niches and crannies of the great building where previously Gnoxies might have lurked, nobody seemed to breathe. To break the moment was unthinkable. Clifford still had his hands aloft, as though the performance was dangling from his baton tip. After an eternity, he dropped his arms, bowed his head, and then, in one swift movement, swivelled round, one hand sweeping along the line of soloists.

The gesture unleashed a tide of pent-up applause from the audience.

They clapped; oh, how they clapped.

The three soloists: Dee, Cuthbert Thwaites and Oscar, were all transfigured into radiance and bowed deeply. Clifford pointed a finger over the orchestra at Bernard Pontdexter, who acknowledged the applause for his few bars of solo as though he alone had made the performance – but then, he had trained the choir, hadn't he? He deserved it. And then the choir got their turn, gleaming and beaming.

Clifford proceeded with the ritual orchestra acknowledgements: leader (a smacker on Mildred Trimble's blushing cheek), other principals, woodwind (Beryl felt like a queen, Evelyn gave a little formal bow, Fred, after his double act on clarinet and the esoteric third flute, scowled good-naturedly, and Stan Bun looked like to burst; poor old Mel didn't get a special mention because nobody could ever decide which horn player was the principal, so the whole section rose), finally the brass – even Sid on the timps.

After that, what then? "*Where is Prince Hamlet when the curtain's down?*" wrote CS Lewis. "*Where fled dreams at the dawn?*" Where indeed? There were those philistines in the audience who thought only of relief from the hard pews and the prospect of a drink down the pub. But for most, with luck, they had been changed. Nothing was quite as it was. Nothing would ever be quite the same again. Something had been created, and the world was renewed. For the better or worse?

Ah, there was a question.

24 Post-Creation

Arthur left the cathedral rather rapidly. He was a mixture of emotions. Relieved, overwhelmed, bewildered and, frankly, knackered. He needed time alone to sort things out, rather than the noise and bustle of the Hippocampus. But he didn't want the others to think he was spurning them or anything. On his way out, he encountered Mel, who was zooming about.

'Bit tired,' he said. 'Going home.'

She seemed to accept it, though with protest. 'If you must, Unk. But make sure you have a little celebratory drinkie when you get home, yeah?'

He took the best lit, most populated route home, along Eastgate, into the High Street and then the short, vaguely straight Groats direct into Market Square. It all felt safe. Nobody, and perhaps more importantly, no *thing* paid him any heed.

The square itself was very quiet. Why he went round the periphery instead of diagonally across to his flat, he afterwards could not explain, but it meant he passed the bench near Stan's bakery, and there was someone there. It was Blind Bella. And yet it was a tall dapper man with a silver-headed cane. And it was both and neither. Arthur felt the awful sensation of being somewhere he couldn't explain and not knowing whether to trust his senses or not. Without volition, he sat on the bench, as far from whatever it was as possible, and tried to shrink into oblivion.

'Are you sitting comfortable, me ducks? Then I'll begin. In the beginning, the earth was without form and void…'

The voice droned on. *I know all this,* thought Arthur. *We've just been singing it. And anyway, I want to be home.*

'…and the Draconi rid the land of Nocti for they were sorely vexed…'

This wasn't right. What about dividing the land from the waters, and light from darkness, and creating all manner of beasts even down to the humble worm on a bottom D possibly?

But the voice was mesmeric. Arthur's thoughts subsided into a vague murmuring beneath a miasma of mist.

● ● ●

From the post-Creation milling about, suffused with the heady realisation that everything had gone pretty damn well considering (bravo us, bravo them, bravo everyone!), from the melee emerged a quartet bound for the Hippocampus. The unique baker-bassoonist, the virtuoso first flute, the awesome horn player – and her boyfriend, or partner, or whatever, Jason.

Jason joined the throng at the bar to order drinks while the others settled for an obscure corner, since their usual table was occupied by mere mortals.

'Well,' said Beryl. 'There we are then. All done and dusted. What's next on the agenda?

'Come off it, B. It was bloody mega-brill. Time to celebrate. Oh, I ran into Uncle Arthur by the way. He says he's knackered and is going home. No stamina, these oldies.'

'Mel, dear, that's insulting. He must be about the same age as me, and I could drink you under the table. Shame he's not here, though. He could tell us what he thought of Oscar from a singer's point of view. I thought the old trooper really came up trumps. "A triumph," the Chervil Gazette will write, mark my words. What a difference in the man. He shone, he glowed.'

'Oscar is fine fellow,' said Stan. 'He has Polish blood, believe me. I can tell these things. But Mr Arthur Davison, yes, I believe he is knackered, as you say. For me, I am used to it, but he, he is beginner. I tell him, "Don't look up," but he does. He cannot help it. It is human thing to do.'

Beryl snorted. 'What are you talking about, Stan? It sounds very mysterious.'

'I speak of these little duckling creatures with hands, and what he calls dragons.'

'What, my Cuddles?' cried Mel. 'What's he been doing now?'

'Stan, I think the excitement's gone to your head,' said Beryl. 'We've just pulled off, as Mel puts it, a mega-brill performance.'

Stan held his hands up in surrender. 'Okay, okay. Forget it. But believe me, Mr Arthur has every reason to be this knackered. I know.' He tapped his temple.

• • •

And what of Oscar? At the end of *The Creation*, the man was feted and applauded by conductor, choir members, everyone he passed, – but only fleetingly. They all then went off with their friends and family and Oscar found himself all alone. He was used to this, oh yes. Throughout his crooning life, he was the switched-on light bulb on stage, but afterwards a nothing, a nobody. Except back then he had his buddies, the band, but even they were a group by themselves and he was never really one of them.

Post-Creation, in the cathedral, there were still left only the last of the departing audience, choir, and orchestra, plus cathedral staff, a few people clearing up, and over there, Walter in his wheelchair and Rupert's wife, who had propelled Walter there. She was keeping Walter to the last so as not to impede the departing hordes. Rupert himself was probably still there too, zooming about somewhere being useful. And then there was Oscar, left behind too. What was he to do? He could go to the Hippo as usual, but today he was a soloist, not one of the lads. And he was pumped up with adrenaline and elation and undiluted pleasure at his achievement. Big-headed and bursting with it.

What he needed was alcohol.

He said to Rupert's wife, 'I'll take the old boy home, if you like. Get him to bed, tuck him in, sing him to sleep. You've done your bit.'

And she, since Walter was only Rupert's uncle, not hers, and since Rupert himself was more than enough of a handful on his own, said, yes, please, and went her merry way.

● ● ●

Jason appeared with the drinks. Beryl sized him up and decided with a twinge of envy that he was All Right, and that Mel was lucky. Mel and Jason. Stan and Mrs Stan. Her and… Just her.

'Stan,' she said, 'did your wife come to the concert? You should have brought her here for a drink.'

'No, no. She work at Pink Pyjama Club. Is not her kind of music for sure, Papa Haydn. In music she is peasant.'

Jason said he knew the Pink Pyjama Club. It was, he said, the best dive in Chervil, kind of chic and cool at the same time.

Before long, Jason and Mel decided they should go on there, go and see Mrs Stan pole-dancing. What a contrast to Haydn! Stan had never actually been to the club, he said. He was an early bird. A baker had to be.

'Come on, Stan, come along with us,' said Mel. 'Give her a surprise. It'll be awesome. Come on. Go wild, let your hair down.'

They all looked at his polished billiard ball cranium and he beamed. 'Yes, yes, Miss Mel. I will. It is time for Bun to know who he married. I am up for him, as you say.'

So that was decided. Beryl however had misgivings. Being honest with herself, the idea of a night-club scared her witless, but she didn't want to be seen a kill-joy. She needed an excuse.

'Mel, Stan, I'm sorry, but for me it's a school night. Don't forget I open on Sundays now. I need to be responsible. Or I might start baking sponge cakes with garlic and chilli butter-cream fillings. And Victoria, what would she say?'

'Victoria?' said Mel.

'My cat.'

'B, don't be silly.'

'No, really, Mel dear. I'll give it a miss. It's just not me. You all go on. Have a great time, and I'll expect a full report.'

So off they went, while Beryl went home. Alone.

And another thing, she thought as she walked, *what about poor old Arthur?* Stan seemed serious when he said Arthur had every reason to be tired out. She remembered Arthur had had that fever a couple of months ago when he hallucinated. What if it had flared up again?

She decided to go through the Market Square on her way home, even though it was hardly direct. The square looked like it usually did, not that she often went through there at night. Sadly, she realised she had no idea whereabouts Arthur's flat was, apart from that he looked down on the square. She gazed at the windows of the upper floors. Some had curtains drawn and lights inside. Some were dark. It was pointless.

So she carried on home, walking rapidly through the couple of alleys she had to traverse to reach Northgate.

• • •

Meanwhile, Oscar, subterranean bass soloist (and yes, he had achieved the low D, albeit almost subliminally), and Walter, lately uncertain tenor of the Chervil Choral Soc, made their way round to Bishop's Close, the one pushing, the other riding. There were frequent stops, for Walter had secreted his hip flask beneath the rug over his knees, and the two of them shared a tot several times on their mere hundred-yard journey. By the time they reached the door, they were also well into their party piece of *Oh for the wings of a dove*, rendered in their respective falsettos.

Inside, Oscar did indeed get Walter into bed, after various other bottles had been very well sampled. It only took half a verse of *'Tis the last rose of summer* before Walter was quietly snoring.

• • •

Beryl opened her front door, entered, and closed it behind her. As the noise of the city shut off, she was left in a void. The stillness sapped the elation of the Creation out of her.

She poured a gin, the cupboard now no longer locked. There was no tonic. She took a sip and grimaced. Water, that would have to do instead. At the kitchen sink she stopped, looking long and distant out of the window into the darkness.

It need not be thus. Suddenly decisive, she took her watered gin into the living room, and sank into an armchair. Then rose. Then paced. Then extracted Hattie from the cupboard. But Hattie was not the answer.

Then she rang Mel.

The merry hubbub coming down the phone, presumably the usual ambient sound of the Pink Pyjama Club, was almost painful. She asked Mel for a phone number. She wrote it down.

She took a long swig of gin and water, holding it in her mouth for ages before swallowing it down.

From the best armchair, Victoria was looking at her. The voice implanted itself in Beryl's head. '*Do you know what you're doing? Have you thought about me?*'

To which Beryl replied aloud, 'Not really. Let's just see how it goes. And don't bully me.' She tried to read Victoria's expression, which in a cat is hopeless.

'Nothing ventured...' she said to the world at large, and rang the number that Mel had given her.

• • •

Since Oscar felt mellow and now in the mood for conviviality, he left Walter sleeping like a baby at home and decided to walk along by the river Cher to the Duck and Grouse, a pub which he felt would be free of concert goers and so a fresh audience for his wit and repartee. The night was chill and the sky clear, star-speckled here away from the street lights. Euphoric, he gazed up at his fellow stars, as he saw them, fit companions for one such as he, when he saw one shoot across the sky. And then another, and another, zigzagging, coruscating, a crown imperial. He experienced a blinding, revelatory light, and in one moment of ecstasy, felt himself complete for the first time in his life, felt a constriction tighten around his chest, and fell to the ground.

Achievèd was his glorious work.

It would be the next morning when an early dog-walker would discover him. Far, far too late.

• • •

After his strange experience at Bella's bench, Arthur found he was back in his flat, an infinite pool of calm. In front of him, he had spread out his drawings for Mel's book. Cuddles picking his nose. Cuddles hanging upside-down from a ceiling lamp. Cuddles sitting on a large iced cake flicking silver balls at a fireman who was just coming in through the window.

Gnoxies. An evil creation. Now confined to the page, Arthur hoped. With luck and the chubby dragon patrol. Or was that all fancy? Escapism from the real world threats of global warming, worldwide plagues, extremists, deranged oligarchs, and greed and lust for power?

Should he destroy the drawings? Burn them as Stan had told him to with the Grand Square-Scape? Banish them to oblivion? But if Gnoxies didn't really exist in the first place, what was to stop them resurrecting?

No.

He, Arthur Davison, who might or might not have created their possible concrete manifestation, was, if so, in his small way, God over this tiny bit of creation. Or perhaps god with a small "g". Or *a* god. A *minor* god. Don't get too big-headed, Arthur. But if so, he could decide to dispense divine clemency, and consequently the Gnoxies would all be grateful and behave themselves, so the drawings could be allowed to remain. After all, Gnoxies were cute. Everyone said so. And Mel might decide to carry on writing the story. And if necessary, there were always his chubby little dragons who could sort the Gnoxies out again. Never mind what Stan Bun had said about dragons. If they were dragons. For Stan was right, how did he truly know what dragons looked like? Perhaps they were projections of some hidden alien power…

Oh, his brain hurt.

He unearthed his bottle of dry sherry, his first aid kit for bouts of melancholy.

'It's all this living alone,' he said to his picture of Cuddles picking his nose. 'It gets to a chap. He starts imagining things. But maybe that's how creativity starts.'

Arthur sighed. A long, long, heartfelt sigh.

And then the phone rang.

Postlude

Stanislav Bun, baker-bassoonist, looked at Mr Arthur Davison with his curious stare. He wagged a finger. 'Gnoxies. Gnoxies no more. Is good. But, ah...' His sigh was long and copious. 'The dragons. They are problem.'

'Yes,' said Arthur. 'Yes. Oh dear.'

'Is life,' said Stanislav. '*Lekarstwo podczas, cięższe niż choroba.* That is what we say. Cure is very often worse than disease.'

Arthur sniffed morosely. 'Oh dear, oh dear. And I fear it is all my fault. A problem. Oh dear. But what can I do about it?'

Stanislav spread his ham-hock hands wide. 'You must begin again. Is only way. Go back to the past. Create it new. Maybe next time better.'

Arthur said, 'That's not possible. I mean, isn't it against the laws of...'

Stan pointed to the bacon bun oozing butter on a plate in front of Arthur. 'That is not possible. I, a Pole, probably the only baker-bassoonist ever, to produce the best bacon bun in the world... Is not possible. And yet I have done it. Eat, my friend, eat and drink and think, and maybe the impossible will be. Is on the house,' he added, directed at Merrylin behind the counter.

And off he went into the stainless steel depths of the bakery.

Arthur Davison ate, and as the butter and bacon fat dribbled down his chin, he reflected, and the impossible occurred. He went back home, pausing at WH Smith's en route to purchase a paper shredder. In the flat, he cut his Grand Market Square-scape into suitable sized pieces and shredded them into a tangle of impenetrable noodles. Then he prepared new drawing paper, spread it on his wallpapering table, secured it with tablecloth clips and began again. This time he would create a new world, with no likeness to what he saw outside. Any whimsical beasties he populated it with could go and plague that new world, and much luck to them. This time, maybe all would be well. He could even include a humble worm, complete with a bottom D and prehensile lips. *Poor old Oscar,* he thought. *Such a shame. But what a character.*

He felt bold and resolute. And tonight he was going out for a meal with Beryl. Who'd have thought it? At *Provocation* in Not Martins Square, where the menu featured foraged plants, and rumour had it, road-kill. Daring. A new world indeed! Whatever next?

About the Author

I used to write Computer User Manuals, but having retired, now prefer to replace writing facts that nobody reads with producing whimsical fiction that people can enjoy. I live in Abergavenny, which should be known as the Rome of Wales, because it has seven hills and a few Roman remains.

My flash fiction pieces have been published in various e-zines, such as Reflex Fiction, Kind of a Hurricane, The Dirty Pool, Fiction on the Web, Chronicle Stories, and the Peeking Cat Poetry Magazine.

In a previous existence as a Maths teacher, I wrote and directed two full-length plays, and I've composed a number of musical pieces, mostly for choir, which have received performances in widely-flung places around the world. They are freely available from my web-site, www.musicolib.net, or through the Choral Public Domain Library (ChoralWiki – www.cpdl.org/wiki/).

In my writing, I seek to bring a wry touch to the commonplace activities of everyday life – "in the ordinary is the extraordinary." Frequently, angels and bad-tempered mythical beings such as garden gnomes creep in, despite my best endeavours. Hence the collection of short stories, **Away with the Fairies**, fifty-five fantastical tales, where they have generally taken over. The collection is also published by The Deri Press.

My **Tangle Tales** are stories set in the fictional small city of Chervil and its mediaeval heart – the Tangle. Characters may reappear. The first, **Of Mouse and Man**, tells the tale of Brian Ellis, who, when his mother dies after fifty years of belittling him, is faced with discovering who is. A rather mysterious fellow student from long-ago university days comes to Brian's antiquarian bookshop with a proposition. It is destined to give Brian a purpose and a way forward.

It is a whimsical story of one man's inner turmoil and his path through it, with much humour, even more food and drink – and a therapeutic cat.

Creation is the second Tangle Tale.

The third promises to involve two small boys, the Bishop and Chapter of Chervil Cathedral, and an incompetent fairy. Coming soon to The Deri Press!

Oliver Barton
oliver.barton@talktalk.net